To John Kelly and Bob Goldsborough,
Friends of the City

THE EL MURDERS

BILL GRANGER

WARNER BOOKS

A Warner Communications Company

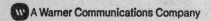

For man knows not his time: as the fishes that are taken in an evil net, and as the birds that are caught in the snare; so are the sons of men snared in an evil time, when it falls suddenly upon them.

—*Ecclesiastes*

AUTHOR'S NOTE

The intention of this book is to tell the truth. The book tells a story of Chicago and politics and the criminal justice system as it really works. Some of the language, some of the racial jibes recorded, some of the criminal actions described—in and out of the courtroom and the justice process—will offend readers who wish to believe that such things do not happen, such words are not used, and that no good purpose is served in recalling them in any case.

—*Bill Granger*

1
THANK GOD
IT'S FRIDAY

They worked as runners for different brokerage houses in the Chicago Board of Trade. They had been friends before they had been lovers, before Brandon Cale was sure that he was a homosexual.

The bell closed down the exchange at 3:00. It was late and nearly dark already because they were in Chicago in the middle of winter. Daylight was very short and weak. The sun was pale and some weeks went by with nothing but clouds in the sky. It was the end of January.

Brandon Cale was the same height and same slim build as Lee Herran, but Brandon Cale seemed diminished when he was with the other man. They were twenty-two and both had come to the city from middle-class homes in smaller towns. Brandon came from Decatur, Illinois, where he had not been certain he was a homosexual. He had suspected it for a long time before he was certain. Lee made him certain.

Lee Herran grew up in Barrington, which is a suburb northwest of the city that has a mix of rich and middle-class people. His father was a certified public accountant and never talked to him anymore. It didn't bother Lee very much to be separated from his father.

There was a certain excitement that built all Friday afternoon that was separate from the grinding everyday chaos of the stock exchanges. The end-of-the-week syndrome of expectation built pressure in the low-paid runners and clerks and secretaries. They looked forward to the weekend freedom and a chance to spend too much of the money they accrued all week. Mondays always came up blue, but all that was forgotten on Fridays.

Brandon met Lee as usual after work in the lobby at the Jackson Boulevard entrance of the Board of Trade building. The building is at the heart of the financial district in the south end of the Loop. The building sits like a tall stone chair at the foot of LaSalle Street.

Brandon's eyes were pale blue and his features were very pale, which made his hair seem very black. He looked as though he had once been sick and never fully recovered from his illness. His cheekbones were high and when he blushed, which was often, they colored faintly. He had a brother back in Decatur and he didn't say much to him anymore, now that he knew about Brandon, but he didn't cut him off either. He went home for Christmas and they all endured him and pretended that he was not a homosexual and that he was not living with another homosexual on the Near North Side of Chicago. Once his brother, Michael, the eldest, said it was a good thing their father was dead. It was the only hard thing he had said to Brandon on the matter.

Lee Herran was wearing a sober navy cashmere topcoat and a gray Alpine hat that made him look younger than he was. He had been waiting for a couple of minutes when he saw Brandon come out of an elevator and cross the marble lobby. He smiled at Brandon. They sometimes ran across each other on the trading floor during the day or they sometimes managed to have a bite of lunch together, but mostly they never saw each other until the end of the day.

They nodded to each other the way old friends do when they meet as expected, but did not speak. The lobby was alive with people clattering across the polished marble floor to the bank of revolving doors. The heavy doors swished continuously and brought puffs of cold air back into the overheated lobby.

"Binyan's?" said Lee Herran, as he always said on Friday afternoon.

"Binyan's," Brandon said, smiling, as he always did.

Lee Herran pushed on the door first and it slid around and Brandon followed.

It was very cold. The city had been buried in winter for six weeks and still the cold was an unexpected cruelty and still the wind was unexpected when they went out into it. The wind slapped around the canyons of buildings. Police traffic whistles filled the air, above the sounds of traffic snarled on LaSalle Street, edging through the maze of short streets. They stood still on the sidewalk for a moment, trying to catch their breath in the wind.

"God, you can't breathe for a minute," Brandon said. He turned his face away from the wind and took a backward step.

"I never get used to it," Lee Herran said. They bent in the wind and went to the corner and then south to Binyan's on Plymouth Court. The bar was upstairs on the second floor of the old restaurant, with its wood-paneled walls and clublike atmosphere. Women rarely were seen in Binyan's because it was a male preserve for the traders and brokers and bankers who huddled there and talked about the deals of the day. The bar was at the windowless west end of the second floor. It was U-shaped and small and was already filling up. The steam heat banged up through the pipes and the bar was so overheated that some of the drinkers were red-faced and perspiring.

Lee Herran slapped his gloved hands on the bar to attract the attention of one of the two men in white shirts who were working the bar. He and Brandon weren't regulars—the place was too expensive for their salary levels most of the time—and they waited until neither bartender could find any way of ignoring them further.

"Myers's dark and cola," Lee said.

"And you, sir?" the bartender said with exaggerated politeness.

"Cutty Sark and soda," Brandon Cale said, and blushed.

Lee smiled at him as the bartender turned away. "Cutty Sark. I think I stopped drinking Cutty Sark when I was a freshman at Northwestern. I mean, Brandon, you're in the real world now. Cutty Sark. I mean, that's something you'd drink when you were a freshman in college."

"You always say that," Brandon said, the blush lingering on his pale features.

"I want you to be as sophisticated as I am and you insist on stumbling back to your hick origins," Lee said. He said it in a familiar, ragging kind of voice that was only faintly serious. He liked Brandon just as Brandon was and they both knew it. And they both knew that part of Lee's appreciation of his friend and lover was to put on the voice of the pompous ass taunting the hick.

They were in a good, smiling mood when the drinks came. They drank them too quickly and ordered another round. It was good to be in a warm bar in the middle of winter in the Loop in Chicago on a Friday afternoon with your pockets full and the expectation of the weekend all before you.

Lee Herran had ruddy skin slapped red by the wind and open good looks and a smile of fellowship that charmed men and women. He was handsome, just as Brandon Cale bordered on being pretty. He told good stories and he knew gossip. He had been a homosexual since he was fourteen. He told Brandon about nearly everything, after they were lovers.

They had been roommates to pool living expenses before they had become lovers. Brandon did not even know that Lee was a homosexual until Lee told him. At least, that is what they both said they believed now. Lee never brought his friends to the apartment. Later, after a few months, when they were both drunk and when Brandon knew that Lee was a homosexual, they had become lovers. Lee thought he had not wanted to seduce the other man. Lee said that Brandon was very beautiful. He said it then and other times.

They always stopped at Binyan's for two drinks on Friday afternoons before they headed to State Street and caught the subway train to their rooms on the Near North Side. They did this as a ritual to begin the weekend. They would stand at the bar and they would decide if they would go to the show at the Biograph Theater that night or the next and if they were going to try the new French restaurant on Broadway and if they were going to get those canvas chairs in the Great Ace or wait awhile on it. They talked of the inconsequential things that would fill their weekend. As they always did. Everything they did after work on that Friday was exactly what they always did on Fridays after work.

Except it was very cold outside. Except they were reluctant to leave the bar after two drinks this Friday. Except Brandon had been promised a raise on the next paycheck and that was reason enough to celebrate. They had a third round and then a fourth, and they talked so loudly that the bartenders stared at them.

They were both hungry and it was just 6:30. They decided to go to Gordon's on Clark Street, just north of the river. But they wouldn't have gone to Gordon's if they hadn't had the good luck to find an empty cab right on Van Buren Street, down the block from Binyan's. If they hadn't found the cab, they would have walked the short block to the State Street subway and taken the El home and been in their apartment by 8:30 P.M.

There were so many elements of chance that changed their Friday afternoon routine so that they were still downtown much later at night than they had expected to be. Later than they usually were.

All this would be noted in the police report that followed and underlined by one of the officers, as though the change in routine might have had some significance.

2
MARY JANE
CALDWELL

Two days before that Friday night, at 3:10 Wednesday afternoon, Mary Jane Caldwell had gotten off the El train at the Jarvis Avenue stop on the far North Side.

She was a student at Loyola University and went to her seminars on the Rogers Park campus at Devon and Broadway twice a week.

She had a very bad cold and her nose was red. It was a long, pretty nose and she had the face of a china doll. Her eyes were gray and lazy. When she looked at things she stared at them for a long time, the way a cat will stare at something. She knew she was good-looking and that pleased her more than anything else. She was in graduate school because she thought she wanted to be a political economist.

Absurdly, she had fallen asleep in the warm car while the El train was still in the subway beneath the Loop. She had dozed in that half-awake way that commuters count as sleep on trains. She dozed and her body swayed back and forth to the rhythm of the train in the tunnel. The El train plowed north across the city, through the stops, rattled from side to side, grinding hard on the tracks in the subway tunnel and then climbing the steep steel hill at the point north of North Avenue where it rises out of the tunnel and becomes the elevated train.

When Mary Jane Caldwell missed her stop at the Sheridan-Loyola station, there was nothing to do but to get off farther north and take a southbound El back to Sheridan Road. She got off at the Jarvis Avenue station. She crossed the wooden platform of the El stop to the southbound-tracks side. It was so stupid to have slept through a stop in the middle of the day. She felt foolish, as though anyone cared.

She stood on the platform alone, in the cold, and looked down the tracks and did not see a train. She shivered in her coat and turned away from the wind. She felt bone-cold. And then she saw the first one open the wooden door that led to the steps and station below. The first one stood there for a moment with the door open, and then the door widened and she saw the second one. They stood in the doorway and stared at her and they were smiling. She turned away from them and faced the wind. The wind hurt. She shivered again. They had dark skin. One must be a Negro, she thought, and the other one might be, the other one might be something else, and she thought: O God, get me out of this, I love You, help me. They both wore olive-drab field jackets. They came onto the platform. One pulled down a ski mask. They stood on each side of her and didn't say a thing. And then the first one, the lighter-skinned one, took out his knife and showed it to her, and she said another prayer.

She saw the doors that led to the stairs and they were between her and the stairs. She stood very still for a moment.

The first man said, "I want your purse."

She gave it to him.

The second man said, "We're going to do it, you know, both of us. You know that."

"No," she said in a soft and frightened voice. "Please don't do this. Please take my purse." She said a prayer that began: O my God, please don't let this happen.

"Come on, come on down to the waiting platform," said the first one.

She screamed. Her voice trailed out of her mouth on a puff of steam in the cold clean air. It was the middle of the afternoon. It was the middle of the goddam afternoon.

"Come on, bitch," said the first one, and they cut her on the arm. She wore a heavy coat and the knife did not go deep into her skin but it was enough to scare her even more.

"Come on," said the second one.

They pushed just inside the door that led down thirty-one stairs to the waiting room. There wasn't anyone on duty in the ticket cage of the small station at this time of day. She didn't know that.

The first one pushed Mary Jane Caldwell to her knees inside the door of the stairwell and unzipped his trousers. She saw what he was going to do. She closed her eyes and felt him against her face.

When he was finished, the second one did the same thing.

They were talking about it, laughing to each other, making noises to threaten her. She thought she might be able to stand it if she didn't look at them.

They raped her after that. She didn't fight them. They hurt her and tore her clothes. She wore slacks and they pulled her slacks off and the one with the knife cut off her panties. She wore a wool sweater and they pulled it off and cut off her brassiere. She was cold and hurt and crying. She was naked and they were laughing. After they both raped her, one of them said they might as well kill her. The other one said, "Shit, let's get going out of here." The first one said they ought to kill her. The second one asked her if she would tell the police about them. She said she wouldn't. She said she swore before God she wouldn't, honest to God she wouldn't. The first one laughed and told her to take him again in her mouth. She did what he told her to do. She was on her knees and crying, her body hurt and she was doing this terrible thing but she did not want him to kill her. O my God, she thought, I am heartily sorry for having offended Thee. And I detest all my sins because I fear the loss of heaven and the pains of hell. She said the words of the Act of Contrition and the first one discharged into her mouth. The second one said they should get out of there, fuck the broad, fuck she gonna say to anyone?

The first one said the second one was right. The second one

said they should just get out of there. And they were suddenly running down the stairs, banging through the empty waiting room, out onto the street.

She lay on the stairs for a long time, crying. She was cold but she thought she couldn't move. She was covered with bruises and dirt from the dirty steps they had pushed her against, from the dirty wooden platform. She felt hurt and broken. After a time, she realized she was still crying but that there weren't any tears in her eyes. She wrapped her coat around her dumbly and saw her dirty, torn clothing strewn on the steps. She buttoned the coat but she still sat on the steps, barefoot, unmoving.

She thought of herself as a little girl in a dainty dress at a party long ago because she wanted to feel sorry for what she had been. She couldn't make any tears.

The police report said a passenger entered the station about ten minutes after the assault and discovered Mary Jane Caldwell sitting at the top of the stairwell, staring down the steps, making noises like a person sobbing but without any tears. The report said the passenger ran back down the stairs and found a pay telephone in the waiting room and called the police. The first two uniforms arrived at the scene approximately twenty-one minutes after the assault, according to the preliminary police report. They reported that the victim had stopped crying.

3
MR. CUTLER

It was Friday night.

"Mr. Cutler. Don't forget your briefcase, Mr. Cutler."

Mark Cutler was very drunk and it was nearly 10:30. He had been drinking in the Loop since he got the check at lunch. Lunch was a long time ago. This place was the Corona Cafe and he was at the bar and Phil the bartender was waving a black case at him. It was his own goddam briefcase, for Christ's sake.

"That's my briefcase," Mark Cutler said. He reached across the bar for the case.

"That's what I said," said Phil. "I said don't forget your briefcase."

"My briefcase," Mark Cutler said. "I almost forgot it. It wouldn't be a good thing to forget my briefcase."

"What you got in there, you got money in there?" Phil said.

"You know what I got in there?" said Mark Cutler, heaving his fat moon face across the bar so that he was very close to Phil, so that the bartender could smell the vodka stench.

"I got a cashier's check. Client gives me a cashier's check like I don't trust him to give me money. Cashier's check, good as cash if your name is my name, which it isn't." He bit off the words deliberately because it was very difficult to speak. It had been difficult in Riccardo's down the street, at the bar, trying to tell the woman in the red dress and the nice wool melton coat that he wanted to take her home with him. He really didn't want to take her home. He wanted to fuck her in a motel room or at her place. He never wanted anything so bad in his life. He knew that if he had gotten her out of Riccardo's, he would fuck her, that was all there was to it. She didn't understand. They threw him out of Riccardo's. It was humiliating. But he took his briefcase. A check for $4,398. Incredible.

"You're tired, Mr. Cutler," said Phil. "Go home. Go to sleep."

"OK. I'll go home. As long as I got my briefcase."

It was 10:32 on Friday night and he was very cold and drunk and there wasn't a single cab in the cab line that usually sat in front of the Corona on Rush Street.

He waved at a Checker that pulled up across the street, but the cab driver shook his head at him.

"Taxi," he said.

"I'm off duty," the driver said. "Where you going?"

"Belmont. Belmont Harbor."

"No, man, I'm off duty."

"The fuck you ask me where I'm going then?"

"Hey, fuck you too, Jack."

"Jagoff. I got your number."

"Fuck you, Jack. I'm off duty."

"Hey, fuck you. Fuck you, motherfucker."

"Hey, fuck you, Jack." And the cab pulled away.

The girl in the red dress and blue melton coat had said he was drunk and now this jagoff blew him off and Phil practically tried to steal his briefcase.

Mark Cutler tried to stand very still but he kept moving to keep his balance.

This was a bad situation.

There was Marilyn to face when he made it home. There was Saturday to face. Saturday would be a bad hangover and Marilyn would add to it, Marilyn would keep telling him that if he didn't drink so much, he wouldn't feel so bad. Marilyn was a genius.

He crossed Rush Street and walked past the city parking garage to the corner and then walked west to Wabash Avenue at the point where the street dips down back to ground level. Across the street was the bulk of the ornate Medinah Temple. He rested at the corner and waved at a passing Yellow cab, but it was full and it shot through the intersection against the lights. It was so damned cold.

He staggered down the deserted length of Grand Avenue another block to State Street and decided to try the subway. He was trying to stay alert now. He was going down the steps, through the pay cage, down more steps to the concrete platform. The subway tiles sparkled white in the tunnel. The ceilings were rounded and there was a bum sleeping on the wooden bench on the wall. There were two candy machines that had no candy in them. He was hungry. He sat down at the end of a bench and waited and wished he had a candy bar.

The subway tunnel was quiet for a long time.

Then he heard steps on the stairs and turned to look at the entrance.

The steps sounded for a long time and he heard voices echo from the hidden stairs.

He had a briefcase with a cashier's check in it. Jesus Christ, this was stupid. He hated the stupid fucking El, the stupid fucking city, the stupid fucking way he made a living. It was so stupid.

He saw the two emerge from the stairwell. They were white at least. Young white guys. They were talking to each other and one of them was making faces and talking in an exaggerated way, as though he was imitating someone else.

The drunk on the bench said, "Shut the fuck up," and turned over to go back to sleep.

The two young men laughed.

"Subways aren't for sleeping," Lee Herran said in a mincing voice. He was drunk because he never talked like that unless he was drunk. Brandon giggled and blushed and swayed a little because he was drunk as well.

"Shut the fuck up," said the drunk. "You fucking fairies."

14

"Hello, sailor," said Lee Herran to make Brandon giggle some more.

Fags, Mark Cutler thought. He smiled. He smiled at his own foreboding when he had heard the sounds of steps on the hidden stairs.

Couple of fruits, he thought.

He was smiling when the train rumbled into the station and shuddered to a stop. The three men crossed the concrete platform and the doors clicked open and they got on and left the drunk sleeping on the wooden bench.

A lot of time would be spent trying to find the drunk mentioned in the preliminary police report, but he would never be found in connection with the matter.

4
ON THE
A TRAIN

At 11:31 on Friday night, the four-car A train for Howard Street on the North Side roared into the Chicago Avenue subway station and squealed to a stop.

The doors clicked open and the black conductor in the third car stuck his head out the window and looked left and right to watch the passengers get on and off.

Raoul and Willie took the front of the second car and Slide came on at the rear.

The fourth passenger to get on was a black woman who had white hair and big arms and carried a paper shopping bag. She had waited on the platform for fifteen minutes with the three of them at the other end, looking at her. She had given them a look. She gave them a look that said it all and they didn't mess with her.

Raoul and Willie were laughing when they got on, jiving with each other.

Slide never said anything.

"She's too tough for me," said Raoul.

The lights above the opened doors were red. The conductor pulled the lever and the lights turned green and the doors slammed shut. He pulled the lever that made a sound signal in the engineer's compartment at the front of the train, and the electric train jerked forward.

Through the dirty glass windows between cars, the conductor, whose name was Sylvester Rose, saw Raoul and Willie and Slide stand in the aisles for a moment, as though they were surveying the car. Bad boys, Sylvester Rose thought. You could tell bad boys.

He leaned to the microphone built into the wall of the car and announced the next stop:

"Clark and Division. Clark and Division. Clark and Division will be the next stop. Smoking is not permitted on the train. Division Street." The voice was distorted when it came out of the speaker system.

Sylvester Rose stared at the three of them standing in the car though there were plenty of empty seats. Through the window, his broad brown face was serene; his eyes were rimmed with red.

The train pulled into Clark and Division, the stop beneath the west end of the old nightclub district. Along Division Street, thirty feet above the subway tunnel, the meet-market bars were crowded with single people and married people who wanted to live single for the night. It was too early and lonely for them to go home. The platform was empty. Sylvester Rose opened the doors, looked up and down, closed the doors and jerked the signal to the engineer. The electric train lurched ahead.

"North and Clybourn. North and Clybourn. Clybourn is the next stop. Smoking is not permitted on the train."

Willie lit a Kool cigarette in the next car and smiled.

Slide nodded to Raoul. They stared at the dude sleeping in the seat halfway down the car. A white dude with one of those raincoats with the brown liner on the collar and the little doodads on the belt.

Raoul wiped his hand carefully over the front of his olive-drab field jacket.

The white dude had one of those furry Russian hats on top of his fat head. He was definitely sleeping. He wore black leather gloves folded on top of the briefcase on his lap.

Mark Cutler began to snore.

The black woman with white hair sat at the far end of the car.

She faced the three youths who were staring at Cutler. Willie kept smoking his cigarette and staring through the glass windows between cars at Sylvester Rose. Willie had strawberry hair matted by dirt and a very pale face. Raoul was light-skinned and Slide was as black as the ace of spades. "We're patriots, you know," said Raoul once. Raoul said clever things off the top of his head, without even thinking about it. "We're red, light, and blue. Lookat Slide. He's the bluest nigger I ever seen."

"He ain't nothing," Willie said loud enough for Raoul to hear because he was staring at Sylvester Rose in the next car, figuring him out, testing him about the cigarette smoking because some of the CTA conductors had more guts than brains and would fight about something like smoking on the train. He was figuring what Sylvester Rose was willing to do about them if they thought to do anything bad.

Raoul nodded. He wore a black beret with a broken, plastic sweatband. His unlined field jacket was zipped shut.

He glanced at the two faggy-looking dudes on the right, near the front doors of the car.

Raoul smiled at them.

He wanted to catch their eyes but they wouldn't look at him.

The train began a screeching slide around a long curve as it turned north and west toward Clybourn Street on the edge of the Cabrini Green public housing projects.

The train built speed on the long curve and the three of them were forced by gravity to lean against the curve. Raoul braced his behind against the edge of one of the seats. Slide glanced at Raoul, but Raoul wasn't paying attention to business. Business was the white dude sleeping in the middle of the car. Raoul had this crazy smile.

Willie wasn't looking at them. He was braced with his hand on one of the metal poles at the exit doors, his cigarette hung on his bottom lip.

"Come on, man," Slide said.

"Shit," said Raoul. Raoul smiled at the two white boys but they wouldn't look at him. That made him feel good. He knew white boys like that in St. Charles reformatory, little white boys with little white asses, learn to do what they told.

"Stick to business," Slide said.

Raoul said, "Aw, man. Be cool now."

That was Raoul, always fucking around, now wanted to fuck around with a couple of boys look like sissies, when they had a sleeping dude with a package on his lap, a guy that has to be in trump from Jump Street. Look at that coat. See myself in that coat. Getting colder all the time, fucking hawk is biting, got to get trump for yourself to stay warm, survive. Or you end up in spring when the snow melts and you're under it like a dead pigeon.

Raoul turned then. He had pockmarks on both sunken cheeks. His skin was sallow. He was skinny, smaller than Slide in build, probably shorter than Willie, but he was harder than Willie and maybe he was harder than Slide. He was mean enough to run them both.

And Willie didn't count.

"Dude, man," Slide said. "Be stickin' to bidness."

And Raoul smiled because it slowed everything down enough to make Slide understand that Slide was not running Raoul.

The train careened into Clybourn Street station and shuddered again and stopped in a squeal of brakes.

Sylvester Rose stuck his head out the window and looked left and right. Just once there would be a policeman getting on the train, he thought. Supposed to be transit police, where the hell were transit police?

Sylvester Rose held the doors open and the coldness of the station permeated the warmth of the cars. He waited.

But nobody moved and Sylvester Rose punched the buttons and the doors closed. He signaled the motorman again and the train lurched forward in that sudden way of electric vehicles.

He closed the window. Too damned cold and too many hours in a day. He leaned to the microphone built into the stainless-steel wall of the compartment:

"Fullerton. Fullerton. Fullerton is the next stop, change for the Ravenswood. Smoking is not permitted on the train."

And he looked back through the windows between the cars at Willie, who was staring back at him, the cigarette dangling from his bottom lip.

Punks. Bad boys.

He sat down then for a moment as the train began the rush to the end of the tunnel. He was too tired. He stared at the three punks standing in the next car. So what if he went into the next car, what difference would it make? It wouldn't make any difference.

He had worked three hours of this shift after four hours off. The long day started when he took his daughter to school. That was eight in the morning. She always said she wanted to ride the bus with the other kids but he knew the CTA buses and Els and he drove her to school every morning and picked her up every afternoon. He worked the four-hour morning shift and then had eight hours off until the night shift. A lot of the engineers and motormen and drivers still worked the traditional CTA split shift that ensured enough trains and drivers at the morning and evening rush hours.

He thought of his daughter as she would be when she was older, living on the North Side, riding the A train home at midnight, sitting in the next car with three punks standing and grinning and deciding on something bad to do. He thought of how afraid she would be.

He closed his eyes because he was so tired.

Raoul walked over to the sleeping dude and reached for the attaché case without a preliminary.

He removed it in one motion from the gloved fingers.

The man in the absurd Russian fur hat awoke.

Raoul smiled at him.

Slide took the hat then and put it on his own head. It was warm and felt good to the touch.

Mark Cutler blinked at the youth with the pockmarked face and black beret and field jacket, who was grinning down at him. He saw the case. The case with the cashier's check.

"Hey, man," he began.

His words slurred. He tried to concentrate. Again: "Hey, man, that's my case."

He started to rise. Slide was behind his seat and pushed hard on his shoulders. Slide forced him back onto the greasy green-vinyl seat.

"That's my fucking case." He tried to turn in the seat. "You got my hat."

"I ain't got your hat, what you say I got your hat, I got my hat," said Slide.

"My fucking case," said Mark Cutler. He was confused and was becoming afraid.

Raoul turned and stared right at Brandon Cale, who was staring back at him. Raoul smiled at Brandon and Brandon looked away. The train screamed through the tunnel.

"You, trash. Get outta here, trash."

Raoul and Slide looked at the black woman with white hair and black hate eyes.

"Mama," Slide began.

"Don't you 'mama' me, trash, get outta here, be leav' that white man 'lone."

But she did not move. She sat still and held her shopping bag tightly between her legs.

"My case," Cutler began again. "I'm an attorney."

"You fucking too drunk, dude, be carrying a case, we carry it for you," said Slide.

Raoul held the case out of reach. He said, "Don't you listen to the conductor, man? He said that sleeping is not permitted on the train. You been sleeping and now you guilty. We're gonna be taking the case off you. You know, it's the law."

"Gimme my fucking case, you fucking scum—"

"Man, you watch your mouth," Slide began, slapping Cutler on the side of the head. The blow was hard. Cutler's face reddened.

And Raoul popped open the attaché-case locks and turned the case upside down.

Legal pads and papers floated to the floor.

The train roared out of the tunnel and began its ascent to the trestles thirty feet above the street.

The papers floated and no one spoke or moved.

The train rose above the night city and the grid of streets strung with orange anticrime lights.

"Jesus," said Raoul. "Look at them law pads. Dude *is* a lawyer. . . ."

In the third car of the train, Sylvester Rose called the motorman on the two-way, and the motorman said the radio to call the police was broken and that most of the radios were broken and there was nothing to be done, he had complained about it at the yards. The motorman told Sylvester Rose to keep his compartment locked and that there was nothing to do.

"Lookit," said Willie.

They all looked at the check on the floor of the car. Raoul picked it up. "Four thousand three hundred and ninety-eight dollars," he said.

Slide smiled in his Russian hat and said nothing.

"Cashier's check, it's good as cash—"

"Gimme my money," Cutler said.

Brandon and Lee stared and did not move. They had been placed beyond the footlights for the moment.

"What you do to get a check like that, Mark Cutler," said Raoul, reading the name on the check.

"I'm an attorney, I—"

"Shit, a fuckin' lawyer, man, you said that, I'm sick to death of lawyers," said Raoul.

"Lawyer rob you and the next thing, you inside and he outside laughing," said Slide.

"Fucking lawyer," Willie said, joining chorus. Everyone was waiting.

The train crossed Armitage Avenue. The twin stone spires of St. Vincent de Paul loomed to the west, above the three-story Victorian houses and flats of the Lincoln Park neighborhood. The winter streets below were quiet and empty. The train flashed above the houses on the iron trestles.

"Gotta go, Raoul," Slide said. "Motorman be calling the pohleese."

"Gotta go," Willie said.

Slide reached inside Cutler's pocket. Cutler grabbed his

hand. Slide hit him like a lazy bear and Cutler's ears rang from the blow. Slide took out the wallet.

"Take the money, gimme my cards—"

"Fuck you, lawyer, you lucky we let you live, you a fucking lawyer," said Slide in a lazy growl.

Raoul held the check between thumb and forefinger. "Keep the wallet," he said. "We gotta cash this check."

"Need identification," Slide said, smiling, not meaning it.

Raoul turned to the footlights. "You like this, Mary, you like this?"

Brandon blushed violently in that moment and turned away to the window, looked at the streets below.

Always fucking around, Slide thought. Always fucking around. Like a sissy himself. He slapped Cutler again on the head. The lawyer formed tears in his eyes.

The train slid into the Fullerton Avenue El station and stopped.

Sylvester Rose hit the doors. The doors all flicked open. There was nothing to be done.

The cold wind swirled into the car and the papers scattered.

Raoul said, "Fuck, get outta here."

And they were off, suddenly, running onto the wooden platform, and Willie slipped on a stubborn patch of ice. Raoul laughed, it was all right, better than they thought. Man, this was a fantastic night, he wasn't even cold, and Slide was wearing that crazy Russian hat and the two Marys were scared shitless. Fantastic night.

They ran down the steps two at a time, their footsteps echoing in the stillness. The wind died. All was calm and empty in the city all of a sudden.

At the bottom of the stairs, before they went through the steel combs of the exit turnstile, Raoul paused. He felt it, he wondered if they could feel it. Slide was smiling and staring at him. He felt it the way he'd feel it sometimes in craps, doubling and doubling, the bones going down the way they should, feeling those bones against the wall when they hit, knowing what the spots are going to say before they stop rolling on the sidewalk.

The train overhead began to grumble forward. In a moment, it flashed out of the station.

"Why we wait?" Willie said. But Slide said nothing.

And then they heard the footsteps on the stairs coming down from the platform.

"They comin' after us," Willie said.

"Shut up, asshole," Slide said. Slide knew. Slide knew Raoul a long time. Slide knew Raoul was going on instinct. Raoul's eyes were shining like he was drunk or high. Slide knew that Raoul was on a roll.

Raoul pulled the knife out of his field jacket and it was open, the light shining on the blade.

Raoul said, "Hey, Mary."

And plucked Brandon Cale by the sleeve. He pulled him into the shadow beneath the El tracks.

"Jesus," Brandon Cale said, his eyes wide, all the color drained now, his pale-blue eyes staring wildly. He saw the knife. Lee saw the knife. They all stood, saw the knife and watched it flash in the light of the orange anticrime street lamps.

"Don't move, don't say a thing," Raoul said in a soft voice. He was very close to Brandon. He held Brandon with his arm around his neck, a little behind him. He held the knife pressed to Brandon's cheek. "Don't move and don't get marked, Mary."

Brandon waited.

"Take the wallet," Raoul said.

Slide reached into Brandon's pocket and pulled out the wallet and slipped it into his field jacket.

"Take the money," Lee Herran said. He was very afraid, but it was not for himself in that moment. "Take the money."

"How about a kiss, Mary?" said Raoul, and he licked Brandon's ear and Brandon wriggled in the arm lock in that moment and Lee Herran stepped forward.

Raoul's knife blade cut Brandon's cheek because of the movement.

"See, I told you, Mary," Raoul said. His eyes were shining and everyone saw that. Everyone stared at his eyes and the knife blade and the blood on Brandon's cheek.

"Come on," said Slide, to be sensible, to think about how this might end up.

"You fucking Puerto Rican scumbag," Lee Herran said. His voice was flat, the words were flat and individual. Everyone stood still. Lee stepped forward. Raoul poked the knife point at him and the blade tore at the fabric of the topcoat.

Lee Herran hit Raoul in the face.

Raoul's arm dropped and Brandon, off balance, fell to one knee.

"Come on," said Slide, as if this was a dream he wanted to end. *Come on.*

Raoul said, "You fucking fairy princess."

Lee Herran had not meant to hit him.

Raoul pushed the point of the blade toward Lee's chest and held it there, resting against the fabric of his torn coat.

There was a smear of blood on Raoul's lips. He tasted his own blood.

"Bitch," Raoul said. "Son of a bitch, man made my mouth bleed."

Crazy eyes, thought Slide. "Let it slide," he said. Softly. "Let it slide."

And Raoul did it in one motion, the knife pushing through the fabric of the coat, through the corduroy sports coat beneath, through the cotton of the Brooks Brothers button-down shirt, through the nipple of Lee Herran's left breast.

Lee Herran stared at Raoul's shining crazy eyes.

Brandon looked up from one knee. All stood still, a freeze-frame from a ballet, with Raoul's arm out straight in front of him and Lee's arms wide, standing and staring.

"You just killed him, man," Willie said with wonder. He had only seen one man killed before.

Raoul's gray eyes became clear again. He pulled back and the knife slid back and Lee fell slowly to the ice-streaked sidewalk and the three of them were running then, pushing through the turnstile onto the street, running across Fullerton and then under the El tracks, their footsteps fading. Then there was stillness and cold. Then Brandon thought he heard another sound. It was his own screaming.

5
NUMBER 41

"You know how many this makes it?"

"I don't know," said the second cop.

"Depending on what they do out in Area Four tonight, this makes it forty-one. This is January twenty-sixth."

"Did you hear they got a pool in Area Five?"

"Is that right?"

"I heard it from Foley. The lieutenant found out about it and he didn't like it, but what was he going to do about it?"

"Is it for the year or what?"

"I guess for the calendar year."

"All homicides?"

"Yeah. It would be too complicated to sort out the murders and the others. There could be too much cheating."

"Yeah," said the first cop. "You know cops." They were standing on the sidewalk, by the police car. They had been the second team on the scene. They were from Town Hall District station on Halsted Street, which is contained in Area Six.

It was 12:30 A.M. Saturday.

The description of the killers was already on the street. The witness, Brandon Cale, was in the overheated street-level station, where a fire department paramedic was treating a cut on his face.

Sergeant Terry Flynn of Area Six Homicide stood over the body of Lee Herran, while Caffrey from the coroner's office gently probed beneath the clothing of the dead man, searching for wounds. There was wet blood on the front of the dead man's coat. The dead man was turned almost facedown on the sidewalk. His arms were bent under him, stiffening in death.

They stood protected a little from the wind by the El structure above and the south wall of the station itself. The street-level CTA station was warmed by a space heater that blasted out pockets of too hot air into too cold air spaces. Some of the policemen in the station were too warm. Their faces were flushed and their leather jackets were open and their light-blue uniform shirts were stained with sweat.

The two patrolmen behind Terry Flynn talked about the pool in Area Five on how many homicides would turn up in the city in the new year. One of them held the body bag. It was a matter of waiting on Flynn, who was in charge of the murder scene. It was cold and it was the middle of the night and there was nothing to do until Flynn let them close the scene and take the body to the morgue.

Terry Flynn stared down at the body of Lee Herran. The year that had ended twenty-seven days before had contained 812 homicides. He half listened to the two uniforms behind him and he stared at the body because he was trying to see the way it went down by the way the body was twisted in death. He had not talked to the witness yet.

Terry Flynn was dressed in a dirty trench coat with a cheap liner. He had bought the coat the year before at Field's and neglected to have it cleaned for too long, and now some of the stains of wear were imbedded deeply in the fabric. He wore a white shirt and a tie because all the officers in Homicide were "expected to dress like gentlemen." That was according to Homicide Commander Leonard Ranallo. Homicide was elite, Ranallo would explain to anyone who listened. Ranallo would not have been surprised to see Flynn's dirty coat because he was under no illusion that Flynn was a gentleman.

Flynn opened his twenty-nine-cent Woolworth's school notepad and took a pencil out of his shirt pocket and wrote down something. He had blue eyes set hard in a red Irish face. It was the kind of face that seemed to go looking for a fight and that implied a lack of patience. In fact, Terry Flynn was more complicated than he appeared to be.

"Just like a real detective," said one of the uniforms standing behind Terry Flynn.

Terry Flynn grinned at that. "You're watching a pro; it's an honor for you." Terry Flynn was a sergeant and the detective in charge of the murder scene and the commander of the moment. But he never let responsibilities weigh on him. He grinned at the uniform because it was something he might have said.

Lee Herran had fallen forward. His head had been bruised on the concrete. Lee Herran's eyes were open. His eyes were clear and blue. A good-looking kid, Terry Flynn thought.

Terry Flynn knelt.

He turned the body gently.

He looked at Caffrey kneeling next to him. They might have been at prayers. There was a lot of blood.

"Single wound," Caffrey said.

"A lot of blood," Terry Flynn said.

"Right through the heart, I would guess. Lucky hit," Caffrey said.

If it had been anyone but Caffrey, the remark would have been ironic. But Caffrey had no time for ironies. He was deeply involved in the business of violent death. It was all technical with him. He had been among the dead so long that he felt more comfortable in their presence. He smelled of the old morgue on Monroe Street, of the sweet chemicals and the odors of putrefaction. There was a move to upgrade the coroner's office into a medical examiner's office and to call the morgue the forensic institute. It would probably happen and it would still be the morgue and Caffrey would still be a coroner.

Sergeant Ernest Buchanan from Town Hall District station loomed over Flynn. Flynn rose and turned to him. He had been the first on the scene because he had been on his way to the Seminary restaurant down on the corner of Halsted Street for lunch. There had been no way for him to duck the call.

He was a large man with a face like boiled beef.

He knew Flynn. They had gone to the academy together and come up on the same promotion list. They had never been friends.

"Fags," said Buchanan. "Fag killing."

"Is that right?"

"The other one. The witness. Crying like a girl."

"How do girls cry, Ernie?"

"Come on, Terry."

"This was a fag killing?"

"These guys lived together. The dead one and the other one. You know. So maybe they were hitting on the killers, you know. Street kids react funny. The one inside says the killer, the shooter, he grabbed him, began to paw him. You talk to him, you're gonna find out they knew who these guys were."

"Just boys being boys, Ernie?"

"Terry, you're a pain in the ass."

"I know. Everyone tells me." He grinned. "I just don't really give a shit."

"So what do you think it is?"

"I know what it is. On the way down, I got it on the radio. CTA beef turned in when the train they were on got into Belmont Avenue station. Our three friends robbed some guy on the train and then waited down here to do more robbing. We got everything but fingerprints on these guys."

"These guys will be easy to find," Buchanan said.

"Yeah. Anything to make our job easier." He turned and looked at the body again. "Two of them wearing field jackets. I didn't know so many guys were in the army."

"Every street punk's got a field jacket."

"Yeah," Flynn said.

"That goes with what the witness said." Ernest Buchanan said it reluctantly. "You know, about these punks hassling people on the train. I didn't know there was a beef turned in yet."

"Yeah. Conductor named Rose and some guy named Cutler. Said they took a check from him. I didn't understand any of it but I didn't see the report."

They were standing over the body, talking, and Terry Flynn looked down then and saw that Lee Herran's dead eyes were staring at the sidewalk. He didn't like that, to be standing over the body, talking to Ernest Buchanan. There was no dignity in any of it. "Close it," he said to Caffrey. They understood. The two policemen who had been discussing the homicide pool in Area Five took the body bag and slapped it down on the sidewalk next to the body of Lee Herran. They lifted the body and placed it in the bag. They zipped the bag from toe to head. They lifted the bag and started to carry it through the station.

"Can't you go another way?" Terry Flynn said. "The witness is in the station."

"We can't get it through the turnstile. We'd have to walk it through the turnstile."

"Jesus Christ," Terry Flynn said.

"You can't figure fags," Ernest Buchanan said. "I been in Town Hall three years. Wall-to-wall fags over east, by Broadway. Fag heaven. Fags hanging from the trees. And kids, young boys, like someone's kids, selling themselves. Hang around the drugstore up by Diversey and Broadway. Between the nigger hookers and the fag hookers, I mean, it's a wall-to-wall meat market up there. Regular whores and fag whores and it's all who gives the best blow job. Whole fucking world seems like that sometimes, it drives you crazy."

"Just so you don't take your work home with you," Terry Flynn said.

They thought they heard a muffled scream or sob come from the station. The uniforms were carrying the body bag through the station to the squadrol waiting on the street. The police squadrol would take the body to the morgue. In Chicago, the fire department transports the living, the police get the dead.

"You're an asshole, you know that," Ernest Buchanan said.

"Yes. I know that. What's the name of the witness?"

"Brandon Cale. C-A-L-E. Cute name, huh? Like a girl's name."

"You been in Town Hall too long, Ernie," Terry Flynn said. Terry Flynn's blue eyes were dangerous now. He was tired of

Ernie, tired of winter, tired of working nights, tired of death.

"I just can't stand fags," Ernest Buchanan said.

"No kidding."

"You're an asshole, you know that?" Buchanan had a limited and vehement vocabulary. He sometimes repeated slurs in case the listener hadn't heard them the first time.

"Maybe I'll see you in Huey's someday on Madison Street and you'll say that, and maybe you'll wish you hadn't said that, Ernie," Terry Flynn said. He said it so softly that the threat carried weight between them and they both felt it and they both backed off.

Terry Flynn went into the station. It was too hot. He started to sweat and opened his coat and he wiped his face with one large hand and ran his thick fingers through his red hair. He lit a Lucky Strike and looked at Brandon Cale.

Cale had cried, Buchanan said. But Cale's eyes were dry now and they were wide and pale blue and as dead as Lee Herran's eyes.

Brandon Cale sat in the ticket cage used during the rush hours. The second ticket cage opposite was occupied by a large black woman who stared at him. The ticket seller was Leona Johnson and she had not wanted them to bring the witness into her small overheated domain and had resisted opening the second ticket cage to give Brandon a place to sit and wait while he was being treated. The police had ended up calling the night CTA supervisor before she acted. While that small drama had gone on, Brandon Cale had stood in the shadows by the shuttered newsstand, staring and not seeing the cops arguing with Leona Johnson. He only saw Lee Herran fall. He only heard Lee's voice. They had been on the train, the doors were open, the punks had fled down the steps. "It's all right," Lee had said. "They're gone," Lee had said.

Terry Flynn's bulk was framed in the narrow entry of the ticket cage. The paramedic from the fire department had put a bandage on his cheek.

"You done?" Flynn said in a low growl that spoke of beer and cigarettes and long hours.

The fireman nodded. "He should go to Henrotin, get that stitched, get a tetanus."

"I don't want to go to the hospital," Brandon Cale said. His voice was soft. He stared at the large frame of Terry Flynn.

"Cut like that can scar you, kid," said the paramedic who was not really old enough to call anyone "kid." He closed his bag. "The other thing is the knife. These fucking dopeheads, you don't know about the knife. How clean it is."

"I don't want to go to the hospital," Brandon said. The voice came from somewhere outside him, Brandon thought. It wasn't his voice. He was still behind the present, with Lee Herran, still sitting on the El train with the doors open, deciding if it was safe.

It's not safe.

The paramedic brushed past Flynn out of the cage and Flynn waited a moment. He said, "I'm Sergeant Flynn with Homicide. I'm sorry we had to carry the body out through the station but there was no other way."

Brandon blinked, listened, the words did form some meaning. He blinked again.

"Robbers. I think they were only robbers. At first," Brandon Cale said. His voice was soft but it was deep and it would deepen with age. He began to tell what had happened on the train in the thirteen minutes between Chicago Avenue station in the subway, when the three had boarded, and Fullerton Avenue station on the elevated.

"I told Lee not to get off. I said, 'Let's go to the next stop, we can get off and come back, what if they're waiting for us.' I had this feeling. On the train. They . . ."

Flynn said nothing. He waited. Matt Schmidt had taught him that in Homicide. You never speak unless you have to. You wait. You make the silence part of the question. You have all the time in the world.

"He called me 'Mary.' You know. On the train."

"Did he do anything?"

"He was smiling. A crazy kind of smile."

"Which one?"

"The light one. Might have been a Negro with light skin. He

wasn't white, I don't think. Maybe he was Italian. No. I know now. Raoul. His name was Raoul. That's the name I heard. I just thought of it. I didn't tell anyone that before, I didn't think of it."

"It's OK. You'll remember other stuff in time. You just let me know. It doesn't matter if you remember everything right at the same time, just so you remember it right."

"Raoul," said Brandon Cale, repeating a magic word.

"Did you ever see them before?"

Silence. There was a heaviness of waiting between them. The space heater *tick-tick-ticked* to itself as the fan whirred on and waited for the gentle *bumph* of the gas ignition. Leona Johnson, her face curious and angry, stared from her cage into their cage.

"No." Weary. "No." Silence. "No, they look like the kind of people you see all the time on the street. You just never look at them close because then they say, 'Hey, you lookin' at something?' You know?"

"Yeah. I just want you to think about what they look like, about whether you saw them before, whether they could have seen you before. You or Lee Herran. If they might have known who you were."

"I don't know." Silence. "I can't think. Oh. Lee called Raoul a Puerto Rican. Scum. That set him off. So he was a Puerto Rican."

"Maybe. Maybe that's so."

"I remember things in little bits and pieces. I remember we're sitting on the El. If we only had stayed on the El. Jesus Christ, if we only had stayed on the El, what would it matter if we went a couple of blocks out of our way, there was another train, if we only stayed there . . ."

"It wasn't you. It wasn't that," Terry Flynn said. The growl was low, almost soft. "It happens and there's nothing you can do about it."

"Lee did it because 'Raoul' had me around the neck. He wanted to . . ."

Terry Flynn waited. It was very hard to do it this way. Matt Schmidt had shown him how to do it. It was a technique, like learning surgery and the best way to slice open a belly. Like in Nam, learning how to set a booby trap. It was a technique and

33

he saw that Brandon was shivering but he had to wait and say nothing.

"He licked my ear. He called me 'Mary' again."

"Are you a homosexual?" Terry Flynn said.

"Yes," Brandon Cale said.

"Why did Raoul know that?"

Brandon looked up, blinked. The eyes were wide, still. "I don't know. I suppose. I suppose I look like a homosexual to him, I suppose." The words were bitten off, the deep voice was a little deeper.

Terry Flynn merely stared.

"A fag," Brandon Cale said. "Like one of the cops said. One of your cops said."

"What do you do?"

"Do? About what? What do you mean?"

"Where do you work?"

"At Kidd and Blethold. Traders. At the midwest Stock Exchange. Lee works at Blye and Levin. We got to know each other down there. We always took Friday night to go to Binyan's, for two drinks, drink with the big shots. But it was too cold tonight. We had four drinks there. Or five. And if we had gone home. . . . And instead . . ."

He unfolded the story in a slow and broken and painful way. Circumstance piled on circumstance to put them on the train at that time, on that night. Brandon Cale turned each circumstance over as he laid it out, as though to see a reason why all these particular circumstances on this particular night conspired to put him and Lee in danger of their lives.

Flynn listened, and sometimes he wrote something down in a notebook and sometimes he merely waited, holding the Lucky Strike in hand, letting the blue smoke curl up to the ceiling of the old, shacklike station. It was past one in the morning. Now and then someone would enter the station, see the police standing around, push past them, stare at Flynn and Brandon Cale, pay a fare and go through the doors to the tracks above. The space heater went *bumph* and the hot air poured into the room.

Ernest Buchanan chased some of the cops back to patrol.

The scene was breaking up. Caffrey was on his way back to the morgue where he would open the body of Lee Herran and examine the wound and write a long report on the cause of death and file it with the other reports and go on to the next body. Buchanan lingered at the cage where Brandon Cale told his story, and he stared hard at Brandon for a long time. He broke a silence at last.

"Why would you get involved, kid? I mean, get involved with something like this?" Ernest Buchanan said. His face was screwed into a question. His eyes looked truly puzzled.

Brandon stared at him. "You mean, why be a fag? That's what you mean? You said this was a fag thing."

So it was Ernie Bucktooth, Terry Flynn thought. He looked at Ernest Buchanan. A credit to his race.

"Sergeant? Can I have a word with you? Just wait here a minute, Brandon." He used the first name in the overly familiar way of all policemen. He took Ernest Buchanan gently by one arm. He turned Ernest toward the station door. They stepped outside onto the sidewalk. There were two police cars still parked at crazy angles on Fullerton Avenue, Mars lights flashing blue in the chill night air. There were still a few gawkers but not many people hung around because of the cold.

"Sergeant," Terry Flynn began.

"I just wanted to ask him."

"This is a homicide, Sergeant, I don't give a flying fuck what you wanted to ask him. You want to know about queers, go read the Kinsey report."

"I never heard of it."

"Why the fuck are these cops all around here still? This a fucking convention?"

"That's my business—"

"No, asshole." Softly. So no one but Ernest Buchanan could hear. "You get on the fucking street and send these boys back to their nice warm squads and get the fuck out of my life."

"Really, *sergeant*? Really, Sergeant Flynn?"

"Really, Ernie. Really."

They waited, felt it between them again, let it go. Buchanan turned and realized he had not lost any face except one to one with Flynn and he thought about the consequences because Terry Flynn was crazy, Terry Flynn would just as soon start something right there on the street, rolling around on the sidewalk, a couple of sergeants heading very quickly for a review board. But there would be another time and place.

In less than five minutes, the squads were gone, the fire department ambulance was gone, the coroner's car was gone, the evidence technicians were gone. Only Flynn's battered Dodge four-door sedan unmarked police car was sitting in the no-parking zone in front of Fullerton station. There were bloodstains left on the walk by the turnstile but no one would notice them in the morning, and in a few days the thousands of feet that scraped through the station every twenty-four hours would have scrubbed them off.

"Come on," Terry Flynn said to Brandon Cale.

"Where are you taking me?"

"You wanna get coffee?"

"I don't want nothing. I want to go home." And then he stopped and he realized it was exactly what he did not want. He stood very still and Terry Flynn watched him. Terry felt the sense of being alone that had come over Brandon in that moment. Terry had not seen Karen Kovac for three weeks because of the hateful overnight shift, because Homicide Commander Leonard Ranallo was riding Terry, pushing him to ask for a transfer out of Homicide, and Karen Kovac was a person on a telephone and not real anymore. He could feel a sense of being alone in winter in a hostile city, even though he had lived in Chicago all his life.

"I know that's what you don't want to do right now," he said.

"You're right. I couldn't stand it."

"I know a place, we can go there, we can have coffee."

"I don't want any goddam coffee," Brandon Cale said. His voice was large and deep and he felt he was on the edge of something. He stood very still because he was right at the edge.

"Good," Terry Flynn said. "I know a place that doesn't have coffee too."

6
ON THE
STREETS

Raoul picked up the Quaaludes from a guy who seemed to be waiting for him at the northeast corner of Humboldt Park. The guy was a walking drugstore. The old city park was in the heart of the Puerto Rican corridor that ran out from the edge of Lincoln Park's gentrified neighborhood all the way to Cicero Avenue.

The 'ludes brought them happiness or something just like it.

At least the 'ludes helped them to see the killing with a whole new perspective.

It was just after three on Saturday morning and Lee Herran had been dead for three hours.

Even Willie was getting into a new perspective on murder. 'Ludes usually just made Willie happy so that he'd want to sleep or fuck the first pig he saw. Now Willie was getting into it.

"Good, feeling very good, very positive," said Slide in the car.

"I told you I knew this was a fabulous night," Raoul said in that voice that strummed like the higher chords on a guitar. "Fabulous."

"Fabulous," Willie agreed in the backseat. He was really understanding the whole thing in a whole new way.

Brand-new cream Cadillac, a Seville, had less than a thousand miles on it, sitting right out there where someone could take it, on Webster Avenue just west of St. Vincent's Church. Imagine. Brand-new, smelled new inside, the way a car smells. Willie did this thing where he was sniffing the leather seat, said he could describe the girl who sat there. It was so funny they laughed until they were out of breath.

Slide was just half down in the front passenger seat, his eyes resting nicely on the scenery. City streets in a warm car looked good and empty and open like fields. Everything was orange light and orange shadows. Slide had to admit it wasn't the worst thing after all, about sticking the fag. Wasn't the worst thing that could happen. And Raoul knew how to pick some wheels, he could drive, sucker could really drive. Handled it like he owned Caddies all his life.

"You drive like you owned a Caddie all your life," said Slide.

Raoul felt oddly proud that his close friend Slide would say that. Buddies from St. Charles reform days. "I dunno," Raoul said with humility born of pride. "It must be some gift, I always could drive, you know, handle the big-ticket items on the road, but in the city, dig, I drive cool, never got a ticket."

"It's good you got no ticket 'cause you got no license," said Willie.

Willie was funny tonight, Slide thought. Like sniffing the seat. Willie was never funny and it showed what kind of a night it was turning out to be. Like Raoul said, a fabulous night.

"I got me a license, dude, it just ain't renewed is all, I been busy," Raoul said. They were cruising east along Division Street. The seats were littered with bills and the wallets. Raoul had the cashier's check neatly folded in the pocket of his field jacket.

"Man of affairs," grunted Slide.

"Check it out," Willie said, giggling.

God, it was funny, that kind of night. Willie handed the bottle of Myers's rum to the front seat and Slide poured some on top of the 7-Up in his McDonald's paper cup. There were still ice cubes in the cup.

"So what's the dude's address?"

"I tole you before," said Willie. "Now I got to find it again."

Willie had the wallets. Most of the cash was gone. There had been more than a hundred dollars. They still had the credit cards. They had the 'ludes to pay for and they picked up one of the PR hookers off North Avenue down by the brewery and drove around for a while to one of the driveways to the deserted factories along Clybourn, off the river. She did Raoul twice; Raoul said he was in love with that mouth and Slide was even laughing that the bitch had a mouth on her. She got scared after a while because they all were really into all kinds of things. And it was dark. She was a tough mama but these were tough boys. She said she wanted some green finally like they said, and they kicked her out on the street and Raoul said he'd cut her tits off. And he was laughing. He said he'd killed somebody just that night.

Slide didn't like that.

"You gotta big mouth, Raoul," Slide had said.

"Bitch has got a pussy mouth," Raoul said.

Willie said, "Wasn't thinking about her, Raoul, you be thinking of that pussy mouth on that dude you wanted, the one you cut."

"I cut both of them Marys," Raoul had said.

"You wanted both of them."

And that was when they started thinking about the address in the wallet, the address where the Mary must live and how he was the witness that they had killed the other one. Not that the other one didn't have it coming, making those slurs.

Slide had been cool inside St. Charles, by himself, not playing any games. When Raoul came in, some of the gangs wanted to make him a sissy. Raoul had a sissy look to him, he was small and light, and Raoul got out of it by being crazy. It was all an act with Raoul. That's what Raoul said to Slide later, when they were friends, when they did some shit together. That's what Raoul said but sometimes Slide was not so sure.

Raoul said he wanted to kill the other one.

Slide thought about it. It didn't seem like a bad idea. Kill the other one and that cleans it up. Besides, a couple of fairies, who gives a shit about them anyway?

"You don't want to kill him, you just want to fuck him," Slide said now.

"Yeah. That too. You think I'm crazy?"

"You crazy, Raoul."

"Ain't nothing sillier than a crazy nigger call a crazy spic crazy."

They laughed at that as well.

Willie always laughed with them but he was always a little late in laughing and a little on the outside. He understood that was the way it was going to be. Willie was white trash from Kentucky, the way Slide put it. He had been around four years. He'd been inside once, in County Jail, not St. Charles, waiting trial on attempted rape, though Willie knew there wasn't no "attempted" about it, he just did his thing too fast. He'd been scared of spooks when he came to Chicago first time, there were so damned many of them and they weren't like niggers down home. But this one nigger on the tier inside County had taken him under his wing, which was all right because the nigger gangs wanted his ass. He had to make adjustments a bit for the big nigger who took care of him, but that was to be expected to save his ass.

"He live on Lill Street," said Willie.

It was just after 3:30 when they pulled off Sheffield Avenue north of DePaul University—less than a block from the Fullerton Avenue El station—down Lill Street. Lill was a short street that ended at Racine in a children's playlot. There were two-flats and homes on the block and at the end of the block was a large apartment building.

Raoul tooled the Cadillac into a space behind a battered Dodge sedan.

"So, you thinking you want to do this," said Slide, who was trying to think around the idea in the face of feeling so good from the 'ludes.

"I'm thinking," said Raoul.

"That boy'd be surprised to see us again," Willie said. "Twice in one night."

"Twice in one night," Raoul repeated with a silly look on his face.

"Let check me the boy's name in the hall," said Raoul. The engine was running, the car was warm. Raoul opened the door and got out and slammed it. He walked around the front of the big car and crossed to the sidewalk. Dirty snow was piled in ice hills at the curbs. He stepped lightly on the crunchy snow. He entered the apartment building and checked the mailboxes. He sauntered back, smiling, his beret worn cocky on his head.

He opened the door and slid in.

"Brandon Cale. And Lee Herran must be the dude I stuck."

"He's there," Willie said, letting the breath go out of him.

They thought of it.

And then Slide's eyes went wide and he spoke very quickly, *"Get out of here, man, get outta here now."*

Raoul was shocked alert. He knew Slide. Slide was cool, Slide never talked like that, he was cool enough to let things pass, which is why he was called Slide. But when it came down to it, Slide knew he could move.

Raoul dropped the car into drive with a clunk and hit the gas and twisted the wheel, and the Caddie squealed from the curb down to Racine, slid through the stop sign, and headed north toward Lincoln Avenue.

"All right now." Slide's soft voice. "Be cool now. Everything cool."

"What'd you see, man?"

They were all holding their breath, they were waiting on Slide.

"Car," Slide said in a soft voice. "Car we was behind on Lill. I was staring at it and I didn't see it and then I seen it."

"What was it?"

"Poh-leese. Motherfuckin' poh-leese. Dodge we was behind. The Dodge was a poh-leese car and I didn't see it. I was staring at the plate. Begin Z and an A, always poh-leese plates, that was an unmarked car, the poh-leese upstairs waiting for us. Poh-leese up waiting with that fag for us."

"Sheeeet," Willie said in a whistle.

"Poh-leese," Slide said.

"Waiting," Raoul said. "Boy telling them about us. Poh-leese waiting."

Slide smiled then. "Or knocking off some of it they own selves."

And they all smiled at that, to think about cops doing that.

7
KAREN AND
MARY JANE

Karen Kovac dressed in the gloom of her bedroom. The heat was banging up through the steam pipes to the radiators in all the rooms of the apartment. Her son was still asleep in his own room because it was Saturday morning and he had no school. Since he had started high school, he slept all the time. Tim was growing as well, alarmingly fast. He was taller than Karen. He was nearly as tall as Terry Flynn. Tim was thirteen.

Karen Kovac pulled the zipper up on her gray skirt and then sat down on the edge of the bed to slip into the black leather boots. She cleaned them every night, wiping off the salt liberally sprinkled on sidewalk and streets all winter long. They had to last this one more winter.

The pistol was kept in a locked drawer in her vanity table. The ammunition was in a locked box inside her closet. She loaded the pistol and put the .38-caliber nickel-plate Smith & Wesson in her black leather purse. The purse also carried her identification, keys, money and handcuffs. She carried the can of Mace in the pocket of her tan raincoat with the heavy liner.

She put on lipstick as the last thing before putting on her coat. Her lipstick was bright red. She looked at herself in the mirror of the vanity and formed her lips. She had high cheekbones and cloudless blue eyes that seemed to see things too clearly. She had been working days in Special Squad for three months, and now she had been dispatched to this rape thing because all the papers were writing too much about it. She didn't like this kind of investigation. She felt too alone on it.

And there was not seeing Terry anymore. It was all to do with Leonard Ranallo. Ranallo had transferred Terry Flynn off Special Squad into Area Six because Area Six was shorthanded. But every area in the department was shorthanded and Matt Schmidt knew what it was about but there was nothing he could do about it.

Leonard Ranallo had it in for Terry Flynn and if he could push Terry Flynn enough, he could push him right out of Homicide and back into uniform.

They had last seen each other once three weeks before when their days off coincided. They had spent the day making love and talking to each other. They had been lovers for two years and it wasn't going anywhere, which suited both of them. At least one of them.

The purse with the pistol was heavy. She dropped her lipstick in it and the tube clattered against the pistol barrel.

It was raining mixed with sleet. The morning rubbed gloom against the windows. She went to the windows in the living room and looked down on the dismal courtyard with the bare trees below and the brown patches of matted dead grass. It was a three-story building in the shape of a deep U opening to the quiet of Kostner Avenue. They had lived in the second-floor apartment for seven years. Since the divorce. She and Tim. She crossed the living room, compulsively straightening the stacked copies of *Time* magazine on the coffee table. She went into the hall and listened for a moment. She opened his bedroom door.

"Going," she said.

"Mmmphfh," he groaned, turned, pulling the covers off.

She crossed the room and dragged the covers across his body. Gangly and dangly. Little Tim. "Going," she said softly.

"Mmmm," he said in his sleep.

Mary Jane Caldwell lived on Wellington Avenue in a large, anonymous apartment building two blocks west of the Belmont

Harbor section of Lincoln Park. Karen Kovac took the Drive along the lake down to the Belmont exit and turned west. The lake was coated with ice that extended out nearly a mile. Beyond was the gray and open sea. A final freighter of the shipping season through the St. Lawrence Seaway was heading south toward Calumet Harbor. The freighter was painted against the gray horizon, flat against the flat gray clouds, an apparition in the rain and sleet that fell lightly on the city. Sleet wasn't the worst thing; snow was always the worst thing.

Mary Jane Caldwell opened the door after Karen repeated her name. They had talked twice before, in the hospital. It had been pretty bad in the hospital. Mary Jane opened the door after turning three locks and dropping a chain.

In the case of rape, there are tests that are not pleasant. Karen Kovac was there from the beginning and she knew what the procedures were. There was nothing to be done about it and Mary Jane had resented her indifference. Karen had been too tough. They both knew it after a while but they both seemed locked into roles they didn't wish to play. Mary Jane Caldwell had been fearful and the role grew on her long after the fear had ended. Karen realized she wanted to put Mary Jane's problem a little distance away from herself because she could find it too easy to sympathize with her rape. There were rapes and there were rapes. They were all different, but this one could have touched Karen Kovac if she let it touch her. She just had to be hard with Mary Jane and the woman resented it.

The doctor wasn't too gentle; he put distance between himself and Mary Jane as well. There is the matter of combing through pubic hairs for signs of foreign hairs. There is the matter of the pelvic examination, the matter of finding traces of sperm. There are a number of procedures to be followed and they were all followed, and at the end of them Mary Jane Caldwell began screaming. She screamed, and when nothing could be done about the screaming, they had to restrain her and give her a measure of sedation and affix IV tubes to her to feed her. She slept for a restless day and night. When they thought she wouldn't scream anymore, they let her go home. It was Friday afternoon when she went home.

Now it was the next morning, Saturday, January 27.

Mary Jane Caldwell opened the door of her studio apartment.

It was a large and light room. There was a kitchenette behind sliding doors on one wall. The bed was a studio couch full of red pillows. It had not been slept in. Karen Kovac saw these things very quickly and smiled and said she would like coffee when Mary Jane asked her.

Mary Jane was dressed in jeans and a heavy baggy sweater and her dark hair was pulled straight back from her very Irish, very handsome face. Her eyes had life in them again.

She had a large bruise beneath her right eye where she had been hit. There were bruises on her body as well. She walked stiffly to the table where a Mr. Coffee machine sat. The doctor had explained that the soreness would take a while to go away. He said it was like the soreness some women had after childbirth. He had said these things not to be callous or unkind. She had asked him if she might be pregnant. He had said probably not. He explained to her that it was the usual procedure to give a massive hormone injection after a rape. He had given her the injection while she was hysterical. He explained it very simply. The hormone injection would probably destroy an impregnated egg in her if the egg had been fertilized. And that depended on her time of month. He explained it all as simply as a kindergarten teacher explaining the alphabet. This was intended to soothe her. She thought about that, about taking a shot to have an abortion. She used that word, *abortion*. The doctor had been distracted and he had said, yes, he supposed it was an abortion, he never thought of it that way. There was still a chance she might become pregnant. He said it was a matter of wait and see. He said she should have a full pelvic examination again in another month or sooner if there appeared to be an infection or any unusual discharge.

Now on a rainy Saturday in dirty winter, they sat at the table across from each other. The table was by the window. The table was plain wood stained dark and there was a pot of flowers on it.

"My father came last night but I didn't want him to stay. He called me this morning."

"How was it?" Karen asked.

"I didn't sleep, if that's what you mean."

"Yes." Karen paused and stared at Mary Jane's eyes. They seemed very bright, very intense. "You had pills. You should have slept. You can't not sleep."

"No. I'll sleep. In the afternoon. While it's light. I sleep when it's light. I can't sleep when it's dark. I fell asleep yesterday in the afternoon and I woke up and it was nighttime out."

Karen Kovac watched her. She could think of nothing to say. Mary Jane sat very still and her eyes were very bright.

"You'll get over this," Karen said. She did not want to say it.

"No," Mary Jane said. "You never will get over something like this. I see it now. I understand what it must be like for other women. I really understand it now. I never—you know?"

Mary Jane almost smiled but there was no warmth. Her eyes were hard and they were pushing at Karen. "I was a virgin. What do you think of that?"

Karen said nothing again because that was the only answer.

"A virgin. I knew what I was. I mean, I knew I was a virgin but no one else knew. I grew up in Algonquin. My father—my father is an old man." She said this very hard. "A lawyer. He was a lawyer. He made a lot of money. He didn't want me to move down to Chicago. He said it wasn't the same city it had been. He said it was dangerous. You grow up in a little town like Algonquin, I mean, you don't really know. You watch these people on television, on the news, these horrible people, these scum . . ."

The word jarred Karen. It was a learned word in Mary Jane's vocabulary.

"I had boyfriends. You might be surprised. About not going all the way."

The vocabulary was so strange to Karen. She blinked and saw Mary Jane more clearly.

"I could touch them," Mary Jane said.

Karen wanted to shut her eyes and put her hands over her ears. Karen sat still.

"They want to feel better," she said. Her voice was very cold now. "Wet their pants even." And the smile faded in and out. "Do you think about it? I mean, about men, about what they really are? They just want satisfaction. Release almost. That's what they want. It's not so much pleasure they want, they just want release, they'll do anything for it."

"Mary Jane." She had to stop this. The voice was too cold, too even. "We have some photographs downtown. We'd like you to look at them."

It was as though Mary Jane had been in a reverie. She moved, her eyes shifted, she stared at Karen as though seeing the policewoman for the first time.

"You do this all the time," Mary Jane said.

"Not really," Karen said.

"But this is what you do."

"Yes."

"So you get used to it."

"No. You try to stay away from it so that it doesn't get to you. But that's not the same thing as getting used to it."

"I really want to kill them. I could kill them myself. I used to shoot, I used to have a gun—I was on the high-school team. Imagine having a shooting team in high school. I used to wonder if I could shoot something real, other than a paper target. My father grew up around guns, he loved them. He used to hunt. He's too old now. He took me hunting with him and when he killed the deer, it made me sick. I tried not to be sick but it made me sick. That pleased him, I think, to make me sick."

"I understand."

"Are you a virgin?"

"I have a son."

"But then you don't know," Mary Jane said. "I really wish they could be killed."

Cold rain streaked the windows. The little morning light was too small for the room.

"My father wants me to go home with him. Stay with him. I know what that would be like. He would look at me all the time just the way he looked at me when he took me deer hunting that one time. It gave him pleasure to see that I was sick from killing that deer."

"Maybe you should go home for a little while. This apartment . . . It's too lonely for you now."

"When I was naked; the policemen who came saw me naked. They looked at me. It was the same look. The look my father gave me when I was sick. That's the way they look at you. The way men look at women, even their daughters."

"No," Karen said.

"But you know it's true," Mary Jane said, her voice strong and stubborn. And Karen felt frightened. By the voice. By the shining eyes. And because she knew that it might be true.

8
BETWEEN
US

Lee Herran was eight hours dead.

Saturday morning was sleet and rain and dawn held off.

It was a mourning rain and it fell straight down in large drops and splattered on the flat city roofs.

Eight hours and no arrests. It should have been easier than it was turning out to be.

Terry Flynn sat crumpled inside the Dodge at the curb in the no-parking zone in front of the Snow White Grill on Clark Street. He sipped the scalding black coffee in the Styrofoam cup.

Coffee without cream was just hot water, he thought. He was carrying fifteen pounds too many and black coffee was part of the price he was paying. He had worked out twice this week in the gym at Area Six, especially on the punching bag. He thought the bag was Leonard Ranallo and it let him hit harder.

In a little while, the street colored gray. It was as light as it was going to be.

On the seat next to him were the morning papers. The January 27 *Tribune* had a story on page three, the *Sun-Times* had a story on page one. They had descriptions. They had wanted an artist's sketch, but the police art department was closed down on Friday night. They would have to wait until Monday morning for a sketch. And the sketch would end up looking like ten thousand dudes wearing field jackets.

His shoulders ached in the rain. He had noticed the ache first when he was in Vietnam that long and terrible year. He had noticed that the rainy season made the ache worse and made his feet itch and turn red and blister. It was something about the rain.

Karen was supposed to be off today but now she was on a special. A rape. So it was another week they wouldn't see each other.

Terry felt the way he had felt sometimes in the army. There was a kind of waiting you had to endure until something opened up. He was better at it now than when he was younger. Matt Schmidt had taught him waiting in the three years he had been connected to Matt's Special Squad, in the time he had met Karen, in the time he had become her lover.

Lover.

He rolled down the window and threw the cup out and it splashed on a passing blue-and-white squad. The squad stopped and backed up and the cop in the front passenger seat rolled down the window.

It was Hauptman.

"You fucking slob, you don't respect the star or the office, at least respect city property," Hauptman said.

"Pigs. Is that Kelly? Hey, Kelly, when did you and The Boy Wonder get out of Area Two?"

"Two months ago. I like Town Hall. I hear you picked up that killing at Fullerton. That wasn't even our district but that dumb fuck Ernie Buchanan pulled it."

"I know. I saw him. Always a pleasure to work with the flying Scotchman."

"What are you doing sitting here? You waiting for a free hooker to come in out of the rain?"

"Yeah. I feel lucky."

A horn sounded behind the double-parked squad. The two uniforms ignored it. The horn sounded again and then sped around.

"Asshole," said Kelly. "He's got the whole fucking street."

"People are inconsiderate," said Terry Flynn, who felt better. He had spent the night with assholes like Buchanan or with broken people like Brandon Cale. He felt better talking to Kelly and Hauptman. They were all right. They had all worked together in better days in Grand Crossing District down on the South Side, when it seemed the sides were drawn cleaner and easier.

"We got the description at roll call but I'm surprised our three players haven't shown up yet," Kelly said.

"Of course, they sound like every three-legged alligator on the street," said Hauptman.

"It was a fag killing is what Bucky says."

"It was a straight hit," Terry Flynn said. He had taken Brandon to a bar on west Fullerton, at the edge of the Puerto Rican neighborhood where no one knew either of them, except the bartender knew right away that Flynn had to be a cop. He walked into a place like a cop. They had drunk beer and Flynn had tried to talk to Brandon and to get him drunk at the same time. But nothing worked. He took Brandon home to the place on Lill Street. He said he'd be in touch with him. He saw that Brandon wasn't drunk enough to sleep. He had wanted to find out if Brandon would do something crazy like kill himself. He had decided that Brandon wouldn't kill himself. At least, not the first night.

"Two guys were fags," said Kelly, who did not approve of homosexual conduct, blacks, liberals and the *Chicago Daily News*. "The victims were fags."

"Not the guy on the train they robbed. They took a cashier's check off him," Terry said. "I went to his place at four in the morning, he's catching zees, his wife is more than happy to wake him up for me. A stone bitch. The guy on the train is a lawyer named Mark Cutler."

"Cutler?" Hauptman said. "I went against him two months ago on an armed-robbery beef. It's the same Cutler, it's got to be."

"Big guy, fat face."

"The same dirty motherfucking son of a bitch," Hauptman agreed.

"Jesus Christ, watch your language," Kelly said, meaning no irony.

There was another horn behind them, this time from a bus.

"Go around, you goddam nigger," Kelly said.

The bus lurched around the double-parked squad and the driver hit the horn as he passed.

"Assholes," Kelly said.

"He drives a bus because he wants to be Irish," Hauptman said. Hauptman liked Kelly because Kelly was so transparent. Every needle stuck deep. It passed the time for both of them.

"Cutler talked to me, said he saw the two queers get on with him at Grand Avenue. There wasn't any connection between the victim and the players," Terry Flynn said.

"Yeah. Well. I wouldn't ride the fucking El at night. Three rapes in three weeks on the CTA, two on buses and that one a couple of days ago up at Jarvis station up in Rogers Park. Was it Thursday?"

"Wednesday. Karen got the case."

"Ah," said Hauptman in a mock voice. "De big Special Squad strikes again. De big SS, as in Super Sucks. Your old stomping ground. How do it feel for you all to be just a peasant again, Terry? Just out here in the field with us foot soldiers?"

"Feels great to be leading you men again," Terry Flynn said, smiling. It felt much better all of a sudden, even if it was a bad day full of rain and he wouldn't be seeing Karen. Kelly and Hauptman put everything in perspective. He had felt, for a while, talking to Brandon Cale about life in Decatur and what he did on the stock exchange and how he had met Lee Herran, that he was going too close to the edge, that he was getting dizzy and that the night was closing around him.

"I hear that Ranallo had you sent up to Six," Hauptman said in that mischievous way, putting the needle in. "They were even talking about it down on the South Side."

"Yeah, fuck him," Terry said.

"And the loo put you on the dead shift," said Hauptman.

"Yeah, and fuck him too. He just wants to suck up to Ranallo's wienie. Fuck the dago."

"You've got a lot of hate in you, boy," Hauptman said.

"Yeah. Well. It's been a long night and it doesn't look like it's getting over."

"Hey, baby." Hauptman leaped into black dialect. "You shift is over, baby."

"It's over when it's over," Terry said. "I got to see a man in headquarters about these guys. I don't see how these guys can still be on the street."

"They look like all the other players," Hauptman said. "You get so all the players look alike."

"But this wasn't what Bucky said it was," Flynn said. "You just pass it around, would you? Kelly? Tell everyone this was a John Q, an innocent, that bought it, that it didn't have anything to do with anything Bucky thinks about in his wet dreams. I'd appreciate it. I don't want it put in the dead-letter file and I'd appreciate it."

Hauptman looked away. "Sure," he said. Fun time was over. Flynn was being serious again. "Sure," he said, as though speaking for Kelly. "I don't take Bucky serious anyway. Nobody does."

"No. But with his mouth, he puts the case in a bad light right away, and a week from now we're not going to find these guys because nobody's gonna give a shit about it."

"You give a shit."

"I just need to clear it," said Terry Flynn.

"You turning fag?"

"Yeah," Flynn said. "Three weeks without seeing Karen, I got to do something."

"I can let you have Kelly's *Penthouse*. He takes it in the bathroom with him," Hauptman said.

Kelly blushed and Flynn smiled. The needle went deep with Kelly, no matter what you said to him. But he never resented it after. That's what made it all right about Kelly. "That's a lot of crap," Kelly said.

"Between us," Flynn said, "I'd like to clear this real fast.

This is an easy one and that's why I think it might get lost."

"Yeah," said Hauptman. He was suddenly bored by it. Another horn behind him. "Fuck the motoring public," Hauptman said. "See you 'round, Terry."

"See you, Ter," said Kelly.

"Yeah," said Terry Flynn, rolling up the window.

Sergeant Leroy Sims was not in a good mood. That was part of his professional demeanor. He was big and black and he liked to scare people. He had worked in Gangs Intelligence Unit for three years. He told Terry Flynn he thought he knew who he was talking about even before Terry Flynn finished.

It was still raining. It was mid-morning. Leroy Sims had been awakened at home by Flynn at 6:00. That had put him in a worse mood. He wasn't due into the unit until 10:00. He had agreed to compromise on 9:00 A.M. Which is why Flynn had been sipping his breakfast coffee on Clark Street an hour earlier, waiting for the appointment with Sims.

"That's gotta be my boy, Raoul," rumbled Leroy Sims. He had a thin smile. "Raoul be a bad dude."

"Is that right?" Terry Flynn had called Leroy at home because Leroy owed him for a couple of things they never talked about. It was enough that Leroy knew and Leroy was willing to come down early to do the favor of looking through his files and his memory of bad dudes who might have killed Lee Herran nine hours earlier at the Fullerton El station.

Leroy Sims went to a green metal file case on one ghastly green wall in the dirt-streaked office. GIU was in a room on the southwest side of the police building at Eleventh and State streets. You could see the El curling toward the South Side below the sixth-floor window. In the summer, when it was hot and all the windows were open, the El twisted on the tracks below and you could hear it all day long, until you had to get out of the building just for a little quiet.

The file drawer was full of papers mashed into manila folders. Some of the papers were flimsies of arrest reports and there were GIU "street cards" on suspected gang members and anyone else stopped by a curious policeman. There were a lot of small photographs clipped from arrest pictures. The city was crawling with gangs, it had always been that way; only the faces and nationalities had changed. The old Irish and German gangs had grown up into politics and churchgoing respectability. The old Italian gangs had formed the crime syndicates. The new gangs were black and Latino with a few white supremacists in the Nazis around Marquette Park on the southwest side and in the suburban motorcycle gangs.

"Raoul Macam," said Leroy Sims, dropping a folder on the table between them.

Terry Flynn felt the tiredness drop off his shoulders. The name woke him up.

He opened the folder and stared at the photo of the man who had killed Lee Herran.

"Raoul be a mean-looking dude," Terry Flynn said. "Got them bad eyes. Look like he cut you."

"Raoul ain't as bad as the dude likes to look," said Leroy Sims. "Fact, he's pussy. Was running with the Divine Assassins for a while, that was a PR gang ran around the east edge of Humboldt Park, did some Sunday shootups about two years ago. So we came down on them. Sixteen months ago, right at the end of summer. Busted their ass. Remember that?"

Terry Flynn smiled. "All you wieners in GIU got your pictures on page one in the *Trib*, crawling over the building roof, looking for secret entrances to the pillbox. You looked like building inspectors."

"Was a Jewish synagogue, you know, when the neighborhood was Jewish."

"What other kind of synagogue is there?" Terry Flynn said.

"Say what?" Leroy paused and did his stare. "They had armor plate fastened to the walls. God couldn't break in there."

"But GIU did."

"Yeah. God don't go to places like that." He smiled. "Raoul is eighteen now or nineteen, he did time in St. Charles on a juvenile petition."

"He still in the gang?"

"Naw. Divine Assassins ain't what they thought they was. He drifts in and out. We picked him up on that one bust, the big one, we scared the living shit out of him, that's why I remember him. He was a crybaby, didn't like no lockup time atall. The chicken hawks were on his pretty ass inside. The only thing he had going for him was acting crazy. He'd get into this kind of state so he'd be putting out that he was crazy, you know what they say about crazy people—"

"Don't fuck with crazy people."

"Had Raoul in here. We banged him around a little with telephone books and he was ready to sing the National Anthem. Of Canada."

"So where the fuck is he now?"

"Hangs up round Wicker Park and he deals a little in Humboldt Park. He had a crib on North Avenue for a while. I bet he wasn't there now."

"You make the other two?"

"Naw. The white boy got to be some white trash. I never go into Uptown myself but you check with Foley, Foley is on medical now but he be back on Tuesday, I think. Foley'd know. Description of the black dude isn't that good."

"You mean all you people look alike?"

"Yeah, we do, but we try to dress different to tell us apart."

Terry stared at the picture of Raoul Macam. "Must be a million dudes out there in winter in field jackets. Uniform of the day."

"Some of them even got them the hard way."

"Wonder if the black guy is a vet. Had a First Cav patch on his jacket. The witness described it but he didn't know what it was."

"They were sissies, huh? That sounds like Raoul. I thought Raoul a little bit of a sissy but you never know, you put them inside and they'd turn John Wayne into one kind of a sissy or another if they kept him inside long enough."

"Nice system we got in this country," Terry Flynn said.

"Yeah, well, the answer to that is: Don't get inside and you won't have to worry."

"This was an armed-robbery beef on the sheet," said Terry.

"Yeah. We reduced to simple robbery, he was only fifteen, they made it that to put him in St. Charles. Otherwise, the SAO said they might have lost him."

"Pussy prosecutors," Terry Flynn said. "Says he stuck up a hot-dog stand with a .44. I thought only Wyatt Earp had a .44."

"Very antique piece. Said if he'd pulled the trigger he'd have blowed his own head off. Got a hundred sixty-five dollars."

"That much? I always thought there was money in hot-dog stands."

"Lot of it was from you, probably. That year I spent with you down in Grand Crossing, I must of seen ever' hot-dog stand on the South Side. Can't even look at a hot-dog stand today."

Flynn blushed. He liked Leroy well enough. Leroy had been standup. So had Terry, especially when Leroy got the brutality beef. That had surprised Leroy a little, to find out how standup Terry Flynn could be.

"Funny 'bout the white dude. Wonder if it was someone one of them knew inside someplace. We got segregated gangs usually."

"This isn't a gang, Leroy, these are just your usual alligators."

"They been working the Els before?"

"No one knows. Maybe this was their virgin act. I'd like the show to close on opening night."

"Man, the way I see it, you got ever'thing. You got descriptions, witnesses. You oughta clear this."

"I oughta been in pictures. Buchanan was at the scene first. Now I'm getting feedback, it gets hazy, it sounds like this is some kind of a fag killing but it isn't a fag killing. This is straight-out old-fashioned bopping off an innocent. Except I hear from two guys I know now working in Nineteen that they heard this was a fag killing, so who's going out of his way for it?"

"I know how it is."

"Yeah."

"See, I'm black, so I know."

"I forgot you were black."

Leroy Sims grinned in a menacing way. "Yeah, Terry, you forgot."

"I just knew you were the other guy in the tac car didn't like hot dogs."

"Yeah."

Terry Flynn smiled. It was no good working bullshit on Leroy. "Besides, you already became a hot dog when you went to GIU."

"Yeah," said Leroy, the eyes glazing. They both waited for Leroy. Then Leroy said, "Raoul stuck a guy in St. Charles, it's in there somewhere, but there weren't no charge because of the way it was, the guy was supposed to be trying to rape him. They added to his time, there was a concealed-weapons beef, but the guy recovered."

"The witness says the guy grabbed him, was messing with him sexually," said Terry Flynn, putting it all down. "Wanted to kiss him up, the other guy, the dead man, he does a standup and he gets stuck for it."

"Standing down there in the cold, how those boys think about sex instead of being warm?"

"Yeah."

"See," said Leroy. "The thing is, maybe Raoul is a pussy, but when you start acting crazy, sometimes you stop acting. I don't mean crazy."

"I know."

"Sometimes you just get crazy."

"He got crazy last night."

"Wait and see. When you get him. See if he don't use it. At court. When you get him."

"One step at a time."

"You think everyone's gonna drag on this?"

"That's why I'm putting in the hours, Leroy. I don't want them to walk away from this because it's just another hit. Number forty-one and it's still January."

"They were fags. I mean, the two dudes they hit on."

"Yeah. But straight. Straight jobs, worked in the stock market or something. Straights. Pay taxes. John Q's."

"Yeah," said Leroy, thinking of something else.

Terry Flynn waited.

"Learns them they can't pass for white," said Leroy Sims.

But Terry Flynn said nothing.

9
JUST THIS EASY

Terry Flynn felt the tiredness so deep in his muscles that he knew no amount of coffee and cigarettes could revive him. But he kept at it because he felt it was slipping away too easily.

The first call went to Lieutenant Shaffer, the Area Six Homicide commander. He said he was staying on the matter into his own hours; Shaffer reminded him that comp time was frozen in the new police-department budget. Flynn said he had to stay with the case and Shaffer said that Flynn could do what he wanted but that he was still on duty at midnight Saturday as usual.

Shaffer was a good enough man but Flynn knew that when Leonard Ranallo decided to do a number on Terry Flynn, he let Lieutenant Shaffer know that it might be good politics not to protect Terry Flynn too closely. So Flynn was on the dog shift, so Flynn had been edged out of his preferred leave time. Two days a week, Terry Flynn was watch sergeant, guarding the desk in Area Six police headquarters on the northwest side. Those were the hardest nights of all but he was damned if he would quit Homicide and give Ranallo the satisfaction.

The second call was to Brandon Cale.

The telephone rang for a long time. Flynn held the greasy receiver in his large left hand and stared at a Federation of Police calendar on the wall opposite and tried not to count the rings.

Finally, Brandon picked up the phone. His voice was slurred with sleep.

"Sergeant Flynn. You doing all right?"

"I'm all right."

"I'm sorry I woke you up but—"

"It doesn't matter. I sat up all night until it was morning. I couldn't sleep in the dark. The bedroom . . . I sat up all night." He broke off a moment and then resumed. "I was sitting in a chair by the window. I must have finally fallen asleep."

Terry Flynn squinted in his tiredness. His eyes were red and his shoulders had a steady aching that wouldn't go away.

"I'm down at Eleventh and State," Flynn began.

"That's police headquarters, isn't it?"

"Yeah. I'm down here and I been looking at pictures and I think I got a picture for you to see. The other thing is, I wondered if you could come down here? And look at some other pictures?"

"Yes," Brandon said. "I appreciate this."

Flynn blinked again. The light was sullen neon in the windowless large anteroom to the records section. The light hurt his eyes. "Yeah." Flynn never could find a way to take thanks or a compliment. "Yeah," he tried again, as though it might be an answer.

"It'll take me forty-five minutes."

"OK, you just come in the lobby and wait for me and I'll take you up," Terry Flynn said and hung up. He turned with the thought of going to the cafeteria. And then he thought: The hell with food. He needed a beer.

He walked out to the elevator bank and pressed DOWN and leaned against the wall and stared at his shoes. He didn't even see her.

"We can't go on meeting like this," Karen Kovac said.

The tiredness lifted like a smile. Terry Flynn turned and saw her in her winter blue-wool coat open over her skirt and blouse, her hands in her pockets, smiling at him.

"Hello, Karen," he said. "Jesus Christ, it's great to see you."

"I thought you worked nights."

"So did I. I've got to stay with this one. I was going down. You want to go down?"

"What kind of a question is that?" she said. She made him smile again. Her voice had a brittle charm to it, as though she spoke very precisely in a foreign language. It came from being the youngest in a large family and growing up when her immigrant Polish mother and father were getting old. She had one language for them—clear and slow English—and another for the rest of the world and, in time, the two languages merged.

"I'm talking about a beer," he said. "You don't think I'd want you in the police department's official elevator, in the event it ever comes?"

They had been accidental lovers. Everyone would agree they were not made for each other. Terry Flynn had no great ambitions in the department and Karen had nothing else. She had been the first woman on Homicide and her affair with Terry Flynn had not fit into her plans. For that matter, she probably was not his type either.

"I was thinking about you," she said. "I won't have a beer but I'll have an orange juice with you."

"That stuff will kill you, Karen. All that acid."

"Beer for breakfast," she said.

"It's long past breakfast for me. I'm waiting on a witness, to show him some pictures."

"I'm doing the same thing. In there." She nodded toward the records department. "She's looking for the men who raped her."

"Oh, yeah." He said it slowly, his eyes going flat. He didn't want to talk to her about his troubles and he didn't want to hear about hers. He could talk out the case later in a cop bar but he didn't want to waste the time with her.

The elevator bell rang and the doors *whooshed* open. They got inside. The elevator was damp and warm and full of people and they stood very close to each other. The air of the elevator was an overpowering mix of human odors, sweat and perfume.

The doors opened. They crossed the wide lobby dominated by a statue of a nineteenth-century policeman with his arm raised like a traffic cop's. The statue was dedicated to the seven policemen killed by a bomb in the Haymarket Riot of 1886. The statue had been on the site of the Haymarket on the west side for a number of years, until the late 1960s when radicals bombed it three times. It was moved into the police headquarters lobby for safekeeping.

They crossed to the street. The rain was slowly turning to sleet and to snow. The walks were wet, the air foggy and gray. They went to the Blue Star Lounge, the cop bar for the "rubberguns" who worked in police administration and never had any war stories to tell.

"What are you working on?" she said as they sat down at the dark bar.

"Homicide on the El. Last night. Three guys knifed a John Q at the Fullerton El station." He was abrupt, putting the matter aside.

"I heard about it. It was in the paper this morning."

"Yeah," Terry Flynn said.

"Another El case. A rape. You know about it?" she said, referring to her own investigation.

"Yeah." He tasted the beer. It wasn't as good as he thought it would be. He lit a cigarette. "How's your victim?"

"Better, I think. I don't know." She stared at the glass of juice. "I feel bad about it. When it happened, I mean. When they brought her in. I just put it aside, you know? My professional manner. My cold-fish act," she said. "You can't let it get personal, can you? I mean, it was too easy to get involved with her, she felt so awful, she was in shock, the bastards really did it to her."

He nodded and didn't speak and didn't look at her. A couple of cops, he thought, trading war stories.

"She started screaming, they had to restrain her at the hospital, drugs, everything. This is the first I've been able to talk to her since I talked to her right after. We lost two days. I don't know. You think your scum might be the same scum?"

"Sure, why not," Terry Flynn said. His voice was so cold and distant that Karen looked up, startled.

"What's wrong, Terry?"

"I don't know what's wrong. I'm tired. I saw you, I wanted to talk to you, I didn't want to talk about three-legged alligators."

"All right," she said, just a touch of chill in her voice now. "We can talk about anything else. You want to talk about when you can get a reasonable day off?"

"What's reasonable, Karen?" Yes, he thought, they were going to fight. They were both walking into it and they both knew they were going to do it. "Reasonable is when you have a day off?"

"Don't do it on my account," she said.

"I'll show you my schedule if you'll show me yours," he said.

"You really are an asshole sometimes," Karen said.

"You're the second guy today said that. It must be true if it's that obvious to everyone."

"Well, you work at it."

Silence.

"I've got to get back to Mary Jane."

"The victim?"

She got up.

"Karen."

She looked at him. Her cloudless blue eyes didn't have any mercy.

"I didn't want to fight with you. I was fighting all night. I'm sorry."

She stood and looked at him for a moment. "None of it's easy. Not for me either," she said.

"How's Tim?"

She softened. "All right. Sleeping. He sleeps all the time. I think he must be sick."

"He's not sick. He's a teenager. That's all teenagers do, eat pizza, smoke dope and sleep."

"He doesn't smoke dope. He better not smoke that stuff," she said. "He better not smoke at all."

"Fuck it," he said. "I'll call in sick tonight. How about an all-night-long?"

"I'm on this thing. I'm working tomorrow."

"Jesus," he said, meaning nothing. "Jesus."

"Terry." She touched his hand. "I picked up Mary Jane this morning, I talked to her a long time, I started feeling different about it. About her. So what if you're supposed to be professional and all that bullshit? I can't do it. I can't let it slide off me like that."

"I know," he said. He didn't look at her. He looked at the stein of beer with the sour taste and he talked in a low and tired voice. "The victim was a fag. Just a kid. Had a job, regular guy, he gets in the territory of three scumbags and he gets killed and Buchanan—you ever meet him?—he's on the scene, he does this bullshit because he has a fag hangup and he wants to dust this off and it keeps making me madder and madder to the point where I see this homicide is going to be in the dead-letter office if I don't press it." He paused in the rambling monologue to light another cigarette. He glanced at her with serious eyes. "No, that's bullshit too. There's no way we don't get these guys, these assholes have muddy footprints over everything. But I want to get them. Just hammer them down fast, right now, and get it over with so I can go back to my regular homicides, the shine prostitute who held back on her pimp and the Puerto Rican shooters putting holes in their arms and in their bellies in Humboldt Park. The regular stuff that's just interesting like a chess game and not the stuff that gets to you. A couple of kids ride home on the El and they don't know they're not supposed to ride home on the El, they don't know the city belongs to the animals after eight at night, I could see Buchanan saying, 'Hey, you fruits, don't you know better than to get in the way of three bad dudes looking for action on the A train?'"

He stopped talking and the silence picked up the conversation for a moment.

Her eyes weren't cold anymore: "And me. That's what this thing is about. Jesus, Terry, what they did to her? A Catholic girl, a real princess, I bet she said the rosary at night. Like raping a nun. And they were going to kill her."

They were talking it out now, letting the war stories sound off, getting the bad feeling out of their systems.

"All right," he surrendered. "What about your animals? Who were they?"

"One is black, that's for sure. Army field jacket. Tall—"

"Bingo," said Terry Flynn.

"Yours too?"

"Bingo," said Terry Flynn.

She let herself get excited. "The other is lighter. The other one might be black, some kind of PR. Skinny. He was the knife man."

"Ba-da-bim, ba-da-boom," Terry Flynn said, borrowing street sounds from the old Taylor Street Italian neighborhood. He put a fist on the bar and let it lay there. "It doesn't sound right but it might be."

"Both of them wore army field jackets."

"So did my boys. I've got a good photograph, my witness is coming down in less than a half hour. Maybe it's the same guys for both of these things." He smiled suddenly. "Maybe I can get back on Super Sucks with this."

She blushed at the nickname for the Special Squad.

"It couldn't be this easy," she said.

Terry Flynn smiled. "Sure it can. Sometimes it can be just this easy."

10
VICTIMS

Brandon Cale was even more pale than he had been the night before. His hair was uncombed and his blue eyes were without depth. He wore a blue parka with a heavy furlike collar. Terry Flynn was waiting for him in the lobby. They passed the security desk and took the elevator up to Records.

The room was large and dirty. File cases bulging with arrest reports, dispositions, unsolved cases and thousands and thousands of arrest photographs filled the huge room and made it seem cramped and closed.

Mary Jane Caldwell sat at the scarred oak table with cigarette burns on the edges of it. She had stared for a long time at the photograph of Raoul Macam and she had said nothing. When Karen Kovac finally prodded her with a word, Mary Jane looked up:

"I don't know. I really thought I would know, I knew I would never forget them, either of them, nothing about them. But now I don't know. I'm looking at this face and it's a face."

"Maybe it could be," Terry Flynn said.

She stared at him coldly for a moment. "I didn't say it wasn't," Mary Jane said. "I just said I don't know."

And now it was Brandon Cale's turn.

Terry Flynn had left Mary Jane and Karen to meet Brandon

in the lobby. Now he took him to a gunmetal gray desk on the far side of the room, away from the women, and told him to sit down. Terry Flynn had thirteen photographs, selected at random. Only one of them counted.

Brandon unbuttoned his parka and took off his gloves and rubbed his hands back and forth slowly as he turned the photographs over and stared at the faces of strangers. The photographs were all taken at the time of arrest. In some of the photographs, the flashbulb had captured a kind of light in their eyes so that the faces appeared to be demented. The photographs contained front views and profiles and sometimes the front view would be fearsome and the profile would seem comic, revealing a weak chin or an absurdly large nose.

Brandon turned the photographs over carefully, as though afraid of seeing something he did not want to see.

Terry Flynn stood behind him, the tiredness held at bay now by the tension of the moment. Mary Jane didn't know, which might mean anything. It was important that Brandon know.

He turned the photograph over and saw Raoul Macam, front view and profile.

"Him," said Brandon Cale without hesitation. The voice was deep and soft. "Him," he said again, almost to himself.

"The one with the knife."

"Yes," said Brandon Cale.

"The one who stuck—who stabbed Lee Herran."

"Yes," said the voice, shaking now. "Yes. Him."

"Raoul Macam," said Terry Flynn, making the name his, inscribing it in mind to make it more real.

"Him. Raoul. They called him Raoul. I told you that. It was him. You've arrested him."

"No," Terry Flynn said. "That's an old beef, that picture. No, we got to arrest him again. But we're going to do it, there's no problem with that."

"Jesus Christ." Brandon shuddered. "I'm looking right at the son of a bitch, the dirty bastard." He used the words oddly, as though he never used them at all. "You are going to get him?"

"No question, no question now," Terry Flynn said gently,

feeling very pleased with himself. He had gone the extra mile times before and it usually turned out to mean nothing. "I'd like you to look at some other photographs as well. We've got one identity. Maybe you can get the others."

"Yes," Brandon Cale said, still holding the police photograph of Raoul Macam. "What will happen to him?"

Terry Flynn looked at Brandon. "We'll charge him. Murder. There's no doubt of that. Murder in the commission of an armed robbery. It's a good beef."

"Will he be killed?"

Terry Flynn frowned a moment and looked down at Brandon. Was he a bleeding heart, even at a time like this?

"I'd certainly like him to be," Terry Flynn said.

"So would I," Brandon said. "I'd like him to be killed and I'd like him to think about being killed before it happened. I'd kill him myself if they wanted, if they wanted someone to throw the switch or whatever they did."

Terry Flynn said nothing. It was good, it was exactly what he would have wanted in a witness. They would catch Raoul and the others and do a dance with the state's attorney's office and the prosecutor in the case would want to know how good the witness was, was the witness ready to take the stand and take the endless delays and take the grilling in the hostile courtroom? Did he have enough hate in him to see it through? Yes, Terry Flynn thought, the answer was going to be yes. Brandon was hating well.

He brought over more books of photographs of young black men and young white men who had committed crimes or who had merely once been arrested on a misdemeanor charge, yet had had their moment before the police camera.

The room with all the files containing all the records is depressing and overheated and lit harshly by fluorescent lights strung across the ceiling.

Terry Flynn crossed the room and signaled to Karen Kovac and nodded his head. Karen followed him out of the room into the anteroom. She leaned against one dirty green wall with her arms folded across her chest. She stared at him.

"Absolutely, positively," Terry Flynn said. "And he wants to fry the guy as well."

"I talked to Mary Jane. She wants it to be the one. But maybe it isn't."

"Well, we tried," Terry Flynn said.

"It's like she was in school," Karen said. "She takes it so slowly, so seriously, as though she were studying for an examination. She stares at them and she wants to remember every one of them so that she can be afraid again when she's alone, when she's on the street."

"It's a bad one," Terry Flynn said.

"Worse than most," Karen Kovac said. It was perfectly true. They both had worked long enough to know there are different crimes because there are different victims. The young Mexican girl who claimed rape in Pilsen turned out to be the neighborhood punchboard but, in that one case, she had truly been raped. No one had sympathized with her and yet, she had seen the case through and the rapist had picked up seven years. There was a grandmotherly type, nearly seventy, raped in her bedroom in an apartment building in the seedy Uptown neighborhood. When they found the rapist, months later, he had confessed in tears to a series of rapes of elderly women. The court-appointed psychiatrists had argued that the rapist was insane and the argument had carried the day because many of the old women did not want to go to court to press their cases. The rapes had humiliated them, the intimacy forced on their old bodies had robbed them of nearly everything they owned in empty old age because it had taken their dignity. The trouble with Mary Jane Caldwell was that the rape had been worse than a bad incident in her life; even Terry Flynn saw that when he spoke to her. The hostility was only beginning for her and it would bank for a long time and grow as hot as a slag heap and glower all winter and, perhaps, all her life.

"At least she isn't jumping to take the first one we give her," Karen Kovac said, staring at Terry but not seeing him. "I hate to tell her in a few days that maybe we won't be pressing this one full-time and that there will be some other murders or rapes that have a greater claim."

"It was Wednesday," Terry Flynn said. "Saturday. You're already running out of time."

"Dammit. I know it," she said.

Both of the victims, at separate tables far removed from each other, went through the photographs in the books for a long time. The rain changed at last to snow and the front blew through and all the streets were filled with plowtrucks and salters struggling to keep the main roads open. The snow came off the prairie and blew down on the sprawling city and strangled it slowly in the soft white blanket. When it was the middle of the afternoon and there were no more photographs to be seen, Brandon Cale and Mary Jane Caldwell left, separately, and went to separate homes alone. And Karen Kovac checked in with the squad and went home alone. And Terry Flynn, finally exhausted, went home and fell asleep on the couch and when it was well and truly night again, he awoke and another day of work began.

11
AT SWALLOW'S

Brandon Cale walked into Swallow's on Broadway shortly after seven Saturday night.

The snow was still falling outside.

Swallow's was a homosexual pub now, but that had not been intended. There were ferns in the windows and it was trimmed in light wood. There was a gleaming brass rail around the light oak bar. A few straights wandered in from time to time and they were neither encouraged nor ignored. Unlike the kink bars and sex bars on the homosexual strip of Broadway north of Diversey Boulevard, Swallow's was merely a trendy neighborhood tavern in the trendy New Town area, where a good percentage of the neighborhood was homosexual.

Everyone had heard about the murder of Lee Herran. Lee Herran had been a regular in the place long before he met Brandon Cale. Brandon had only been in the place a dozen times and he had felt vaguely uncomfortable being there, to be seen by some as Lee's property, as belonging to another man as though it might be unnatural. Brandon's mixed feelings about Swallow's reflected his mixed feelings about his own sexual preference. Lee had been amused by that, by Brandon's discomfort in Swallow's.

Lee Herran's ghost filled the place for Brandon. It was a place to find him and not be alone for a while.

He had returned to his apartment, showered and changed, and thought he would never fall asleep again. Lee's side of the medicine chest was filled with cough suppressants, stimulants and depressives such as Valium, aspirin for his real and imagined headaches, a pharmacopoeia for a hypochondriac. Brandon had been unwilling to take any sleeping pills. His thoughts were dominated by Lee and by the unsmiling face of Raoul Macam. He had gone to Swallow's not to be alone.

David was behind the bar. Brandon sat down at the bar alone. Some of them in the place knew him. They wanted to speak to him but Brandon stared straight at David and David came down the bar and waited for a moment.

David was tall, he had broad shoulders and a fine face in which the bones illustrated the flesh.

"I'm really sorry, Brandon," David said at last.

"I want something, Scotch or something," Brandon said.

"My God, I'm really sorry," said David again.

"Yes." He paused. He tried to find some words that were suitable. "Yes, I appreciate it. I'm in shock." Yes, those words were good enough. He used the words like a man who really has no use for words anymore.

He drank the Scotch slowly at first, letting the smokey flavor sink into him and make his mood. Then he finished the drink quickly and David gave him another and did not take the money Brandon had put on the bar. When your friend dies, the drinks are on the house. Brandon thought that and then shuddered because he did not want to think things like that about Lee or about Lee's friends or about David, who had once been Lee's lover.

David said, "Have they found . . . anyone?"

"No. They have a face. I picked it out. The policeman . . . the detective . . . he seems to be trying hard enough. . . ."

"That's for show," David said. "That's for one day and then you don't hear from them again."

"I picked out one of them. A mug shot."

"Is that right? You picked him out?"

"His name is Raoul Macam."

"A spic, you knew it would be a spic," said David. "I hate them worse than I hate niggers, I swear to God."

"Raoul Macam," said Brandon Cale, using the name as an incantation. If he said the name long enough, the name would disappear and the man with the name would die.

"A spic," David said again.

"I told him I wanted him dead," Brandon said.

"You told who?"

"Sergeant Flynn."

"Flynn. Lovely. Does he smoke a twenty-cent cigar and fart too? I love that name."

Brandon looked curiously at David's mocking face. "He worked two shifts at least, I think. He was there when . . . it happened. And all this morning and afternoon."

"Because it was in the paper," David said. "Listen, dear, I hate to tell you, but cops have less use for us than they do for people who like to bash us. Or who think they can get away with it." David leaned both arms on the bartop, palms down, and the muscles stood out in bunches from the elbow up to the sleeveless T-shirt.

"Jesus Christ, David," Brandon said.

"I'm sorry, Brandon, I'm sorry, I just get hot thinking about them sometimes, I could tell you stories, stories right out of this place," David said.

They were silent for a moment, David staring intently at Brandon.

"I called his father," Brandon said. "I called my brother. My brother hadn't known about it. I called Lee's father and said how sorry I was. I told him I would get all of Lee's things and . . . I said how sorry I was. He didn't say anything to me the whole time. I talked to him, it was hard, I asked him if he had any questions. He said nothing until I said that and then he said he knew everything, he had been contacted by the police, that the chief of the Barrington police had come to the house shortly before dawn and told him everything and that was the last he wanted to hear of it. That's what he said finally. An hour ago. He said he didn't want to hear any more about it, not from me, not from anyone. He said he had been humiliated enough."

"The bastard," David said.

Brandon was not angry. It was part of the intense unreality of everything he had experienced since that moment on the El, watching three crazy people hassle a drunk with a briefcase. When Lee's father said he had been humiliated enough, Brandon had accepted it as something that very well might be said in the strange wonderland he found the world to be now. Brandon blinked at David and David's reaction.

"The funeral is Monday. Naturally, they don't want me to go."

"The hell with what they want," David said.

"No." Quietly. "He has a sister. There shouldn't be a row because of . . ." Brandon stopped and let the words wander away.

David stared at Brandon.

"You have a car, David," Brandon said.

"Yes. You want—"

"They'll bury him in Queen of Heaven. It's west somewhere. Could you drive out?"

"Sure," David said. "Sure."

And then Brandon saw the price of it. To have to tell David the story of what had happened last night and the rage that was filling him, slowly, seeping into every minute that passed since the death of Lee.

12
FUGITIVES

Raoul and Slide slept late into Saturday afternoon. They slept in the storefront off Seeley and Roscoe. The store had been abandoned two months before and the gas was still on and the store was warm. They slept on mattresses on the bare wooden floor. The windows were shaded with newspapers stuck to the plate glass. There were littered remains of Church's Fried Chicken boxes, as well as chicken bones and the remains of some soggy French fries. There was an empty bottle of Wild Turkey on the floor and an empty bottle of Smirnoff vodka and three full cans of Coke and three empty cans.

Willie was gone. He said he had to go. Willie had the shakes bad and he was probably in Uptown right now, doing what he had to do to get straight.

When they woke up at last, it was snowing and cold and they were broke again except for the credit cards and the cashier's check still snug in Raoul's pocket.

Slide had slept on the mattress, covered by his field jacket. The field jacket bore the running horse symbol in yellow and black of the First Cavalry Division. His brother had been in Nam in First Cav. It was his brother's jacket. His brother had worn it the day he held up Pappy's Liquors on East Forty-seventh Street and got shot right in the left lung by a security guard. The bullet hole was right there on the jacket. It was Slide's jacket now because George, his brother, was dead.

"What we gonna do?"

"I need something to fix me up," Raoul said in his lazy drawl, his eyes glittering again. "Need me to get straight."

"Sheet," said Slide, stretching. "I feel like swamp water."

"Where was the car?"

"I dunno where you put it. You was driving it."

"Shit." Raoul shook his head. "I can't remember. Fuck it. Get another car."

Slide smiled at that. "We didn't even fill up the ashtray on the first one."

They sat and stared at each other for a while and didn't speak, as though they were waiting for something. There was a harsh light from a single bulb hanging in the back of the store.

Raoul said, "Car 'round here someplace. Got the motherfucking keys right here. Car must be 'round here. We get the car first. Get the car. Get down to the park, man, do a hit, something. Get some ready. Get some ready, go down to the park, man. Score down there. Score. Then we be set up."

"Who we gonna hit?" Slide said, keying in on the scenario.

"I been saving for a rainy day."

"It's snowing besides. Who we gonna hit?"

"You know San Juan Grocery?"

"I dunno all those spic joints."

"Man, you gotta lot of hate, nigger, calling me names." Raoul was smiling but not really. "San Juan Grocery, been thinking about that place. North Avenue. San Juan be a grocery, you know, but very long in the back. You know. *Bolita* game. Some other shit. They be turning over money, this be Saturday night."

"How come I never heard about this place?"

"Man, I tole you, I saving it for a rainy day."

"You know 'bout this place, ever'one knows 'bout this place. I don't wanna be hitting no *bolita* parlor, them boys bad with guns, they carry some shit on them."

"No, no, man, you don't dig. The ole man, he's got a piece but he keeps it behind the counter, this is very small-time. Ever' place on North Avenue is *bolita*, baby, ever'one knows that. But this is Raoul's private stash, this is the real thing and I knows about it because I plays there." The street accent was dragging, Raoul was playing words with Slide.

"You gonna hit your own place."

"Man's gotta do what he gotta do."

"They know you, you hit the place, man, what they gonna do to you when they get to you? Ain't that big a city."

"Fuck the city, fuckin' city in this shitty weather. We gonna go south, my man. We gonna hit good and score at the park and we be headin' south before we see morning. Drive all day Sunday, we be in Florida. Florida now, I got cousins all over. Go down to Miami, I got people."

"I got no people in Miami—"

"Dig, Slide, be thinking cool," Raoul said, shifting on the mattress. "We gotta be outta this town anyway for a while, we stuck a guy, kill his ass."

"That's what the man say on the radio," said Slide, thinking of the radio in the cream-colored Cadillac, thinking of the sudden downer listening to the voice recite the crime, thinking of Willie ducking out on them the way he did.

"Man, you never seen so much pussy in your life in Miami. Wear those real thin shiny clothes, pussy push it in your face."

Slide thought about that.

"I can deal there. I can get some good shit there. We can put together enough to come back in spring, we score good, all spring, all summer—"

"No more hits—"

"Hell, we do good enough, we don't have to come back. Nobody said you gotta come back to Chicago, fuck it."

"Yeah, but it's all we know."

"Man, you gotta loosen up. We head south. . . ." He closed his eyes to see it better. "Everything be all right by this time tomorrow, we be going through Georgia, all them pine trees, so pretty and it smell so good—"

"Couple of people like us in a Cadillac, going through Georgia. Man, I don't like that thought at all."

Raoul opened his eyes and Georgia vanished. "Well, dude, what you wanna do? You wanna wait 'round for the poh-leese get your ass?"

"How you know they gonna get my ass? What'd I do?"

"You was with me. You hold the guy for me when I stuck him."

"Man, Raoul, sometime you trouble."

For a long time they were quiet again in the large and empty storefront. The wind rattled the plate-glass windows. The day had been a brief and dreary thaw in the middle of winter, full of rain and fog and then sleet and now it was full winter again, back to snow and cold so permanent and deep that it seemed to etch its way into the room through the brick walls.

Slide said, "We gotta do something. Sit here till we freeze to death. OK, man. We gotta do something. I see that." Reluctant. "I see that, we see your game, see what we do."

"All right," Raoul said, smiling because Slide had decided.

"If I had a piece," Slide said.

"Well, we see what we can do," Raoul said.

Slide looked sideways. "Oh, you gonna fix that too?"

"Everything in time, my man," said Raoul as though he had a plan.

But when they found the place where Raoul thought he had parked the car, the car wasn't there.

13
SUNDAY
MORNING

Terry Flynn took off his raincoat when he entered the building. It housed Belmont Avenue police station, as well as the various detective sections in Area Six on the second floor. The police station had replaced the old Damen Avenue station house, which Terry Flynn thought had been a properly gothic horror to inspire the fear of the law in the various criminals who were trooped through the building in its eighty-year history. The new Area Six building was located on the site of the old Riverview Park amusement center, which had been torn down. Terry Flynn would tell anyone who listened that Area Six headquarters looked like a goddam funhouse or a supermarket.

He climbed the concrete stairs to the second floor.

The detective divisions were arrayed in glass-walled offices that opened onto a common central area. Detectives from Robbery, Narcotics, from General Assignment, Youth, and Auto Theft were gathered around their squad rooms in various states of preparation for the coming overnight shift. Terry Flynn knew some of the other detectives in other divisions but, characteristically, he did not say anything to them as he crossed the large bright room. It was snowing bitterly outside; more than six inches had fallen in the time since Terry Flynn had finally gotten to sleep on his couch in his littered apartment. It had taken him too long to drive to work in the snow. The city salt trucks were out, massaging the roads with tons of salt that worked into the asphalt and cracked it into potholes each spring.

Terry Flynn poured a cup of coffee into the cup marked TERRY FLYNN on the coffee stand next to the sergeant in the common room, who ran the coffee concession. The sergeant said, "You wanna doughnut? We got doughnuts today from the Entenmann's driver."

"No."

"We got chocolate and plain and sugar."

"No," Terry Flynn said.

"We had glazed but we ran out," the sergeant said, because he never paid attention to what others said.

"No," Flynn said and poured cream in his cup and stirred it with a plastic swizzle stick, courtesy of the Slammer Inn, the police bar across the street.

He crossed the large room to the office that was the preserve of the Homicide/Sex division. In Chicago, the homicide detectives also handle all sex crimes, which means, practically, rape crimes and child-molestation cases. Often, those crimes are tied to homicides anyway.

Sergeant Kaufman was handling the shift tonight. He glanced up at Flynn as Flynn entered the room and said, "Call Tom Kelly at home. I got a message a while ago for you."

"Tom Kelly. What Tom Kelly?"

"I dunno what Tom Kelly. You know a lot of Tom Kellys?" said Sergeant Kaufman, looking down at his department correspondence again. There were always matters to be read at roll call. Every division, every shift, had a roll call, though the midnight roll call for Area Six Homicide/Sex was a fairly casual affair. Especially on Sunday morning.

Terry Flynn called the only Tom Kelly he knew. The telephone rang for a long time and then he heard Kelly's voice for the second time in less than twenty-four hours.

"Hello, Kojak," Tom Kelly said.

Flynn waited.

"I fell asleep, I was watching *Patton*," Kelly said.

"You've seen that movie six hundred times."

"I wish they would make it mandatory in schools," Kelly said. "I wish the scum would have to pass a test on it before they were allowed to fart."

"You've got a lot of hate in you, son," Terry Flynn said.

"So I was sitting there in my own domicile and it occurred to me. The name on the card," said Kelly.

Flynn waited.

"Right at the end of the shift, we were over by Roscoe and Damen, one of your up-and-coming neighborhoods, and we see this cream-colored Cadillac Seville parked sort of funny on the curb."

"How funny?"

"Front two wheels up on the curb, sort of the ass end sticking into the street. That would be Seeley Avenue. It's snowing by now, I suppose you were home in beddy-by."

"By the end of your shift, I was having a well-deserved beer in the Blue-Gold."

"Well, we take a look. Fucking doors are unlocked. It's stolen. We call in, it wasn't on the sheet yet but they had a beef on it. Stolen early Saturday down on Webster by St. Vincent's. Guy was named Parelli."

"Yeah," said Flynn.

"Credit cards in the backseat, stuff like that."

"Yeah," said Flynn.

"I didn't pay attention," Kelly said. "It didn't connect. Hauptman was talking about going ice fishing up at Lake Geneva on his day off. Hauptman is going on about it and he drives me crazy. He is crazy. Hauptman takes his day off to go sit on ice in a lake and fish through a hole in the ice for fish. That is crazy. Eskimos got to do it because they got nothing else to do but it is crazy. Don't you think?"

"The name on the credit cards," Terry Flynn said because he had figured it out.

"Brandon Cale. That was the name of the witness, wasn't it?"

"Bingo," said Terry Flynn.

"I didn't connect because it wasn't the victim but I did finally get around to the paper and I'm reading it and it doesn't identify the witness naturally but then I think I saw the report and I saw the name. I called up and that was the name, so I called down to Six and they said you were coming in and so I figured I'd stay up and tell you."

"Your check will be in the mail," Terry Flynn said. He was smiling. "They towed it?"

"Yeah. I mean, we didn't know. But I called to the pound for you already, I told them that a fucking big shot in the dick division was going to want to see the car, that they should make sure all the tires are still on and the radio and the rest of the stuff that was on the car when Hauptman and I ran across it."

"What about the cards, that stuff?"

"Everything is in Property," Kelly said.

"You give good police," Terry Flynn said.

"Hey, fuck that dirty mouth of yours," Kelly said. "I'll see you around sometime and you buy me a schnapps."

"Two," Terry Flynn said. He broke the connection.

He was smiling still when he walked back into the squad room, but Kaufman had shaped up the roll by then so he put down his cup on a file cabinet and stood at semi-attention in his shirtsleeves, his Colt .357 Python with the short black barrel in a holster on his belt. He had trimmed five pounds in his endless campaign to stay on a diet and he felt better for the two days a week in the gym. He kept thinking he would be thin again by spring, the way he had been when he went into the army nearly thirteen years before. He was getting old, Terry Flynn thought as he stood and half listened to Kaufman mumble through the department bulletins. Old in the service of mankind.

"Sergeant Flynn," Sergeant Kaufman was saying. "You and Quigley make a team tonight, Quigley needs a backup. He's doing that Mendota shooting."

"All right," Terry Flynn said. "I could use some backup myself."

"Is that right?" Kaufman said. He never smiled and never told jokes and never inquired anymore. He was perfect as a desk sergeant.

Quigley said, "You need help on the fag killing?"

"Herran killing," is the way Terry Flynn put it.

"Yeah, that was the fag," said Quigley. Terry Flynn said nothing. They were still in the squad room. Quigley was a full-figured Irishman with a dark scowling face and the eyes of a priest who doesn't believe in anything anymore.

They drew keys to one of the cars and went down the stairs to the lot. It was always a zoo: Teams of detectives searching the lots for their cars of the evening because the previous tenants of the cars never left them in the same place. It was worse in the winter, worse when it was snowing and the wind was blowing.

"Why don't you find the car and bring it 'round?" Quigley said, biting the words against the wind.

"Who made you the Lord High Mayor of Dublin?" Terry Flynn said. "If anyone waits inside, it should be a superior officer. Like me."

They found the gray Dodge sedan parked halfway in a snowbank at the edge of the lot. The snow howled over the Western Avenue overpass and across the lot and slapped at them.

"Fucking snowbank," Quigley said.

"You drive," Terry Flynn said.

Quigley had trouble starting the car and then had trouble getting it out of the snowbank. The tires whirred. He pumped back and forth between D and R and the tires began to smoke but the rocking increased and the car finally lurched ahead to dry pavement.

"Fucking cars," Quigley said.

"You can't live with them and you can't live without them," Terry Flynn said. He could get along with Quigley well enough, as long as it wasn't permanent.

Quigley wanted to go into a shooting gallery in Uptown that had been the last known hangout of Wee Willie Mendota, a sometime pimp, sometime dope dealer and sometime car thief, who had been found on Thursday in a garbage dumpster behind 4314 N. Kenmore with three large round dirty holes in his forehead and three slugs from a .22 in his brain.

The shooting gallery was called Pal Freddy's on the strip on

Wilson Avenue, where southern Appalachian whites and American Indians huddled in their separate, violent bars and wailed about their lost homelands through long northern winter nights.

There were rifles in Pal Freddy's that fired weak shots, and in the back there was a different kind of shooting gallery.

"I don't want to make waves for Wee Willie," Quigley explained as the Dodge sedan chugged north on Western Avenue. "I just want to pass the card around and let them see my face in case anyone remembers who had a hard-on for Willie bad enough to make him dead."

"Wee Willie sounds like he didn't have an enemy in the world," Terry Flynn said to be conversational. He was awake finally—it usually took him an hour or two—and he was watching the mean street with a chill and a good feeling. He knew where he was going tonight. He was going to look at a cream Caddie and then he was going to look around a strange neighborhood for a cream Caddie to be found abandoned in. And Quigley was good enough when it came down to it.

The shooting gallery was brightly lit and it had the usual collection of hard-eyed, sallow-faced young men and women. Terry Flynn and Quigley moved their bulks into the middle of the place and everyone went quiet and stared at them.

"Wee Willie Mendota," Quigley said in his fine baritone made for the pulpit of a solemn High Mass. "You all heard about him."

They stared and said nothing. Quigley went on to tell of his death and to inquire if any of them might have information on who wanted to chill Mendota and he passed around a card that had his name and office number and the star symbol of the Chicago Police Department.

It was over in less than fifteen minutes. It was nearly midnight and Quigley said they might as well eat. They agreed on Miller's on Adams Street in the Loop.

Quigley parked the car in a NO PARKING NO STANDING NO STOPPING TOWAWAY zone marked on Adams Street and crossed to the pub nestled snug in one of the few low-building blocks left in the Loop.

They went to a booth in the back of the place and Quigley ordered a Reuben sandwich and chicken noodle soup and fries and Terry Flynn ordered a large salad with French dressing and a Diet Coke.

"You'll make yourself sick with that stuff," Quigley said, sipping the foam from his glass of beer. "You can't survive winter on salad and pop."

"Save me your sermon, Father Quigley," Terry Flynn said. "I want to lay out the rest of our evening to you."

"I'm all ears, Monsignor Flynn," Quigley said.

"On the Herran killing. I know you know about it because you call it a fag killing."

"It wasn't a fag killing?"

"It was a kid named Lee Herran who runs afoul of a three-legged alligator named Raoul Macam. And before I go on shift tonight, I get a call from Tom Kelly—he's patrol down at Town Hall district—he ran across a car that was stolen in the vicinity of the killing about the time of the killing. And Tom found it with his partner Saturday afternoon in an unlikely neighborhood."

"And you are going on this?"

"No, Father, he found credit cards. Belonging to the witness. So these were the same guys. They iced this Herran kid, they stole a car, they end up at Roscoe and Seeley—"

"One of my favorite neighborhoods. There's a good German delicatessen there, did you know that?"

"I didn't know that," Terry Flynn said. "We go up there and try to find this alligator."

"Is the word, as they say on 'Starsky and Hutch,' 'on the streets'?"

"I hope so. By now. There was a piece in the papers."

"Our clients do not read newspapers. They use them to wipe their asses. Showing, I suppose, some judgment."

The food came.

They ate in the greedy silence of policemen. Policemen on duty eat food as ritual, with reverence, as though they were setting an example to their lessers.

The first tavern they hit at 1:15 was on the corner of Seeley and Roscoe itself, less than fifty feet from where the Cadillac had been abandoned.

Quigley sniffed at the smoke in the dim-lit place. "I think we're the only people in here without police records," he said in that faintly sneering voice that made it hard for him to keep a partner for any length of time. He had been married three times and he wasn't forty yet.

Terry Flynn went to the bar and the girl came down to the end and she looked bored with it all, with Flynn and cops and the people in her place.

"Raoul Macam," said Terry Flynn, and he showed the photograph in the dim light. She took a flashlight from under the bar and looked at it. "Show it around," said Terry Flynn.

She went down the bar. The photo went from hand to hand. People shook their heads. People stared at the two men in raincoats with the snow melting on their bare heads. Quigley had his coat open so that he could be less than a second from drawing the .44 Smith & Wesson widowmaker strapped in his shoulder holster. Hardly anyone in Homicide wore shoulder holsters. They were considered ostentatious, something to be worn by the cowboys in Robbery or Narcotics.

A drunk Mexican came up to them and exhaled tequila breath at them. He said, "What dis one do?"

"Killed someone. You know him?"

"I no know him. I wonder him. Name ees Raoul? He is Mexican?"

"He is Puerto Rican," said Quigley. "Don't lean on my coat, you might leave a stain."

"Puerto Rican," said the Mexican, chewing at the words. His eyes were glazed. "I don't know any Puerto Ricans."

"Yeah," said Quigley. "They're a rare breed."

The Mexican blinked and seemed reluctant to move away. The girl behind the bar brought the photograph back and gave it to Flynn and waited. Quigley gave her his card. It was ritual for both of them. He might get a call and he might not. No one in the place would say anything out loud to him.

They hit two more bars before the 3:00 A.M. Sunday closing. There were a couple of 5:00 A.M. Sunday bars after that. No one had seen anyone or anything.

For a while, around 3:30 A.M., they sat in the Dodge and burned gas at the curb to make heat. They stared out the windshield at the emptiness of Roscoe Street, at the darkened apartments above the darkened storefronts, at the all-night signs blinking neon messages in the darkness to no one. To them. THE COZY LOUNGE. ONE-HOUR CLEANING. FOOD. MEAT. CERVEZA FRIA. OLD STYLE ON TAP. JOHNNY'S TAP ROOM. DINING. COCKTAILS. VIENNA HOT DOGS. ALL BEEF.

They said nothing, they stared at the dark winter street. The snow had stopped around 1:00 and now the street was clear, glistening with salt and water. The snow was piled along the curb and it had been used to bury cars left parked on the street despite the NO PARKING IN WINTER ban against overnight parking on arterial streets. Roscoe reached from the lake a mile east through the old German neighborhood to the shopping center built on the remains of Riverview Park at the north end of the Western Avenue site.

Quigley slipped the car into drive. He left the headlights dark.

They had seen the first figure at the same time.

The second one came a moment later.

Both of them came out of the darkness of Seeley Avenue.

Both wore field jackets.

Both of them.

"Must be a million guys dressed like that," Quigley said. His voice was soft.

"I don't give a damn," said Terry Flynn and he took the pistol out of his belt and put it on his lap and the car prowled along Roscoe, sticking close to the snowbanks covering the parked cars.

"Go ahead and let me look back," Terry Flynn said.

"Lights?"

"Yeah. Just go ahead, go up to the gas station at Damen and we'll turn around."

The car slid past and Flynn stared out the side window at the thin face and he blinked and the car was past the two men.

Two men.

"Was it?"

"Yeah, fuck it, come around and I'll drop off ahead of them."

"I'll call—"

"Fuck, we got no time," Flynn said and he was out of the car as it turned in the driveway of the shuttered Shell station. He slipped on the snow, fell to one knee, was up and on the sidewalk and the two of them still were walking right toward him, as though they didn't see him.

Quigley fought the wheel and the Dodge swung heavily around and came back through the red light at the intersection of Damen and Roscoe and cut west toward Seeley Avenue, a block away. Quigley passed them and stopped and was out of the car, the big piece drawn.

Slide saw what was happening.

There was no place to run. They could jump in between the parked cars, in the deep snow, but the one with the big gun was already talking.

"Police. Hands up! Police!" Quigley said, the revolver hammer cocked.

Slide saw the way it was going down. He thought of his brother staggering out of Pappy's with a bullet through him, right through the coat. The way it was. Fucking Raoul. Fucking motherfucking Raoul.

Raoul jumped for the snowbank and Terry Flynn had the piece out and was less than twenty-five feet from them.

Slide thought about it. Then he hit the snowbank too and struggled behind Raoul between the parked cars for the street.

"Come on," Quigley said, standing in the street. "Come on and make it fun for me." In that voice without amusement, in the cold and glaring tones of a sermon uttered in a darkened cathedral.

Raoul was on the street and he started to run east, he was crazy, he didn't care. He thought of the knife. He pulled it out in one motion and threw it in the snowbank and in that moment, Quigley fired.

The bullet broke Raoul's arm and he was down, still running but with his face in the snow.

Slide put his hands up high.

"On your face, scum," said Quigley in a big voice. Slide knew that voice, knew that cop. He was in the snow, on his face, his hands above his head. He stared at the snow.

Raoul felt the white pain in him, it was all over him. He got to his feet and felt Terry Flynn's pistol at his head.

"Raoul Macam," Terry Flynn said, he was so sure.

"Man, you shot me, you shot me," Raoul said, shock glazing his eyes.

"And you knifed Lee Herran last night and I want the fucking knife."

"I got no knife, I ain't no Raoul whatso," said Raoul.

"You're dying, you scumbag, you want to die like this, like a dog?" Terry Flynn said, his voice coming fast, sweat on his face, his eyes glittering. He was working as fast as he could. The knife. The fucking knife had to be somewhere. Quigley was bent in the snow, cuffing Slide's hands behind his back.

"You're dying—"

"Get me a doctor," Raoul said.

"You're bleeding to death like a dog. Where's the fucking knife? Who was the other guy?"

"I don't know no other guy."

"Who was the other guy, the white boy?"

"Man, get me a doctor."

Terry Flynn grabbed his hair, made him look at the red-stained snow. "That's you, Raoul, you're bleeding to death and I can save you, you gotta talk to me, you're going to bleed to death if I don't save you—"

"Don't save him," Quigley shouted. "Kill the rodent mother-fucker. I'll kill this one."

"Kill your ass," Terry Flynn said to Raoul in a soft voice. It was all said desperately, in the darkness, on the empty street, in pressing tones, in dry, excited voices, in voices of meanness and threat. No one was around. This was the way it was done.

"Don't lemme die," Raoul said, looking at his own blood, feeling the hand in his hair, feeling the gun at his temple. This was getting serious, he thought.

"Where's the knife—"

"Threw it down. Snow—"

"The other boy—"

"Willie. Willie."

"The three of you—where's Willie—"

"Dunno. Went away. Man. I am dying—"

"Why'd you stick him?"

Pause.

Raoul looked at Terry Flynn's large, marble-blue hard eyes.

"He was a fag, man," Raoul said. "Called me a spic, man." The voice full of a life of grievances.

"Yeah," said Terry Flynn in a long and lost whisper. "Yeah." And he wished Raoul was really dying.

II
PUNISHMENT

14
SAO

Raoul Macam did not die on Sunday.

Quigley called backup, and in ten minutes a fire department ambulance and several squad cars and a squadrol were trying to create a traffic jam on Roscoe Street between Damen and Seeley. Lights were on in all the windows of all the apartments on the street. Despite the cold, people had the windows open and were leaning on the ledges and watching the free drama on the street below.

The old-fashioned black-and-red Cadillac ambulance of the fire department took Raoul Macam to Henrotin Hospital, where the emergency-room staff was accustomed to fixing up organs damaged by bullet holes. Macam was in the operating room for an hour and twenty minutes. By morning light, he was in a hospital bed with a tube up his nose and a second tube connected to his arm, and his hands and legs shackled by cuffs to the bars of the hospital bed. A policeman sat in his room and read the basketball scores in the *Sun-Times*.

Quigley and Terry Flynn had Slide manacled to the ring in the wall of the windowless interview room number 1 by 4:30 A.M.

Terry Flynn had his coat off. His trousers had darkened bloodstains from the place he had knelt in the snow. The stains would not come out.

Every policeman on patrol in Uptown was looking for a man

who resembled Willie. Unfortunately, the description indicated Willie looked like several thousand other Southern whites who lived in Uptown.

Quigley wore his coat. He dressed well. His eyes were calm, the unforgiving eyes of a father confessor. He had studied at the seminary at Grayslake and when he lost his faith, he had still toyed with the idea of becoming a priest. He was that kind of man. Instead, he had slept with a member of his parish choir and married her and divorced her after three months, when she would not do certain things that he preferred. He was a hard man to live with, both in marriage and in the department.

The room had a table and four folding chairs and the walls were painted a dull white color. The room was lit by fluorescent lighting in the ceiling.

The room had an intensity because of the lack of windows, because of its brightness. It was intimidating, even without the chain that came from the ring in the wall that was connected by handcuffs to Slide's wrists.

"Walter Johnson," Terry Flynn said. "You named for the pitcher?"

"Say what?" said Slide, staring with hangover eyes at the policeman.

"The pitcher, Walter. Famous pitcher in baseball a long time ago," said Terry Flynn.

"I ain't named for nobody."

"Your street name is 'Slide.' Why is that?"

"Slide," said Slide. "Let it go. You know."

"Why didn't you let this go?"

"I didn't do nothing."

"It's over. We got the witness coming down. Raoul already confessed. He gave up Willie. He gave up you. You wanna hold the bag of shit all by yourself, you be a standup guy."

Quigley said nothing. He stared at Slide, as though he might be examining a butterfly before impaling it.

"Now, you know we got your balls," Terry Flynn said in a gentle voice. "Why don't you make it easy?"

"You didn't even give me my rights," Slide said.

"Christ," Quigley said for the first time. "You know, Terry, you give it too easy to this scum. We should have finished him in the street."

"No, I—"

"I, I, I, your ass, I'm gonna kill the dirty motherfucker," said Quigley.

Slide waited. This was playing, this wasn't real. Except he knew that look in Quigley's eye. Quigley was crazy for sure.

"Slide, you want your rights? You don't know your rights by now? You have the right to tell us everything you know. You have the right to have the fucking book thrown at you. You have the right to try to wiggle off easy if you throw enough shit down on Raoul. You have the right to sign a confession."

"What about my attorney?"

"Fuck you and your attorney," Quigley rumbled. And he slammed his fist hard on the oak table so that it jumped and the loudness of the blow filled the room like a shot.

"Where's Raoul?" Slide said.

"Dead," said Quigley. "Where the fuck do you think he is. We finished him. And I'm gonna finish you."

"He dead, why you wan' me say some shit down on Raoul?" said Slide.

Flynn grinned. "A crafty devil, ain't he?"

"A piece of work," said Quigley. "A genuine piece of work."

The door opened. It was Sergeant Kaufman. "We got the witness," said Kaufman in a dull voice dulled by tiredness.

They walked out of the room. Slide waited. In a little while they took him to room number 2. They put him at the table, facing the door with the small peep in it. He stared at the peep. They talked to him but he knew they would not hit him with someone looking through the peephole. The little fag that Raoul been stupid enough to want to hit on. Simple little robbery on the El and Raoul gets crazy, should have left the sonbitch . . .

In a little while, they took him through to interview room number 1. One of the detectives from Robbery, who was wearing two holsters and two guns, stared at him like a prison guard. Slide stared back.

In interview room number 1, Terry Flynn said: "You were made. Now you want to tell me."

"Raoul did it," Slide said, deciding. "None of me. Raoul want to stick the dude, the dude say he a spic or something. I say nothing. I wanna get out there."

"You were the sensible one," Terry Flynn agreed.

"Yeah," said Slide. He wanted Flynn to understand. "See. Raoul, he crazy. I wanna get outta there. We got what we was coming for, get outta there and go party. But Raoul, I think he's, you know, *marican* he/she himself, he likes boys too, see these boys coming on to him—"

Quigley started. "What?"

Good, thought Slide suddenly, inspired. This was good. "Boys, them white boys, coming on to Raoul. Right on the train. Coming on to him. That why they got off. You don't think they get off if they was 'fraid of us? No, man." Certainty now, the story was fabulous. "Come down the steps, say they want to party, I don't want none of that but Raoul got the money, got ever'thing, I wanna go and they say they wanna play with us, they say they think we cute, man, I ain't no sissy, I seen them boys looking at Raoul and that one boy, that one boy he wants to kiss Raoul right there and Raoul, he loving it, and the other one get jealous and call Raoul this name, you know that ain't right, ain't right no one call no one nigger or spic or scumbag or none of that, that ain't right if you do that on the street, man, you know the street, you gotta be prepared to pay, see, and those boys, that one got the dark hair and sort of pretty face, you know, the one that say he saw me there, well, that one, he comes on to Raoul, I mean, like a fox or something, coming on, he smelled funny like perfume, man, it was sickening, I was inside and I know that, you know, and I don't mess around none with that stuff at all. It was sickening, I want to get away and Raoul say he want to party and I say, 'Man, you gotta split up with me then,' and Raoul gets angry or something, and Raoul's got his arm around this one, like this one was a fox or something and he kissing Raoul, they partying already, and this other dude, this white boy, this white boy says this thing to Raoul and

I say, 'Man, you crazy, that crazy say that kind of stuff,' and Raoul has the knife, see, and I know Raoul, so I say to Raoul, 'Be cool, baby,' but Raoul, see he's already in a quarrel that I ain't no part of so he sticks the dude. Man. Dead. Sticks him and I just sees it. That's all. I just sees it." He paused and wet his lips and his eyes were wide and shining in the intense, still brightness of the windowless room. "Dead."

Quigley stared at him for a long time.

No one spoke.

Slide said, "Can I get a glass of water?"

Terry Flynn and Quigley got up and walked out of the room.

Brandon Cale was sitting at a desk in the large room, waiting. Brandon was hung over, he had gone home alone and slept at last. David had wanted to take him home but he hadn't wanted that. He had gone home and decided something about himself. He thought he would buy a pistol—a thought that David had given him—and that he would be safer with it. He had hunted as a child growing up in Decatur. He was not afraid of guns. He would buy a pistol the first thing. And then he had slept and not dreamed and then the telephone had been ringing and it was Sergeant Flynn and he said they had caught the men, just as he had promised.

Quigley looked at Flynn away from Brandon Cale. "All right, Monsignor," Quigley said. "How do you explain why they left with the robbers?"

"That's bullshit," Flynn said. "It happened the way Brandon put it down."

"But it's an interesting story," Quigley said with a slight smile.

"Where's the fucking asshole on felony review?" Flynn said, turning away from Quigley. He didn't like that smile. He didn't like Slide's rambling story. He took a step back and bumped into Goldberg.

"I'm the fucking asshole you're looking for and a pleasant good evening to you, Sergeant Flynn," Goldberg said.

"I thought you were off felony review," Flynn said.

"This is a very important case," Goldberg said. He had

bright eyes and red hair slightly darker than Flynn's. "Confessions? Police-brutality beefs? What do we have here?"

"We have two scum and are looking for a third. We have a witness and I expect we will have witnesses to the robbery on the El. I think we have murder, we have armed robbery, we have grand theft auto, we have everything to allow the state's attorney's office to let them off with probation," Terry Flynn said. It wasn't Goldberg. He even liked Goldberg. It was losing control of the case now. Now it was up to the lawyers and he never trusted it after it left him. Some of them were his friends in the SAO—maybe Jack Donovan, chief of the criminal division of the state's attorney's office, counted as a friend—but they weren't friends on cases like this.

"Rights were given, of course," Goldberg said. "Does he want a lawyer?"

"No, of course not," Quigley said.

"Do we have a confession?"

"Sort of," Quigley said.

"Confession for what?"

"Confession of innocence."

Goldberg's eyes were amused. "Is this the knife man?"

"The shooter is in the hospital," Flynn said. "Quigley missed. He's got a howitzer in his pocket and he missed the flea." "Shooter" was the common term for the man who pulled the trigger or wielded the knife or the baseball bat.

Goldberg enjoyed Flynn. He didn't like him—he saw cops as criminals in uniform opposed to criminals out of uniform—but he enjoyed him.

"Well," Goldberg said. "I talked to Jack Donovan a little while ago and he said to go ahead with it but to bring in a PD right away. We'll go to appearance this morning and arraignment Wednesday. Bond?"

"Are you kidding?" Terry Flynn said.

"My little joke. What's the status of the shooter?"

"Unfortunately, he'll live," said Quigley. "The light was bad."

"Roscoe Street is not a shooting gallery," Goldberg said. "There is an element to this case you don't know about, though.

And it makes matters a little more serious. I mean, from your point of view."

Which was why Goldberg had been sent down to Area Six at 5:00 in the morning instead of the regular assistant state's attorney who was consulted on felony review before felony charges were leveled. Goldberg was too important for felony review. Terry Flynn frowned as he realized something bad was going to happen.

"Step into my office," said Goldberg, leading them into interview room number 3.

Terry Flynn entered and turned and stared at Goldberg, who closed the door behind him.

"We have a little problem," he said.

"Go ahead," said Terry Flynn.

"DEA . . ." began Goldberg and Terry Flynn groaned at the mention of the federal Drug Enforcement Administration. Whatever it was, wasn't going to be pleasant. Nothing involving the G was ever pleasant, even for policemen.

"DEA," Goldberg began again, "and a special task force with the state's attorney's office—"

"More bullshit coming," growled Quigley.

"—have conducted a six-month investigation—"

"Jesus, I'm standing in it up to my knees," said Quigley.

Goldberg flushed and frowned and soldiered on. "Investigating a drug ring operating on the Chicago Board Options Exchange and the Midwest Stock Exchange—"

"They're selling stock in it?" Quigley said. But Flynn saw where it was leading. He thought a prayer and closed his eyes for a moment to make it count. When he opened his eyes, Goldberg was still there and still talking.

"Lee Herran was under investigation."

"So what?"

"So was his . . . roommate. . . ."

"This is bullshit—"

"This is the DEA," Goldberg said, not meaning it that way. He blushed. Quigley, inevitably, said, "Same thing."

"Anyway," Goldberg said, "there just might be a connection here."

"No," Flynn said. He saw where Goldberg was going. Sometimes he could figure out a conversation without anything being said. "You want to deal with these creeps? The one in the interview room, he already tried one story where the victim and the witness are supposed to be hitting on these scum because they were all fags together. I know the next thing you're going to tell me is that Raoul Macam was a dealer and that maybe there was some dealing going on between Lee Herran and Raoul Macam. I won't even try to point out to you how stupid that sounds on the face of it. I will point out to you that there was a robbery on the El train a few minutes before the homicide. Was that coincidence?"

"It could have been. We don't have all the facts." But Goldberg took a step back.

"Gimme a break," Terry Flynn said.

"It doesn't matter. In any case, we come down to hard charges here. We can talk to these people later, see if they know anything. DEA wants to talk to them. Maybe DEA knows things about the man Mr. Quigley plugged that you don't know. Maybe you don't know that Raoul Macam not only was a dealer but that there was an incident involving him and a runner with the Options Exchange—"

"Bullshit."

"Yeah. I know. Everyone is full of shit except you. It's almost morning, Sergeant, and I'm tired of talking to you." And Goldberg sounded tired.

"So stop talking," Terry Flynn said, pushing it. "What is Jack Donovan going to do?"

"Go along, for now. For now. But we still talk to everyone. DEA still talks to everyone. We all expect cooperation from the police department and in case you forgot, you're part of the police department, Sergeant, you're not running a one-man show. There may be bigger things involved here than you can figure out now."

"I doubt it," Terry Flynn said, as though he had won.

And Terry Flynn was wrong.

15
TERRY AND
KAREN

The unplowed snow was piled in drifts against the apartment-building entrance. Karen Kovac pushed against the door and finally the hard, powdered snow eased and she slipped out of the entrance and found herself in nearly a foot of snow. The snow was almost to the top of her boots.

"Goddam the janitor," she said, and knew that it was not his fault. It was 8:00 on Sunday morning. The snow had fallen overnight.

She lifted her feet and walked giant steps through the snow. Her car was parked at the curb on the side street she lived on and it would have to be dug out. And it wouldn't matter because there was nothing to be done today with all the snow. She had planned to go back to the Jarvis elevated station, where Mary Jane Caldwell had been attacked, and carefully walk a pattern around the neighborhood in larger and larger circles, to talk to people on the street, to see if there was a chance that someone had seen the two men who raped Mary Jane on Wednesday. It was a neighborhood of old people and old people were good watchers.

But no one would be on the street this morning because of the snow.

She reached the sidewalk. Down the street, an old man was

already out, shoveling snow. The street was lined with apartment buildings like hers and a few brick three-flats.

The car that came up the street from the south end stopped across from her. Terry Flynn rolled down the window.

She looked at him for a moment and then crossed between a line of parked cars to the street and opened the door of the battered Ford. She slipped inside. There were empty cardboard coffee cups on the seat and a pile of old newspapers and empty packages of Lucky Strike cigarettes.

"Just like home," she said to him.

"I've been circling the block, there's no place to park," he said. He didn't look tired. His eyes were bright. "I saw your car. You can forget it until spring. It looks like a snow hill."

"A gallant man would have dug me out if he had so much time on his hands."

"I agree," Terry Flynn said. "What are your plans today? You said you're on duty."

"I told Matt Schmidt I wanted to go through the neighborhood around the El station where Mary Jane Caldwell was raped. Around Jarvis station."

"And talk to the old people," Terry Flynn said.

"Yes. You told me they're good watchers."

"Words of wisdom," Terry Flynn said. "You're going to have to wait awhile. Until the janitors get out shoveling the walks. This is broken-hip weather for old people."

"So what do you have in mind?"

"I could be locked up for that."

She smiled. "I have handcuffs."

"This is Sunday," Terry said. "Let's not be too kinky."

They didn't say anything after that for a while. Terry drove as though he might be on patrol and she sat near the passenger door, watching the empty morning streets the way a cop watches. It is the way old people watch.

They drove down the empty shining width of Irving Park Road, going east toward the sun. The sun glinted off the snow and made the city look wonderful and calm and still. The three thousand taverns in the city were closed for Sunday morning and even the drunks slept away the waiting time.

He told her how he and Quigley found Raoul Macam and Walter ("Slide") Johnson and about the absurdity of the DEA involvement. When he was finished, she did not speak. Terry Flynn turned onto Lake Shore Drive and headed south toward the towers of the Loop and the Near North Side district.

"Damn," she said. It was the only thing she said.

After a moment, he said in a gentle voice, "When I saw you yesterday, I just went crazy thinking about you. Can I buy you breakfast?"

She looked at him with her odd blue eyes that were so clear and honest and open they belonged to the face of a child. "No," she said.

He drove and did not look at her.

"I don't want anything. I really want you," she said. "Please."

They pulled into the parking lot of the Ohio Inn motel on Ohio and LaSalle, north of the Loop, and Terry Flynn went into the lobby. The clerk looked out at the car once and shrugged and took the money and gave him a key. He drove to the back of the motel and stopped the engine.

The room was dark because the blinds were drawn. It might not have been morning.

They walked into the room apart, as though they were suddenly shy with each other. Their thoughts of each other had overwhelmed them for a moment.

The room was warm and she sat down on the edge of the king-size bed and took off her boots and stood up. She was shorter than he was. He had taken off his coat and his sports coat and unbuttoned his shirt.

"Wait," he said because the smells of the night—of the interrogation, of the confrontation on Roscoe Street—were suddenly keen to him. "I smell like the job."

She turned away and unbuttoned her blouse. It was such an old-fashioned thing to do. It never failed to arouse him.

He showered and thought of her and felt warm in the shower. When he came into the darkened bedroom, she stood by the door and was naked.

He dropped the towel and held her. His skin was warm and he enveloped her cold body. She trembled because she was cold but she just wanted to stand a moment, with his arms around her, feeling the warmth of him.

He pressed against her. He kissed her deeply and her neck was forced back because she was shorter than he and it was not very graceful and comfortable. They fell onto the coverlet.

"I'm cold," she said at last.

Beneath the covers, he touched her. He opened her legs and felt her wetness.

They made love and it was over too soon for her. She wanted him now and she pushed him down on the sheets and took him in her mouth and coaxed him with her tongue. He pulled her head to him and grew in her and she finally climbed on him and felt it deep inside her. She shook her head to free her pleasure and closed her eyes and her mouth was open and she pressed her hands down on his belly and came in great shuddering spasms.

"Stop," he said then, after she came.

She stopped.

For a long time, he looked at her, filling his eyes with her. Then he began to lick her breasts. He licked the nipples and he licked in the crevice between her breasts until her head was shaking again in passion and she grabbed his head and pressed it to her and he felt hard again against her leg. She opened her legs.

"I love you, Karen," he said.

She said nothing.

It was understood between them about the subject of love and yet they both would break the rules between them, from time to time. Terry Flynn was large and bluff and abrasively honest and he had no more future in the department than a black Communist.

Terry Flynn had spent all his points very quickly. His father had been a wheeler-dealer in the department, though he only made sergeant when he was on the verge of retirement. His father was loud and had smoked big cigars and he had been the bagman for the various shakedown schemes in the various districts to which he had been assigned. His father had tried to teach Terry Flynn the rewards and punishments of a job on the cops—the life brutalized you and yet you had a fairly good chance of making money at it. And the money came from the scum, not from ordinary, honest people, so there was nothing in it to stain your conscience. His father had been an usher at St. Alma's when Terry Flynn was a boy and his father often had whiskey and cigars with the monsignor in the rectory house after the twelve o'clock Mass.

They made love now as though one was cold and hungry and the other was shelter and food.

Terry Flynn was never what Karen Kovac had in mind. She had ambition; she had grown accustomed to living alone after seven years as a single mother following her divorce. Her life was ordered and neatly divided and Terry Flynn occupied one wild and strange corner of it. The trouble was keeping him there.

The trouble was this, she thought as he moved on top of her, as she felt herself releasing in waves that made her body shudder like a boat suddenly beached on a sand bar. The trouble was that Terry Flynn kept insisting, kept breaking the rules.

Now it was after and they fell apart, naked and uncoupled, touching hands with fingertips.

She lay in the darkness, staring at the ceiling, thinking about Terry Flynn who was next to her on the rented bed.

"I thought about my husband," she said.

"That's a wonderful compliment to me."

"I didn't mean that. I used to talk to him about all the things I wanted to do and he would just stare at me sometimes like I said I was the queen of Spain."

Terry Flynn said nothing for a moment. Then, "You think about him."

"No," she said. "I think about him but I'm thinking about

sex. With him. With you. Funny. He's faded. Only sometimes, I can think it is the first time. I was really afraid, physically, but I wanted to do it badly. He didn't understand how much I wanted it, that I was just afraid because I had never done it before."

"I thought of Brandon Cale," Terry Flynn said.

"I know," she said. She didn't know but he needed her to say that.

"That's terrible," he said. "I couldn't help it. I looked at him this morning, in the squad room, he looked washed-out, sort of weak, you know. Is that what it's about? We make love like dogs, top dog and underdog, we make up to each other. I saw this film on Channel Eleven about packs of wolves, the top dog and how he makes the other dogs subservient."

"That's part of it," she said.

"Men don't talk about that stuff," he said.

"Not real men," she said. "Not women either. I guess we're just peculiar."

"It's kinky to think of cops screwing each other," he said.

She laughed in that sudden way that made him happy to hear it. She rolled to him and buried her face in his chest.

He said, "For two days, I've got fag, fag, fag. I got sick of it. I hate being put in a position. Everyone expects they know about Terry Flynn and they don't know shit."

It was true, she thought. It was exactly the way it was. Everyone understood everything about Terry Flynn from the moment they saw him or he opened his mouth. He was a crude, insensitive cop from a family of cops where his old man had been a bagman for the district; he was crude because his voice carried the unpolished accents of the South Side; he was blunt and maybe dishonest and certainly lazy and he was the kind of man who did not represent the highest standards of the department. So thought Commander Ranallo, so thought a lot of people.

But that was what had attracted her. She saw him as he really was. Confused, almost shy, sensitive to the point of pain. And he was speaking in pain now, in the darkness, and she held him because he hurt so much. She never wanted to feel that sensitive to anyone except maybe Tim, and yet she had seen everything he was almost from the beginning, as though his soul were visible but she was the only one to see it.

They fell asleep like that, and when they woke again it was nearly noon.

"Do you think the sidewalks are plowed?" she said to him.

"No," he said. "Not yet."

And they made love again, gently now, with pleasure that had no pain or pressure behind it.

They left shortly after 1:00 on the bright, crystal afternoon. The sky, streaked with airline-vapor trails, was so clear that the city stood out in sharp relief, like a city portrayed on a postcard.

He left her, reluctantly, on Jarvis Avenue in the old Rogers Park neighborhood at the north end of the city. The walks were cleared, the main streets were open, the cars along the side streets were still buried in snow. Here and there, in a cleared parking space, someone had put out wooden chairs and signs warning of death or worse if anyone tried to use the parking space.

"Who said cities are civilized?" Terry Flynn grinned at her. He was tired and his face was stubbled and there was a bloodstain on one trouser leg.

"You go home and get some sleep and we'll try this again tonight," she said, and kissed him. She opened the passenger door and got out on the street side and slammed the door shut behind her.

He watched her cross carefully over the drifts of plowed snow to the sidewalk and then start west to the El station where Mary Jane Caldwell had been attacked. He had wanted to say he loved her again but he was always afraid that at some point it would get too serious for her. She never wanted it to be serious between them, as though breaking up would not be a difficult thing.

"Who can sleep?" he said to her softly, in the car, but she was down the block already and had turned into the station.

He could tell her everything, he suddenly realized.

Except to say he loved her all the times he wanted to say it.

For fear it would be the wrong thing to say.

16
THE SEAMLESS GARMENT

"We've got a problem," Lee Horowitz said.

Jack Donovan waited. There was plenty of time. The problem would come to him.

Jack Donovan sat on the ledge of the tall window that opened onto the courtyard behind the Criminal Courts Building. Across the courtyard was the bulk of Cook County Jail, which was connected to the Criminal Courts Building by a tunnel. The prisoners were shuffled across from the jail to the courts by the tunnel.

Lee Horowitz had commandeered Jack's desk and sat in Jack's chair. It was all right. Jack Donovan always preferred to sit on the periphery of meetings like this, as though he might be able to escape quietly if no one noticed him. It was an absurd and childish thought and he knew it, but he still preferred to sit away from the center of the action.

It was nearly 11:00 on Tuesday morning.

Jerry Goldberg and Mario deVito sat on the leather couch. Mario actually was in the couch, indented heavily in the fabric so that he seemed part of it.

"The problem is both with the sloppy work at the arrest and with the DEA and our own investigation," Lee Horowitz continued. Jack Donovan thought Lee was sounding pompous this morning, which was unlike him. It probably had to do with the federal angle. Lee Horowitz had once worked for the Central Intelligence Agency and he had a picture of himself and President Truman on the wall of his office. He had known Truman, or claimed to.

"I don't really understand the first part of that," Jack Donovan said. "It sounded like a good bust."

Lee turned in the creaky swivel chair and fixed Jack with a hard look and a moment of silence.

"Sloppy. Number one, the shooting. That was unnecessary and it makes our job harder."

"Too bad he missed," said Mario deVito, who had not wanted to be part of this meeting either. He was the assistant designated to handle the prosecution of Walter ("Slide") Johnson and Raoul Macam, and that was why he had to be at the meeting.

"In a way, Mario, you're right," Lee Horowitz said. "Aside from this knifing, I mean. I mean, our investigation and the DEA becomes very . . . sticky . . . because this Mambo person is still around."

"Macam," said Jack Donovan.

"Whatever his name is," Lee Horowitz said. Lee was an energetic man in his sixties with white hair and aggressive gray eyes and a voice that barked out words like bullets. He was first assistant, which meant he was political guru to Bud Halligan, the elected state's attorney of Cook County and a man profoundly puzzled by the nature of his office.

And because Jack Donovan was chief of the criminal division, the political machinations invented by Lee Horowitz would have to be sorted out by him and his staff and made to appear "part of the seamless garment of the efficient criminal justice system." Which is the way Mario had once put it when he and Jack were both too drunk not to tell the truth to each other.

They had all been discussing the way to handle the arraignment of Raoul Macam and Walter Johnson that was scheduled for Wednesday morning.

"The problem is that the chief witness to this stabbing is tainted. He was targeted by our investigation. So was the dead man. And I read the reports, the initial report and the Homicide file on this. I wouldn't know that you could call this murder to start with," Lee Horowitz said. He had said it at the beginning of the meeting. He was getting them used to the idea.

"Bullshit," said Mario deVito, his voice coming deep from within his bulk buried in the soft leather couch. "There was a robbery, first on the train, then a second robbery at the foot of the steps at Fullerton El station. Then the witness was cut and the victim was stabbed. In the commission of a felony. What would you call that?"

"Maybe I'd call it voluntary manslaughter. Maybe the argument is going to be that Raoul Mambo was defending himself. The witness said the dead man attacked this Mambo person—"

"Christ," Mario deVito said with disgust.

Jack Donovan stared at the tips of his shoes and leaned forward from his perch. His back was cold. The window was single pane and the cold seeped in through the dried glazing.

"DEA has talked to Mambo twice—" Lee continued.

"Macam," Jack Donovan said. "His name is Macam."

Lee hurried on. "Talked to him twice. He wants to talk to us. He wants to help us out."

"He's shit, you can't deal with shit," deVito said.

It was Goldberg's turn. "Look, what this is about is bigger than a stabbing that might go murder, might go voluntary, might not even fly, although I agree with Mario that there was a crime here, we have a witness—"

"Who is tainted, who may be involved with the drug-selling scheme on the exchange, who may have been part of the deal—"

"This is an arraignment," Mario said. "We press the charge. We've got enough on them for this."

"But Stacy wants something else," Lee Horowitz said.

They waited for a moment.

"Stacy wants a bondable charge. At least on Macam. He doesn't care about the other one but we make it for one, we make it for both. He *wants* Raoul Macam on the street again.

Stacy says he'll have a short leash, he promises me that. This Raoul has already told enough about the market, about dealing. Stacy is convinced that everything we've been doing is heading in the right direction."

Jack Donovan felt drawn in. He was reluctant. His face was pale and his thin body was cold and everything in his manner was hesitant and even shy. Except when it came time to say the thing that had to be said.

"What does it do to our witness if we go in with a bondable offense and Macam makes bond?"

"Our witness is part of our target, Jack," Jerry Goldberg said. He was in charge of the long-running investigation of drug trafficking on the various stock exchanges in the Loop. The stock exchanges were perfect places to sell drugs. There was a lot of money among the traders who led a fast-paced, high-line existence. There was money for women (or men), for $50,000 cars, for apartments on the ninety-fifth floor of the John Hancock Building and $400,000 town houses in Lincoln Park. And for cocaine and heroin and lesser drugs of choice. "Brandon Cale will get nervous, so good. Maybe we can put pressure on him as well. Maybe we use Raoul Macam to crack Cale to crack bigger fish."

"And why does the state's attorney's office want to bend over backwards for DEA?" Jack Donovan asked, but he was not looking at Goldberg.

"Because for the obvious reasons," Goldberg said in an offended tone.

"What are the obvious reasons, Lee?" Jack Donovan said to the first assistant in the swivel chair.

"White-collar crime," Lee Horowitz said. "It's a growth industry." His mixed metaphors were not always unintended. "We make Bud Halligan an example of the kind of leadership that can lead to higher office."

"Like state attorney general," Jack Donovan said in the same flat monotone.

"Maybe like that. There's no percentage when you've got three terms in as state's attorney and there's an election in two years. What are you gonna do, run again? There's no percentage not to move up the food chain, you might say."

"We go in with voluntary so the guy can be bonded and then we can reinstate and go for the greater charge down the line," Goldberg said.

"Fuck the G," Mario deVito said. "You wanna do this great favor for the G, what do you think they're gonna do for you?"

"It smells nice, doing favors for the federal district," Lee said. "I don't need to tell you, we get heat in this office, we get civil rights complaints about the police, we get all kinds of heat—the rape ladies last week, they're in my office, they think we don't prosecute enough rape cases hard enough and we got rape cases coming out of our ass, which I pointed out to them— heat like that. It's like brass. You know, brass? Brass is brass but you gotta keep it polished. Every day, you gotta take the Brasso and give it a rub to keep the crud off. But once you got it shining nice, what have you got?"

Mario deVito only gaped at him.

"Brass," said Lee Horowitz. "The same old shit. You can rub brass until you're blue in the face and it's still gonna be brass. What you got to do is move up in class. This is a way to do it. It shows we go after the guilty, no matter how big they are. We get a couple of high-rollers on the stock market, it turns out they were doing drugs, then there's all kinds of investigations, I tell you, it will look good for Bud. And it never hurts to prosecute a big shot once in a while, it shows we have even-handed . . . you know. . . ."

As though Lee Horowitz did not want to say "justice."

"I'm against this," Mario said. "Murder takes precedence over dealing drugs on the goddam Board of Trade."

"Is that right?" Lee said. His voice was bulletproof. "Murder is what you call it. This is a homicide of a drug dealer by another drug dealer and maybe it will come down to murder in the end but—"

"Wait a minute, there was an investigation, there weren't any charges—"

"Charges smarges," Lee fumed. "I'm talking about what the

DEA knew. Lee Herran was dealing drugs. Lee Herran would take little trips down to Key West with his queer friends and when they came back, he had dope and he was selling it. But he wasn't the only one and he wasn't the biggest fish in the sea."

Jack Donovan's flat voice broke the excitement in the room. "Brandon Cale is going to get nervous. If he gets nervous, the defense gets stronger. The other charges are armed robbery, which is good for three to five in this case if we don't have anything else. These are punks. Kids. And Brandon is a homosexual, his testimony has to bring that out, bring out about Lee Herran. Homosexuals are not the most popular people to your average jury of twelve."

"One thing first," Lee said. "The story is dead in the water. We did our arrest, the papers buried it because they know this is fags involved now. The cops aren't going to beef on this."

"One cop will," Jack Donovan said, thinking of Terry Flynn. He had known Terry Flynn in other cases.

"Make it bondable," Lee said as a final note. He got up from the chair. "I want him to walk—"

"They'll both walk, you can't do murder on one and voluntary manslaughter on the other," Mario said.

"Wrong again. You get the beef to fifty thousand dollars and where is Walter Johnson going to come up with five thousand dollars bail?"

"But Raoul Macam is going to find five thousand dollars, right, Lee?" Jack Donovan said in a voice so soft it had to be an accusation.

"Sure," Lee smiled. "He's got friends he didn't know he had."

17
WEDNESDAY

The arraignment took twenty minutes on Wednesday morning and when it was over, Terry Flynn slammed out of the courtroom on the fifth floor of the old Criminal Courts Building and took the stairs down to the ground level. Quigley took the elevator. He knew where Terry was going. He found him at Jean's, down the block from the court building. It was just 11:00 in the morning and Terry Flynn drank a shot of Christian Brothers brandy and swallowed a first long draught of beer. Quigley ordered a gin and tonic without lime. It was going to be a long afternoon.

Raoul Macam was surprised to find himself bonded out by 3:00 in the afternoon. Life was very surprising, especially since he had started to trust and talk with Richard Stacy of the Drug Enforcement Administration.

Slide spent the afternoon in the day room on tier four, watching a soap opera on the black-and-white screen, listening to the others in the common room talk about the various sexual attributes of the various women on the soap opera. He kept thinking about what had happened in the court at the arraignment. He kept trying to figure it out.

Karen Kovac dressed carefully in the morning. Her son was most surprised to see her don the black wig. She said she was working on something. She never talked to Tim about the business of the job, more for her own sake than for his. She needed separations in her life; she realized it was what she had always wanted and why her marriage had not worked and why she would never marry Terry Flynn. Terry Flynn was her lover and he was here; and Tim was here; and the job was here. All separate and clear and bearable.

It was a week to the day since the attack on Mary Jane Caldwell at the Jarvis Avenue elevated station. Karen Kovac had a hunch and she was superstitious enough to act on it, to the extent of explaining it to Lieutenant Matt Schmidt in Special Squad. He suggested that Sid Margolies go along with her while she acted on the hunch. Margolies was a taciturn and reliable detective, who had been in the police department about two years too long.

Sid Margolies drove the blue Plymouth north on Sheridan Road toward the Jarvis station. It was just after 11:00 in the morning.

"Tell me the theory," he said to Karen Kovac, who sat next to him.

"I've stomped through that neighborhood for a week and there isn't any sense to it, to them being there at that time, on that El platform. There's no high school right there, there's nothing. So who are these kids? I don't know. But maybe it has something to do with the day of the week."

"That's not a theory," Sid Margolies said. He was offended by the lack of logic. He was a careful and logical man who took note of the details. He would have made a good accountant. Which, in an odd way, made him a good detective. He had a thin, worn face and dark skin and weary eyes. He had been in Special Squad for four years and he had been sorry to see Terry Flynn transferred out. Terry Flynn was everything Sid was not, which made them work well together.

"I know," she said. "It's all I've got. I talked to the victim yesterday again, for a long time. She's in trouble, Sid."

"She should have counseling," said Sid, who believed in such things.

"I told her that. I even called up the rape ladies. But she doesn't want to talk to them." The "rape ladies" was the slang designation for the women's coalition in the city that pushed for vigorous rape prosecutions, as well as offering counseling to rape victims.

"She's inside herself. She said she spent Sunday with her father. She said she could see that her father thought it was her fault," Karen Kovac said. She stared straight ahead, out the windshield, at the narrow canyon formed by the high-rise condominiums on either side. The street was the extension of Lake Shore Drive north along the lake to the Rogers Park neighborhood. The day was gray and the snow piled along the curb was dirty. The windshield was dirty and streaked by the wipers.

"Is that true?" Sid Margolies said after a while.

"I don't know. She said it about the policemen who found her. I don't know. I wasn't the one who was raped."

"Purse snatchers. I mean, there's a lot of old ladies in that neighborhood," Sid said, blurting out an idea formed apart from the conversation.

"Yes," Karen Kovac said. "I did some work on that. There have been a dozen reports in the last month. So maybe that's it, they're guys working the neighborhood on a schedule, because most of the reports around Jarvis station came on Wednesday or Thursday. Not all of them."

"They might not all be the same guys," Sid said. "They work one neighborhood and then leave it and work another neighborhood."

"But not on a regular schedule," she said. "There were three reports on a single day and it was a Sunday, two months ago."

"So maybe this is a theory and maybe it isn't," Sid Margolies said, as though he had to decide.

"It's something worth a try."

"Worth a try," Sid said, because you're supposed to go along with a partner.

"The wig looks right, doesn't it?"

"I don't know what the victim looks like. I don't understand that part of it—"

118

"Maybe they want to see if this woman uses that station all the time. Or on Wednesdays."

"They can't be that stupid," Sid said.

"Come on, Sid. They were stupid enough to attack her in broad daylight, right in the stairwell of an El station. They aren't so bright."

"They aren't that stupid," Sid said.

18
JARVIS

The decoy operation was a complete failure and Karen Kovac admitted as much to Sid Margolies. She had caught cold, standing on the El platform at Jarvis Avenue, waiting for a miracle.

She and Sid had been given two-way radios—for which they signed out—but one of them refused to work and so they had been out of touch for most of the afternoon. Sid sat in the car at the end of the block and drank coffee from a Thermos bottle he always kept in his locker at work for use in assignments like this.

For five hours, they saw only the few old men and old women and the occasional housewife who used the Jarvis station pass through the wood-and-glass entrance.

At 4:30, she was ready to go home and stand in a hot shower for a couple of hours. She removed the pistol from her coat pocket, where her hand had kept the pistol warm, and put it back in her purse. She closed the purse. And the kid who had just gotten off a northbound A train grabbed the purse in that awkward moment and pushed Karen on the slippery platform boards.

The kid hit the entry door while Karen felt herself falling.

He took the steps two at a time.

Karen shouted. Her ankle felt dangerously weak. She crawled to her feet. A man helped her stand.

"Police!" she shouted.

"It's only your purse, lady, it could have been worse—"

But she pushed herself away from the helping hand and staggered to the door. The kid was already turning down the last flight of stairs.

She didn't have her gun. He was wearing a field jacket.

She forced herself to the rail and took the stairs as fast as she could. Her ankle threatened to collapse on her every time she stepped on it. She grimaced in pain.

The kid was through the station before she made the first flight of stairs.

He slipped on the packed-down snow in front of the station and caught himself and started running east.

That was the mistake, as Sid Margolies told him later. If he had gone west, it might have taken Margolies too long to force the car out of its spot in the packed-down snow at the curb, over the hump of snow along the parking line and into the narrow street after him.

As it was, Margolies simply opened the door of the unmarked squad as the kid ran into it.

He was down, the purse was spilled open, he saw the gun that came from the purse on the snow. He shook his head.

Sid Margolies had a conservative black Smith & Wesson .38 Police Special in his hand as he stepped from the car and placed the muzzle gently against the youth's left ear.

The kid flinched.

"Don't even shiver," Sid Margolies said carefully. "Where's the woman?"

"I didn't do nothing," the kid said.

"Don't ever lie to a policeman," Sid Margolies said in the same, flat, almost uninterested voice. He was sweating because he did not see Karen on the street. This was her purse, that was her gun on the snow.

"Where is the woman—"

"Man, I didn't do nothing—"

"She's a policeman—"

And the kid said, "Oh, shit."

Margolies blinked.

"Fucking purse, she's gotta be a policewoman, you guys got nothing better to do than try to trap purse snatchers? There's criminals out there," the kid said, and Margolies only blinked again.

And then he saw Karen limping down the sidewalk toward them.

He took the pistol away from the youth's left ear and stood up straight. He realized he felt light-headed.

His name was Rodney Rodriguez and he said he was a juvenile, which no one listened to.

They had him in an interrogation room in police headquarters at Eleventh and State streets. It was dark already though it was not yet five in the afternoon. Margolies and Karen Kovac and Lieutenant Matt Schmidt were all in the interrogation room with the prisoner.

Rodriguez sat by a window laced with a fine wire grill. Seven stories beneath the window, he could see the Dan Ryan Line elevated train curving between the last tall buildings of the south Loop, twisting into an escape route south and west to Chinatown.

They were waiting for Mary Jane Caldwell to come home from her classes. A policeman was at her apartment building and another had gone to the campus of Loyola University to see if she could be intercepted at her class. It was that important to them.

The excitement was infectious. Even Matt Schmidt, whose dour face and impeccable blue suits and white shirts and dull ties spoke of an old-fashioned homicide detective who had seen everything, was caught in the unspoken fever.

Karen hobbled back and forth on her sprained ankle, wrapped in an Ace bandage.

"How long you been doing this again, Rodney?" Sid Margolies said.

"I been doing nodding," Rodney Rodriguez said.

"Rodney, I told you not to lie to a police officer."

"I ain't lying to you." He looked with sullen eyes at both of them. "You got nodding better to do than set up me for a stinking little thing like this?"

"Someone has to catch you," Sid Margolies said.

"Aw, man." He paused. "You gotta smoke?"

"Smoking isn't good for you," Sid Margolies said.

"What are you, a fruit or something?"

Karen Kovac hit him without a word and even Matt Schmidt seemed startled by that. Rodney went spinning out of the wooden chair that he dragged over on top of him, because he was connected to the chair by handcuffs. Karen pulled him up by his hair and put him in the righted chair again. He stared at her with hatred. And a little edge of fear in the brown sullen eyes.

Matt Schmidt stared at Karen. Her face was white, her eyes were brittle and cold. Matt Schmidt saw her hands were trembling but it was not fear, it was more like rage.

"Where were you last Wednesday?" Karen Kovac asked.

"I dunno. I was around or somethin'. You know. I dunno." The nasal voice was on the edge of a whine. He kept his eyes on Karen and one hand was tensed on the arm of the chair, as though to ward off a blow at any moment.

"I don't want 'I dunno,' I want a place and a time," she said, biting off each word. "I'm not playing with you."

"I say, I dunno, I mean, I dunno."

She made a move and Matt Schmidt said, "Karen." The voice was a whip-crack in the tense little room with gray walls and green linoleum.

Karen looked at the cadaverous face of the Homicide Squad commander and seemed to see the others in the room for the first time.

She stepped on her bad ankle again and felt the surge of pain and winced. She went to the door of the interview room, turned the handle, walked outside.

The hall was cheerlessly lit with rows of fluorescent lamps hung low from the high dark ceiling.

Matt Schmidt was behind her. He closed the door. He took

her elbow and walked with her down to the alcove where the cigarette and candy machines were kept. The candy machine had been broken all week because someone had jimmied the change box. Speculation was that it was a criminal instead of a policeman, because a policeman would have popped the lock with more expertise.

"Don't get that close," he said to her.

"I'm not," she said, turning to him. "I'm so damned far away from it that it makes me mad. I'm getting like everyone else around here, I just don't give a damn anymore about anything, and that little bastard in there, he's got a grievance because he was just knocking me down and grabbing my purse and we shouldn't have had two policemen on a case like that. He's right. There's criminals out there and real crime; we're wasting our time with flotsam. Dammit."

"Too close," Matt Schmidt said. "You've knocked yourself out on this. I appreciate that." The voice had no judgment in it and no appreciation. Matt Schmidt's gray eyes were steady on her, deciding something about her, about the way she looked now and whether she would be any good if the case dragged on.

She stared at him.

"This is a rape case and this may be the suspect or not, but you can't get close to it, not the way you are. Separation, Karen. There's you and there's a rape victim and there's someone who did it and—"

"I'm not a complete idiot," she said in a very cold voice. "This is a rape case, like you said, but it isn't the run of the mill. Mary Jane Caldwell wasn't the neighborhood punchboard. I know about rape. I get lots of practice in rape cases. Remember I'm the token woman in Homicide so I get all the good ones, the real ones. 'Give it to the broad.'"

"Cut the crap, Karen," Matt Schmidt said. "Nobody has time for that much self-pity. You want out of Homicide, get out. Get a job writing parking tickets."

"No self-pity and no pity either," she said. "So we picked up Rodriguez. But if we didn't luck out today, how many more days do I have on this rape case?"

"The case is open."

"But that's because we're slow. We're in the dead of winter and nothing is moving, even the criminals get slowed down. So I have time for Mary Jane because she got raped at the right time of year. But I'm balancing a court schedule on the gang shootings and there's still the Mosconi-Rivalvi murders, and what will tomorrow bring? Maybe a stabbing in the tunnel under City Hall and that will make this place a Chinese fire drill again, everyone running around and shouting, and in all the shouting, we'll lose the Mary Jane case in the card file—something to look into if we get another slow day."

"It works that way."

"It works that way," she answered.

"It just works that way, Karen. What do you want from me? A heart-to-heart? If you promise not to tell Gert, I'll reserve us a back booth in the Well-of-the-Sea down at the Sherman House and I can give you advice and grope you at the same time." The stern face softened. "But I forget. They tore down the Sherman House, didn't they? Never mind. I know a hundred dark bars we can hide in and get drunk together and tell cop stories in and no one will care about us or even miss us."

She tried a smile then. She understood. She nodded her head and the smile opened.

Matt Schmidt stared at her sharp and pretty face. "OK? We'll make a date."

"OK, coach," she said.

"I'm old enough to be your father."

"Sometimes I think you are."

"OK? You understand now about Rodriguez?"

"Yes. I'll be OK. I was seeing Mary Jane, I was feeling her inside me. That's too scary," she said.

"OK. Just so you understand. It's all right to get scared that way but don't let anyone see it. Now go back into the game."

"OK, coach."

"I'd pat you on the fanny . . ." Matt Schmidt said.

Her smile was real and he felt relieved to see it.

"Save it for the dark bars," she säid. "When we tell each other cop stories."

Mary Jane Caldwell was led to the elevator by a uniformed policeman. They rode up to the seventh floor in silence. Karen Kovac was standing near the elevators when they arrived. Mary Jane was pale and her pale features were heightened by the dark blue coat she wore. She wore no makeup. She stared straight ahead.

Karen greeted her and she did not respond.

"Mary Jane," Karen said again.

The gray eyes shifted, focused. Mary Jane's eyes were bright and hard.

"Are you all right?" Karen said, feeling the other woman crawling inside her again.

"I'm all right," she said. The voice was flat.

"We found this one. On the El. He attacked me on the Jarvis El platform."

"One man," Mary Jane said.

"Just one," Karen said. "Are you all right?"

Mary Jane blinked and saw Karen again. "Which one is it?"

"He's a Puerto Rican. Lighter skin. It might be the smaller one you described."

"He attacked you?"

"I was a decoy. He grabbed me. He pushed me, I slipped and fell down. Sid Margolies got him. Detective Margolies."

"He admitted—"

"No."

"Why do you think?"

"The El, the same kind of attack, you know."

Mary Jane stared at Karen to see her better. The headache was coming back. Sometimes it waited for night to come back but sometimes, today, it started in the morning.

"It's called a showup. It's all right. Just be careful. Take your time and be sure. Just take it easy."

Terry Flynn had rounded up a few tactical cops from First District, which was on the first floor of the headquarters building at

Eleventh and State. A lot of tactical cops wore army field jackets on duty. Flynn needed them to round out the showup.

The showup room was at one end of the hall. The method was simple and crude and not at all like showups on television. The suspect and the policemen dressed like him entered the room and stood by the far wall. The witness looked through a one-way mirror in the door that led to the room to identify the suspect.

Matt Schmidt was in the room as well, to maintain order. The five men on the wall included four policemen in field jackets. Rodney Rodriguez stood in the middle of them and looked back and forth at them. He wondered if he was in real trouble now.

"All right, stop fidgeting around and look at the door, everyone."

"Man, why I gotta look at the door?" Rodney Rodriguez said.

One of the tac cops stared at him. "Because if you don't we beat the shit out of you. Right, Loo?"

Schmidt said nothing.

Outside the door, Mary Jane Caldwell looked through the glass. She stared for a long time. Karen watched her profile, watched the stubborn chin and the soft face and the hard eyes. There were lines of strain around her eyes now. "I don't know," she said.

"Take your time," Karen said, holding her breath.

It must be the one who looks Spanish, Mary Jane thought. It could be the same one. It really could be the same one.

She closed her eyes a moment.

Karen stared at her profile.

She opened her eyes and nodded. "The one in the middle," she said.

"The middle," Karen said.

"The shorter one."

Karen stepped to the door, looked through the glass. "Are you sure?"

"Yes." The voice snapped, almost in anger. "Don't you think I would be sure?"

"I just wanted—"

"Everyone patronizes me. I'm not crazy, you know. I was attacked and I ought to know what he looked like."

"Look again," Karen said.

Mary Jane glared at her. She looked again. She looked at Karen and said, "He hasn't changed."

"All right," Karen said, letting her breath out in a rush. "All right. Good." She touched Mary Jane's elbow. Mary Jane pulled her arm away.

"Good," Karen said. "This is good, this is a good one."

She was smiling.

"We got him," she said.

And Mary Jane said nothing.

19
THE WAY
IT WORKS

David said to Brandon, "So what did he say to you?"

"Sergeant Flynn said it stinks but that it might work out. He said the Drug Enforcement people were playing a game; I didn't understand it. He said at least they locked them up. He said it was a long way to the trial and that the charges could change."

"And then what happened?"

"I had to talk after the hearing . . . the arraignment . . . with this man. His name is Richard Stacy and he said he was an agent with the Drug Enforcement Administration. He talked a long time."

"He's the one that said that Lee was dealing in drugs," David said.

They were in the office in the back of Swallow's. Brandon was sitting at the desk with a glass of Scotch in front of him. The color was back in his face. It had been bad, all of it, all day long, and there was a sick feeling in his stomach, as though it was never going to stop being bad.

"Yes. He kept after me. I was in there two hours." Brandon closed his eyes to better see the cluttered room given over to the man from the DEA. The room was filled with cardboard boxes full of evidence from trials, trial records, transcripts. Everything was disorganized and the chair he sat in during the interrogation was broken so that it rocked back and forth as he tried to understand what Richard Stacy was telling him.

"He kept after me. He kept after me. I finally got it. He thought I was dealing drugs, it had all to do with this Raoul Macam. I saw what he was saying."

"He asked you about when Lee went to Key West at Thanksgiving—"

"Yes. I told him I went home. To Decatur. And he said, 'We know that.' I mean, that's just the way he said it. 'We know that.' I said, 'What does that mean?' and he gives me this look and he starts on about me and Lee, he said we were a couple of fruits, that when it was my turn to go inside, I'd be happy to be a princess—"

"Bastard," David said. David sat on the other side of the desk. David sat still and he was not drinking anything. He wanted to hold Brandon in his arms and he thought in a little while he would be doing that.

"Lee liked to go to Key West. It made him relax. He played around. I knew that. I went with him once, I didn't care for it. It was a different crowd down there. People that Lee knew—"

"I know," David said. He did know. Brandon was naïve in so many ways and there were so many things he did not know.

Brandon began to cry and neither of them noticed it at first because the tears were without sound and because Brandon kept talking about Richard Stacy of the Drug Enforcement Administration and how the day of the arraignment of the men who had killed Lee had turned into this kind of prolonged torture with questions about drugs and who was dealing with who and vague threats about what life would be like inside a federal penitentiary.

"He told me—I can't remember when he started on this— he told me, 'You probably hear about federal prisons being country clubs. You probably heard that. It's true they're better than state prisons but they aren't country clubs, you don't see people standing in line to get a membership. And there's no guarantees about federal prison anyway. This can be a state beef just as well. You think you could stand a couple of terms down in

Stateville. You know what they would do to you in a prison like that? You have any idea?'" Brandon shuddered, the words kept on in his head. They went on, and then both of them realized Brandon had been crying all the while he was talking.

In that moment, Brandon Cale felt utterly alone for the first time in his life. He felt isolated even from David. From the moment of Lee's death, when the first policemen arrived, when he stared at the black woman in the ticket cage opposite where he sat in the Fullerton Avenue El station, from the first interrogation by Flynn, he had felt further and further away from what he had considered always to be the base, to be real, the thing he was part of. He had talked to his brother on the phone and the voice had been odd and distant, as though his brother was talking to him across a void that was getting wider. Brandon shuddered, and when David touched his shoulder the shuddering increased. The void was endless. He was lost in a demented wonderland, through a dark looking glass. He stared at David and David seemed far away.

And he heard his own voice at last but it was a distant voice, very small and pleading and faraway:

"What did I do, David?" he sobbed then. "It was Friday night and we ate out and we were coming home and then, just like that, for no reason, one of them cut me and one of them kills Lee, just like that. Just like that, he's dead. Lee is dead. Just like that." He paused and wiped his eyes. "Now he talks about me going to prison. Lee wasn't a drug dealer. I'm not a drug dealer. What are they trying to do? Is this because I'm gay? Is that what this is about?"

"Yes," David said. "Part of it. I thought you understood that."

"Jesus. Jesus," Brandon Cale said.

"Yes," David said.

"And he said he would see to it that Raoul Macam got bail on the charges. He told me that. A federal officer. That animal is going to be on the streets again."

"Yes," David said.

For a moment, there was silence between them.

David got up from the desk and went to the opened safe. He took out a brown paper bag with a heavy object in it.

"I was thinking about it. What you said to me Sunday. About getting a piece. I was thinking about it and I didn't know if it was a good idea for you. I didn't know what you wanted it for. I thought you might even kill yourself. You were in here and you kept talking about Lee as though you were responsible for his death. And then, Monday, when we went to Queen of Heaven and you saw Lee's father and you wanted to explain to him. . . . God, Brandon, I didn't know how it was hitting you. So I wasn't going to get this for you. I had the piece all along but I thought maybe you'd forget about it. You told me you knew guns. You said you hunted with your brother. You know this gun?"

Brandon had no more tears. He opened the paper bag and took out the piece.

It was an automatic with the words WALTHER and the initials PPK on the side.

Brandon handled it. It was light but it had a solid and chilling feel. He turned it over and opened the cartridge.

"You know that piece?" David said.

"Yes. I knew about pistols. When I was a kid, I was a good shot. I was on a team in high school. I knew about pistols. I never kept a pistol, we didn't have money for that kind of thing. We had shotguns. For the vermin. And my father had a rifle, he hunted deer. We ate venison all winter. He would kill a good-size buck and skin it right in the field." He recited the commonplace of his childhood, as though he were thinking about it for the first time in a long time. "I was fascinated by guns when I was a kid," Brandon said. "This is a good pistol. A very good pistol."

"Yeah. Well—"

"How much is it?"

"Gimme three."

"Is it . . . you know . . . stolen?"

"Sure," David said. "You wouldn't get a piece like this for that if it wasn't hot. This is a good piece."

Brandon stared at David. The room was small, filled with folders, boxes, promotion materials from brewing companies.

"I think you need it now. I think you do. But you have to be careful. If there's federal agents involved, I don't want to be involved. I'm doing this for you." David blinked. It was a trick to make his eyes wet. He looked hard at Brandon, at the suddenly softened face. He wanted him very badly. He reached out and touched Brandon's face. Brandon sat very still. David touched Brandon's lips and Brandon opened his mouth a little and David knew. And Brandon knew. Brandon said, "Thank you."

David got up then and came around the desk in the small room. There was nearly no room at all between them.

"Come on now," David said, and Brandon did what he felt he should do, what he wanted to do in that moment to stay the void a little longer from coming all around him and swallowing him.

20
THE
MACHINE

For a long time, Rodney Rodriguez thought he should say nothing at all, that somehow the silence would stop all this from happening. Because it was ridiculous if you looked at it the right way. And it was all a mistake. It was just a mistake.

He was given a lawyer at last and the weary public defender started in with his rights and all the other garbage that Rodney Rodriguez had heard all his life, except that he knew it was all garbage, he knew it from Jump Street.

He spent the night in jail and it was noise all night long. He knew that noise. Jails are always full of sounds all the time. There are sounds of men crying and singing and laughing and screaming. There are shouts and taunts and curses thrown from the darkened cells. There are animal grunts and groans and there are sounds of radios wailing black soul music into the darkness. The jail never sleeps inside; it is like a beast that has to keep wounding itself to be alive.

In the morning, they took him to the courtroom through the tunnel and they still didn't figure it out, it was so crazy. Rape. That was what was so crazy about it.

Jack Donovan assigned Mario deVito to the prosecution at 9:30 Thursday morning. At 10:00, the machinery of justice demanded Mario's heavy presence in Courtroom 602 on the sixth floor of the Criminal Courts Building in the matter of arraignment of charges against Rodney Rodriguez.

Judge Henry Boyle mounted the three steps to his chair at 10:02 and his clerk, a fat man named Leroy Baxter, stood at his table at the side of the bench while the attorneys lined up to file for their continuances. Henry Boyle was bored, he had been bored for twenty-three years on the bench, and this day was like all the others. In fact, it would turn out to be quite a different morning.

Mario deVito made his way to the front of the room and nodded at one of the public defenders.

"Yes, I can put this over to March but why don't you just give me a reason this time, counselor? This is the fourth continuance—"

"Your Honor," began the assistant state's attorney. "The state is ready on this case—"

The lawyer turned. It was Mark Cutler. "Your Honor, I have been unable to prepare this matter—"

"Is that right, Mr. Cutler? What is the excuse this time, counselor?"

"Your Honor, you may remember the matter of an assault and murder on the Howard Street El. I was involved. I was assaulted and I was robbed in that matter and the trauma and the court appearances I have had to make since the matter—"

"Awright, awright, counselor, we'll put it over to March fourteenth. That's Thursday. That's March fourteenth. In the present year of Our Lord." Boyle had a reputation for sarcasm. "Between now and then, don't ride any more El trains, awright, counselor?"

"Yes, Your Honor." Mark Cutler smiled and his client nodded vigorously. It was a simple case of armed robbery.

Cutler nodded to the judge, nodded to his client who had robbed a liquor store nine months previously and gotten $2,313 in cash for his efforts, and put the case envelope in his attaché case—the one that had been opened by three men on that El train nearly a week earlier.

Cutler pushed through the crowded courtroom toward the

exit. Mario deVito brushed against him on his way to the table. They looked at each other as though they should know each other.

"Oh, yeah," Mario said. "Cutler, on the El."

"Yeah. I didn't understand that arraignment yesterday. Why was the murder reduced?"

"I didn't understand it myself," Mario said.

"You're Ginnetti," Cutler said, perplexed.

"DeVito."

"DeVito. Yeah, I know. So what's up?"

"Something about the feds. They want to play games with the slasher."

"Puerto Rican scum, cut my topcoat. Burberry. I paid four hundred dollars for it, now it's got a cut on it."

"Yeah. Well, we all gotta expect losses."

"That's the name of the game," Cutler said in a merry voice. And they pushed away from each other.

". . . putting this over and that is it, counselor. You will be prepared for trial on Thursday, February 28, this is not a game we're playing, counselor . . ."

"Your Honor, I realize that, I have a call in Courtroom 314, Judge Fitts's courtroom, I had no idea there would be a conflict—"

"How much money do you need, counselor? If you can't service all your clients, drop some of them. Don't be greedy," Judge Boyle said. "There's plenty to go around. There's a whole world full of criminals and lawyers looking for each other."

The attorney blushed and mumbled another apology and the clerk was turning to the next matter, and in all the confusion and noise and crowd there was a certain logic to it.

Mario waited patiently at the table while the assistant SA assigned to the court followed through his packet of briefs as the cases came up and were continued to another day. The crowd thinned. The lawyers scattered to other engagements. And then it was the matter of an arraignment hearing.

Judge Boyle looked at the brief and then looked at Mario

deVito and at the public defender, Tom Murray. Murray had been a lawyer for two years. He would jump into private practice in two months if the deal went through with the firm. In two years more, he would own part of his first Atlanta shopping center on a tax-loss limited partnership. He had a schedule and he was right on time.

"Rape, huh?" mumbled Boyle, looking at the docket. He looked at Mario. "Is this the one I read about in the paper about the girl on the El platform up on the North Side?"

"Yes, Your Honor," Mario deVito said.

"Christ, what a bunch of animals," Boyle said. "You. What's your name? That's Rodney Rodriguez?"

"Yes, Your Honor," Murray said. "Client wishes to enter a plea."

"How does he plead?"

"Not guilty."

"Of course," Boyle said in a bored voice. "Who's the state's attorney?"

"Your Honor," began Mario deVito.

"Hey, judge," said Rodney Rodriguez suddenly, standing up. The sheriff's bailiff put his hand on his pistol and came around the bench. "Siddown."

"Sit that man down," said Boyle.

"Judge—"

"Siddown," said the bailiff, and he shoved Rodriguez hard. Rodriguez said, "Hey, you got the wrong man."

"Shuddup," said Boyle. "We always got the wrong man."

"I dinna rape nobody!"

Karen Kovac was there and Mary Jane Caldwell was in a witness room in the back of the courtroom. Sid Margolies sat sprawled on a chair, chewing gum.

"I'm gonna hold you in contempt of court—" Boyle began.

"Dey say I was rapin' this lady, I was no rapin'," Rodriguez said. It was time to start talking, the silence wasn't working at all. "I couldn't rape nobody."

"Why not?" Judge Boyle said.

"I was in jail, Judge. I was in the motherfucking jail, same fucking place I was in last night. I dinna rape nobody and I dinna rape nobody on Wednesday 'cause I was in jail."

It became very quiet.

Mario stared at Rodriguez and Rodriguez stared back at him. Even Murray stopped thinking about the Atlanta shopping center he intended to buy into.

"What about this?"

Mario deVito stared and said nothing for another long moment. "Your Honor, the record shows the arrest of Mr. Rodriguez on January 14—"

"Das right—"

"Be quiet, Mr. Rodriguez."

"Dey say I was breakin' into a grocery. I wasn't but dey say it—"

"Be quiet."

"—shows an arrest but it doesn't show disposition, I mean . . ." Mario stumbled. "Records, Your Honor—"

"Look, I can straighten dis out," Rodriguez said, strutting a little. These people were hopeless. "Look, mon, dis guy and me, we was comin' over for hearings, this guy was my buddy, you know, we was tight inside, so they make a mistake, they bring us out to the court. I was waiting, it was Judge Fitts's court, you can check, and pretty soon, they all done with the cases and we just sitting there in the court. I dunno what happened." He smiled. "It was like a miracle or something. So we walk out. You know. Him and me. He was on a assault, I theenk. You check it out. I mean, you lost the paper, not me. I mean, you let me go."

"Did we let him go?"

"I don't know," Mario deVito said. "When did he walk out?"

"Dis was Friday, mon," Rodney Rodriguez said. "I was in jail right to Friday. If I was in jail, I couldn't rape nobody, no matter what that crazy bitch say."

Mario looked at Karen. They understood that it could happen, that sometimes it did happen, that in the shuffle of prisoners and papers and lawyers and charges and cops and continuances and witnesses back and forth, that sometimes it happened.

"This is crazy," Mario said.

"I suggest a recess until two P.M., and I want this matter straightened out. I mean, I want this straightened out." Boyle rose. Boyle shuffled in his gown down the three steps into the back room.

It was not pleasant to discover that Rodney Rodriguez was speaking the truth.

They brought Mary Jane Caldwell to an anteroom off the office of Jack Donovan on the second floor of the Criminal Courts Building.

Mary Jane Caldwell sat on a wooden chair in the middle of the office with her hands folded in her lap. She stared at Karen Kovac and at the others who crowded into the room for a long time. No one spoke.

Karen Kovac said at last: "He was in jail, Mary Jane. You picked out the wrong man."

Mario deVito cleared his throat, as though he was embarrassed. Jack Donovan sat on a throne of cardboard boxes containing evidence and transcripts from a murder trial the previous fall that had attracted some national attention. There was no place to file the boxes for the moment and so they were stacked in this spare room.

"I thought he was the man," she said. "I did at the time. I thought you wouldn't have arrested him if he wasn't the man. I knew it was him, the other men in the room in the lineup . . . in the showup . . . looked like policemen."

"But he was the wrong man," Karen said.

Mario cleared his throat again.

"I'm sorry," Mary Jane said. "I'm sorry. I made a mistake. In the light, I thought he might have been the man and that I was . . . I was blocking him out of my mind because I was afraid of picking the man, because I was afraid of having to go to court and tell . . . this . . . thing . . . that happened . . . again. I was afraid."

"It's all right," Karen said. She patted her hand. "I'll drive you home in a little while. Wait for me here."

And Karen went into Jack Donovan's office with Mario and Sid Margolies and they all stared at each other, as though they had too much to say and they were waiting for the first one to break the ice and say it.

"This kills it," Mario said. "We can't use her again."

"Why can't we?" Karen said.

"Because she picked out a wrong guy. If she picks out the right guy sometime, if we're lucky enough to find the right guy, then the guy's defense attorney will get him off by pointing out that Mary Jane is an unreliable witness, and since she is the only witness to what happened, we're fucked."

Sid said, "I'm going home. I'll see you guys." He walked out of the office without another word.

"So that's it," Karen Kovac said in a dull voice.

Jack Donovan looked at her. "There's nothing you can do. You can't work magic."

"Dammit, I pushed her into it. I really wanted that to be the guy. I pushed her into it."

"It's your fault?" Jack Donovan said.

"Yes."

"Bullshit," he said. "That's what you get when you get too close to something. That's bullshit. You just keep your distance and get some perspective."

"Is that right?" Karen Kovac said.

"Yes," Jack Donovan said. They looked at each other in that moment as though they were looking at each other for the first time. Even Mario saw it.

"Is that the way you can see it from over there, being a lawyer?" she said.

"Don't talk like Terry Flynn," Jack Donovan said. He sat down on the window ledge. The gray yard below the window was filled with police cars and squadrols. The gray walls of the jail across the yard blended in the dirty grayness of the morning.

Yes, Karen thought. That's something Terry Flynn would

say, and everyone would say, There goes Flynn again. He was a joke to some people because he didn't care what he said or did. He ran by his own rules. He ran by emotions. It was the least attractive thing about him, she thought in that moment.

"What do we tell Mary Jane?" she said.

"We don't have to tell her anything. Tell her we're going to keep working on it. Tell her that her local law-enforcement agency will spare no effort to bring the guilty to the bar of justice where her local prosecutor's office will do the same sterling work in getting a conviction." Jack Donovan said these things in a flat voice. His face was the color of ashes. He stared out the window as though looking for light. "Tell her any damned thing."

"That first afternoon, she was in shock, she kept trying to explain in a calm voice but she would break down, and, finally, they had to restrain her. She was bleeding from the vagina," Karen Kovac said.

"Christ's sake, Karen," Jack Donovan said. "Cut out someone else's heart. I know what rape is. We prosecute a few rape cases."

"This was different," she said.

"Yes," Jack Donovan said. He stared at Karen's certain eyes. She looked very beautiful standing in her blouse and skirt and jacket in the middle of the room, her hands at her sides, very certain and poised. Jack Donovan stood up and kept staring at her. "I know about different. I was a cop."

"Why did you quit?"

"Because of crap like this case," Jack Donovan said.

They both acted as though Mario deVito had left the room. He stood between them and buttoned his coat. They didn't see him.

"It's a long sad story, the way all cop stories are, and there are funny bits too. Some night when we need to get boozy at O'Sullivan's, I'll tell you all about it so you can pity poor Jack Donovan. Pity is a nice ploy in a dark bar," he said. The voice was still metallic. "In the meantime, do your good duty by Mary Jane and try to tell her that we all feel this too and—"

"It's not that cynical," Karen said.

"No," Jack Donovan said. "It's a matter of survival."

"I'm afraid now all the time. At night especially, but it happened right in broad daylight but I'm afraid at night," Mary Jane Caldwell said. She sat at the table where she made coffee for Karen. It was just afternoon and Karen Kovac did not want to stay with her but she could not pull away. Mary Jane was talking compulsively to her.

"I go out in the afternoon, that's the only time. I don't know what—"

"You should get counseling," Karen Kovac said.

"No. I don't want to talk about it. I don't want to talk about it with . . . strangers. I mean, I don't want to talk about it with anyone. It's as though I did something wrong. If you get raped, you had to be part of the act. I can see that in a crazy way. But that's not the way it was. I was raped."

She was crying. She cried a lot. She cried but there were never any tears in her eyes. She merely cried and cried and no one knew she was crying.

"This apartment drives me crazy—"

"You should go home—"

"No. Not that. Not so that everyone would know. I want to be in a city and be anonymous so that no one knows about me. But the city frightens me now. It's funny, isn't it? I've been thinking about getting a gun. I have a firearm card, you know. When I was in high school in McHenry County, we had a shooting club. Do you think I should get a gun? A pistol or something?"

Karen Kovac stared at her. "What would you do with it?"

"To make myself feel safe. To feel safer. To know I have a gun. If I had had a gun that day, I would have killed them. Both of them. I know that now. I always thought I couldn't kill anything—and my father killed a deer. . . . I could kill them now."

"You can't kill people," Karen Kovac said. "You just get in trouble." It was so banal, she regretted it as she said it.

"Look," Mary Jane said, "I can talk to you. I really want your advice . . ."

Karen looked at her for a long time. "If it makes you feel safer, get a gun, I suppose. I don't think I can give you advice about that. I mean, I'm not crazy about the thought that another person is in the city with a piece. But I know what you mean." She thought of what Jack Donovan said. The case was over and Mary Jane didn't even know it.

Or perhaps she did.

Maybe that was what this was about.

21
WILLIE'S
PROBLEM

Willie thought about it a good long time.

When he left Raoul and Slide to find something to make him straight, he knew he wasn't going to be able to think good until he figured out a few things.

He went to Uptown in search of smack and bread. The bread had to come first. He stood on Wilson Avenue east of Broadway for a long time Sunday morning after the killing, waiting for his luck to change. It changed when he saw the old woman crossing Kenmore Avenue, heading north. He watched her because you couldn't tell about old people just by glancing at them; you had to look hard at them, figure out if they were worth it. He figured she might be worth some change, fifty cents or maybe even a dollar. Then he saw her turn into a three-flat building halfway up the block, and he knew his luck was holding because he was half afraid she might be heading for the old people's home on Lawrence and that would mean she would be harder, if not impossible, to bust. To make a long story short, he busted her good and cracked her apartment good. She kept crying and saying not to hurt her. As though Willie had been brought up to hurt old people. He told her to shut up. She had $313 in a cookie jar, a regular old-fashioned cookie jar that said COOKIES on it. Old people. You never could tell what surprises they might have just by looking at them; you had to stare at them and try to see into them.

He went out of town for a couple of days, down to some people he knew in the west suburbs, in Lyons. Lyons was a lot of bungalows on strands of side streets strung out from the high-life bars on Ogden, the bars where bikers went or the places where the hookers hung out and the Mafia types were in charge. Lyons wasn't much in Willie's opinion and the rules in the suburbs, even the sleazy suburbs, were all different from the rules in the city. You had to be careful. Willie kept reminding himself to be careful.

Hung around Lyons a couple of days, couple of the good places where the motorcycle crowd likes to hang out on Ogden Avenue, had a good time and plenty of time to think about it.

There was a problem to think about.

First part of the problem was what Raoul and Slide did and what Willie had no part of doing and would not have done on a bet. That was the first part of the problem.

He sat in a bar in Lyons, where the jukebox was loud and the place smelled stinking from the bad plumbing and bad beer pipes. He took a cocktail napkin and borrowed a pencil from the fat guy behind the bar and he wrote down: *Murder*.

Willie knew enough about such things to know that if there are a bunch of guys together doing some shit and one of the guys does murder, then the other guys get in trouble over the same shit, even if they weren't doing it.

So the problem was not of Willie's making, but maybe it was still Willie's problem.

So, Willie wrote on the napkin, *Witness*.

The witness is the guy ties Willie to murder. Time passes and Willie will be into thinking about summer and going out to the beach and lying around, and smoking some good shit, and then one day, riding the El or something, out of nowhere, it's going to come to Willie and the other dude, the witness dude, coming face to face. It's just going to be. People run across each other all the time.

Or say it comes down to Willie gets caught up on something

else and this dude might see Willie in the papers or on television. Willie did not think he had ever been on television but he would like to be sometime. Everyone wants to be famous.

So if it came down to Willie on television, and the dude sees him on the news at six or something, then he calls the police and says, "That's the guy that killed my fag buddy."

The more Willie thought about it and scratched on the cocktail napkin, the more he thought that it was unfair. He wasn't even involved and it was going to come down to him getting time out of it or living by looking over his shoulder all the time to see if this fag dude might be there, coming behind him.

Totally unfair.

Willie drank seven or eight highballs and then folded the cocktail napkin carefully and put it in the pocket of his heavy wool coat. It was merciless outside, he thought. He hated the suburbs. There was never any street action and everyplace you had to have a car. He had stolen a car in Berwyn the first day and dropped it in Brookfield the second day and now Chester was letting him use his beater. Chester ran a chop shop in Lyons and the car he was driving had so many different parts in it, it was an original. "I make unique cars," Chester said. Chester was funny and a good friend because they were cousins and had been boys together for a while in Kentucky, though Chester was older.

Willie wondered if Raoul had gone to Miami.

He started the car and went to Chester's house and pulled it carefully behind the house to the edge of the garage, where Chester did his work. The house was brick and two bedrooms in a bungalow style. The garage behind the house had room for five cars.

"Chester," Willie greeted him on that Thursday, when he had it all figured out finally. "Chester, old man, I need a favor."

"You got it, cuz," Chester said, lifting his head out of an engine cavity. "What you need?"

"A piece."

"A piece."

"Yeah, a piece."

"Piece you need?"

"Piece to do a job."

"What kind job?"

"A job in the city."

"Kind of piece you need?"

"Piece."

"There's pieces and pieces. You want a sawed-off? There's a sawed-off. You want a piece that shoots good or one that shoots good enough? You know?"

"Sawed-off?" He had not considered the idea. "Sawed-off? That would be a piece all right. That would do the job, all right."

"Sawed-off be clumsy though."

"I ain't gonna dance with it," Willie said.

Chester laughed at that. He liked Willie a lot. He knew Willie had knocked off a piece of his wife's tail—Willie thought he didn't know that but Chester knew—but he didn't care. He liked Willie a lot more than he liked that fat slut.

"Willie, you're funniest damned man I ever heard. You funnier than Jerry Clower."

"That's a compliment comin' from you," Willie said. "I like that about the shotgun. I just wasn't thinking about that but that would do the trick all right."

"Do the trick all right," said Chester. "Do the trick a treat."

"Trick or treat. You right there." Willie smiled.

Chester came around the car he was altering and wiped his greasy hands on a greasy rag. He was sweating. He kept the garage warmer than the house. That's what his wife said. Slut. He guessed he had never really cared for the bitch, even from the beginning.

"I got just the thing for you, Willieboy," Chester said, grinning. He had a nice grin, and at Christmas he liked to dress up as Santa Claus for the neighborhood kids. He liked kids, it was the only good thing about the slut, she made some pretty kids and they were smart as well. Chester had a Santa Claus suit hanging in his closet that he had bought at a costume company. He saw the kids mostly believed he was Santa Claus because he acted so natural in the part. "Got just the thing for you but I want it back."

"You get it back," Willie said.

"You gonna do someone, Willie, is that what this is all about?"

"Yeah. Got to be done. I don't wanna but it's got to be done."

"Got to be done," Chester repeated.

"Yeah. Sometimes you got to do the hard row," Willie said.

"Ain't it the truth," Chester said.

Chester had a Remington double-barrel pump-action and it was good enough. Good enough indeed. Chester was right on when it came down to it and had been since they were boys together in Kentucky, which seemed a long time ago. Willie was twenty-one years old and he felt he had been living an awful long time.

The problem was to really spray the dude when he wasn't expecting it, just let him have it full, for once and all. Willie felt he could do the job. He had killed somebody once, in Kentucky, and he had not felt bad as he thought he might feel. The bastard in Kentucky—it was in Bowling Green on a summer night, outside a package store—the bastard had had it coming. But this case was slightly different in that the fellow really was just a bystander, like Willie had been. Willie had no personal animosity toward Brandon Cale. None at all.

22
I SAW HIM

Tim was with his father for the weekend; they were going to a Black Hawks hockey game at the stadium.

Karen Kovac and Terry Flynn made love in her bed. It was very different to make love in her apartment. Everything in the place was hers and Terry Flynn felt painfully shy to be in a house that was as neat as his mother's house had been. Karen Kovac had a plaque in the kitchen that said something about home cooking being the best cooking, and it was corny and Tim had given it to her at Christmas when he was nine years old. There was a tablecloth on the solid red-oak table in the dining room. A clock counted the hours with a tinny Westminster chime and thin gongs. Karen drank wine at home. Terry Flynn usually brought over a six-pack of Old Style beer when he visited her and they both pretended it was a house present. Terry Flynn hated wine.

After love, for a long time, they lay in the bed in the middle of Sunday morning, talking to each other about many things. They heard the clock chime the hour. It was Sunday in winter and the apartment was warm and the building was winter-quiet in the way an apartment building learns to hibernate during the dark months.

"I've been thinking." She yawned. "I've been thinking about doing something."

The words lay between them on the sheets. He didn't say anything at first. "Doing what?"

"Doing something else."

"Quit?"

"No. Not right away."

"The pay's good," he said. "You get to carry a gun."

"I had a talk with Jack."

"Jack who?"

"Jack Donovan," she said.

He turned and looked at her. He loved to look at her. His eyes were wide, nearly amused. But there was something wrong with her voice. He felt on the edge of something. They were naked and alone in a warm bed and they were on the edge of something.

"I'm going to law school," she said.

"Why?"

"To become a nurse," she said. "Why do you think?"

"You want to be a lawyer?"

"I've been thinking about it. All along. Talking to Jack about it was the last step, not the first. He can help get me into law school. I'm a little over age."

"What brought this on?"

"You talk to me as though I'm a child. What do you mean, 'what brought this on'?"

"People do strange things in winter just to make the time pass."

"This is not a sudden thought."

"Jack told you his song and dance about him wanting to be a lawyer when he was a cop so he could see what it was all about, sort of going to God school to become God," Terry Flynn said. The voice was sullen.

"He had some clout to get me into school. I needed a chinaman," she said. "I think about Mary Jane. And all the Mary Janes."

"And Brandon Cales and Lee Herrans," said Flynn.

She looked at him. Her nakedness was tense. "You've got your way of dealing with it. There has to be a better way."

"Being a lawyer is never a better way," Terry Flynn said.

"Oh, I'm tired of that low intellectual approach to everything, Terry. I really am. It doesn't wear well. I talked to Jack and he was supportive," she said.

"The bastard. He's lost his soul and now he wants to get other people to lose theirs."

"You don't lose your soul," she said.

"It's part of the Chicago Bar Association code. Part of the initiation ceremony when you pass the bar exams, you sign over your soul to the devil in exchange for a condo on Lake Shore Drive and a Mercedes-Benz and a membership in the Chicago Athletic Club."

"Poor is honest, huh?"

"No. Poor is being a crook but having a reason for it. Like that deal they cut this week. The deal to put Raoul Macam back on the street. Only a lawyer could agree to something like that."

She looked at him. "And the law put Rodney Rodriguez out of jeopardy. Leave it to us and we would have just as soon killed him in the street."

"And the world would have been a better place for losing him," Terry Flynn said in a hard and flat way that was looking for a fight.

She got up suddenly and put on a robe and went into the kitchen. She banged dishes around.

He got up slowly and dressed. When he followed her into the kitchen, she was finished banging dishes. He opened the refrigerator and took out a can of beer and opened it.

"You drink beer for breakfast I'll bet," she said.

"Karen, if you want to fight like this, we have to get married. We are lovers, remember? We are people who love each other. We don't do a Maggie and Jiggs."

She turned, her eyes were very angry and deep. "We're not married, Terry. We're never going to be married. I told you what I was going to do, I am going to law school, I didn't tell you to get your permission or anything. I just told you what I am going to do, as if you were a friend. So you say, like a friend, 'Gee, that's great Karen, good luck to you' or you don't say a goddam thing."

The telephone rang. She stood a moment, hating the interruption. She went to the wall telephone and removed the receiver from the hook.

"Yes," she said.

Then there was silence. Her face was drained.

"Yes," she said. "Where? Where are you now? And where are they now?"

Another silence.

"Yes," she said. "You stay right there. I'll be there in ten minutes. Stay right there. If they go somewhere, don't follow them. Just stay there."

She replaced the receiver and rushed out of the yellow kitchen to the bedroom. She began to dress quickly in slacks and sweater.

"What's going on?"

"Mary Jane Caldwell. She sees the two men who raped her, they're in a pancake house at Broadway and Belmont."

"Wait a minute," Terry Flynn said.

"This isn't your business," she said.

"The world is my oyster," he said, and pulled on his dirty sheepskin jacket with the tear in the lining. He took out his pistol from the stiff holster in the pocket of his jacket and transferred it to his belt.

They were in the car in four minutes and Terry Flynn was driving. He pushed the car through the ruts of frozen snow to Irving Park Road and shot through a red light in front of a giant green CTA bus and skidded across two lanes and he was pushing it hard, hitting his horn, weaving around the slower traffic through the jammed-up intersection of Pulaski and Irving Park, where the Kennedy Expressway crosses on a viaduct.

The day was brilliant.

Terry Flynn said nothing, he bit his lip and wrestled with the wheel of the large, light-bodied Ford, with the concentration of a race driver. He felt the adrenaline pumping him and his face was flushed and his eyes were bright.

Seven minutes later they were a block from the intersection of Belmont and Broadway, in the crowded heart of New Town. It was as close as they were going to get in the heavy traffic. Flynn pulled into a bus zone and they got out of the car and they stared at each other for a moment.

"What can we legally do?" Karen Kovac said.

"Fuck legal. You're the one who wants to be a lawyer, you figure it out."

Mary Jane Caldwell was on the corner, in an alcove of a shuttered disco lounge. It was still Sunday morning and the bars were closed.

Mary Jane Caldwell was wearing a bright-blue jogging suit and a woolen cap and a woolen scarf. Her breath came in puffs. Her cheeks were bright.

"I was running in the park, I was coming around to get the Sunday papers, I saw them," Mary Jane said, spilling the words.

"Which ones?" said Karen Kovac.

"The two in the window. That window. There."

"Don't point," Karen said.

"I see them," Terry said.

"You stay here," Karen said. She took the pistol from her purse and put it in her coat pocket.

"What we do is wait for them to come out," Terry said. "I'll go on that side, you go on the other side—"

"No," Karen said. "The problem is still the same. With Mary Jane, I mean." She looked at the woman. "Mary Jane," she said. "We have to get them a different way. I don't even know if this is legal or not."

Mary Jane said, "Anything."

"When they come out, I want you to make sure they see you."

"All right," she said.

"If they don't see you, I want you to call them."

"All right."

153

"I want you to stand on the corner and stare at them. And take your stocking hat off. So that they see you. I want you to stare at them and if they see you, you don't have to say anything. Let them come to you. I want to see if they will say something. I mean, if they say something, we can use it. I think we can use it."

Terry Flynn stared at Karen without expression for a moment. "All right," he said. "Your show."

"Go across, Terry, see if you can get close to them."

Terry Flynn crossed Broadway against the lights and walked past the pancake house where the two men sat and went to the front of the movie theater just south of the intersection and studied the posters. He had glanced for a moment into the window and seen them clearly. They wore field jackets and stocking caps and one was black for sure and the other one was light-skinned and smaller.

They all waited for breakfast to be over.

It was just after 11:00 and the street was filling with pedestrians. It was Sunday morning in New Town and the carnival was coming to life again. The long colorful slash of Broadway crawled through the old neighborhood full of boutiques and fern bars and homosexual hangouts and art-movie houses and old hotels full of old men on pensions and prostitutes on piece work.

The movie poster was for a version of *Farewell, My Lovely* by Raymond Chandler.

Terry Flynn even read the names in small print at the bottom, and he was feeling very cold. The wind was steady and slight and insistent this close to the lake.

They came out of the restaurant and stood for a moment on the corner and looked around, like men of the world surveying their prospects.

Mary Jane Caldwell stepped out of the alcove of the disco lounge. Her hair was loose and long. She stood very still.

They saw her.

One saw her and nudged the other.

They stared at her for a moment.

Then they looked around and one of them stared straight at Terry Flynn.

"Poh-leese!" He yelled very loud and Flynn pulled out his pistol in one movement.

"Police! Hold it!" Terry Flynn said.

But they were across the intersection, going from the southeast corner to the northwest corner against the traffic. The larger one split at the corner and headed north through the heavy pedestrian traffic on Broadway and the second one started west on Belmont.

Flynn saw he could not fire. He began to run after the big one going north along the sidewalk on Broadway. Flynn ran into the middle of the street and started along the center line with his pistol drawn.

Traffic screeched to a halt around the large man running down the middle of the narrow, crowded street.

"Police!" Flynn tried once more but the fleeing man knew exactly who he was.

Karen Kovac did not have to run as far. The second man slipped on a patch of frozen snow on the walk and fell and then got up again but it was enough. She fired point-blank into the brick wall and the bullet tore into the bricks and sent chips of brick flying and that was enough. He put up his hands and said, "Lady, don't shoot me."

"On your face!"

He knew the routine. He lowered himself to the frozen sidewalk and spread his legs.

"Hands high."

She had to fumble in her purse for the handcuffs and when he was cuffed, he said, "Can I get up? It's cold on the ground. I could catch my death." He had an elegant accent out of place with his appearance.

"Shut up, scum," she said. She went through his jacket pockets carefully. "You got any needles?"

"No, honestly. I don't have needles, I don't do dope, if that's what you're asking."

"I get a needle stuck in me and I'll blow your head off," she said in a nervous, barking voice. Her eyes glittered and her face was flushed. She wasn't thinking now, she was going through the routine.

"I have no needles, lady," he said. He paused before asking a question: "You a cop?"

"I got the gun," she said.

"I know, but lots of crazy people have guns. This is a dangerous city."

He was not armed.

A crowd had gathered around Karen, attracted less by the violence that went before than by the curious spectacle of a woman with a pistol standing over a man lying on the sidewalk.

"What'd he do, lady?"

"I'm a police officer, will someone call the police? Tell them an officer needs assistance. Will someone make a phone call?"

"If you're really a cop, let's see a badge," one of the spectators said.

"Will someone please call PO 5-1313 and tell them a police officer needs assistance?"

She stared at the crowd. An old man said, "I'll call, I'll call. You got a dime?"

And someone else said, "Forget the dime, call collect."

Mary Jane Caldwell was next to her, staring at the figure on the ground. "I'll call," she said. She ran across Belmont to the phone booth. In a minute, there were the sounds of sirens screeching a path through the crowded streets of the old neighborhood.

23
LOSING

It was a terrible day.

Terry Flynn ran out of breath and the suspect six blocks away, in an alley off Addison Street near Clark Street.

The man Karen had arrested was named Harry Lemon and he was a native of Kingston, Jamaica, and he said he was visiting friends in Chicago and had a perfectly valid passport, and why was he being treated this way?

They kept at him all afternoon in interview room number 1 on the second floor of the Area Six headquarters building. They ran fingerprint checks through the department and even the FBI.

Harry Lemon had never been charged with committing a crime.

Leonard Ranallo, commander of the Homicide division, was interrupted at Sunday dinner to take charge of the matter and the fact that it involved Sergeant Terrence Flynn did not make it more pleasant for him. He had to forego dessert and he had to act in a civil manner to Flynn. At least, at first.

The problem was that everyone was convinced that Harry Lemon and the man who got away had raped and brutalized Mary Jane Caldwell. Everyone knew that was the reason both men had run when they saw her standing on the corner across Broadway from them when they left the pancake house.

The problem was that it was not good enough.

The felony-review officer from the state's attorney's office was called and he felt he was too inexperienced to make a judgment. He called his superior, who called Jack Donovan at home.

Jack Donovan lived with his daughter in a two-bedroom apartment in the Lincoln Park neighborhood. He lived like a man who always expected to live alone. He lived like a hermit with few possessions and a meticulous life-style. He had spent the last six years of his life closing doors in a house that was too large for him; when his daughter finally left for college, it would be the last door and he would be alone in one small room and that would suit him. His wife had been deranged and ran away one summer night five years before and had never been heard from again. His wife's family blamed Jack Donovan. So did Jack Donovan. To understand all this, you began to understand the constant pain in Jack Donovan's pale face and cheerless green eyes.

He listened to Ranallo on the phone in the kitchen and he had not interrupted his Sunday dinner. Jack Donovan said he would take a cab to Area Six to see what could be done. He didn't think anything could be done.

Jack Donovan was chief of the criminal division of the state's attorney's office, which was the largest prosecutor's office in the United States. It was a political office but Jack Donovan was not a political appointment. He was supposed to hold the office together for Bud Halligan and Lee Horowitz.

In the cab, all the way to Area Six, he thought about Terry Flynn and Karen Kovac and the problem of Harry Lemon.

Karen and Terry were waiting like children when he swept into the office on the second floor. Jack Donovan looked at Leonard Ranallo, one of the most political and ambitious officers in the whole department. Whatever was decided here was not going to be hung on the police department, and that was what Leonard Ranallo wanted Jack Donovan to understand. Letting a rapist go was not going to be Ranallo's idea.

It was nearly 4:00 in the afternoon.

Jack Donovan closed the glass door. Mary Jane Caldwell sat at a desk in the large squad room beyond the glass wall of the inner office. Jack Donovan stared at her through the glass a moment. She looked back at him and he felt the weight of her eyes on him.

"So what do we do?" Leonard Ranallo said. He was a thin man with a hawk nose and large and cold eyes. Karen had told Leonard Ranallo the whole story and, incredibly, Ranallo had been surprised that Terry Flynn had been visiting Karen Kovac at her apartment when she received the call from Mary Jane Caldwell. Leonard Ranallo was a very moral person and to that moment, he had probably believed that Karen was living like a virgin. He thought less of her from that moment, especially for being involved with someone like Sergeant Terrence Flynn.

"We can go through the process," Jack Donovan said. "We can bring the charge. But the minute he gets a lawyer, the lawyer will know that Miss Caldwell perjured herself once before. So he walks today or he walks tomorrow."

"That's what we thought," Leonard Ranallo said.

The office was very small and crowded and everyone looked unhappy to be there.

"What are we going to do?" Leonard Ranallo said.

Jack Donovan stared at Karen for a moment, as though they shared a secret. It was a look intended for her, and Terry Flynn saw that and he was puzzled and hurt.

"Mary Jane Caldwell poisoned herself on Wednesday. Her case can't exist unless there's a confession, and I take it there does not appear to be any willingness on the part of Mr. Lemon to confess. Is that right?"

"We haven't used telephone books yet," Terry Flynn said with disgust.

"Sergeant," Leonard Ranallo said. "This is not a joke. This is not a joking matter. And police brutality is never a joking matter."

Terry Flynn thought Leonard Ranallo was an asshole. So did many men in the department. Terry made the mistake of showing his feelings.

"We let him walk today," Jack Donovan said. "The longer we hold him, the worse it gets. If the newspapers get this, we're cooked. The case has died down in interest from the first attack. There's no pressure on us now to find the rapists. I think we have to let the case die. I know that's exactly what you didn't want me to say but I can't see any other way."

"Shit," said Terry Flynn. "This is shit."

"But I'm not making the rules," Jack Donovan said. "I'm telling you what you already know."

"Resisting arrest," Karen Kovac said. She felt shaken and she was disgusted with herself.

"All right," Jack Donovan said softly. He knew what she was feeling. He could feel it from all of them in the small and crowded room. "If you want to drag it out, there's always a charge. No weapon found, he has a clean sheet on him. Maybe we could cause him some trouble at Immigration and Naturalization. I'll make some calls tomorrow on that. But that's about all I can do."

"Get him deported at least," Terry Flynn said.

"The problem is that he looks so legal," Jack Donovan said. "Why do you think she got it right this time?"

Terry Flynn said, "That's bullshit, Jack. She was there, standing on the corner, and those two scumbags saw her and they made tracks. I got eyes. You see someone you raped, you run because it's got to be a trap."

"All right," Jack Donovan said. "All right."

The room was glum with silence.

"Let him go," Ranallo said to Shaffer.

"Hold him until I take Mary Jane home," Karen said.

"All right," Ranallo said.

"All right," Jack Donovan said.

Karen opened the door to tell Mary Jane Caldwell what would happen next.

24
MARY JANE'S
PROBLEM

Mary Jane Caldwell listened to Karen Kovac all the way home. She concentrated on the words at first; when the words became the same, she concentrated on the tone. This was a good woman, she thought, this was a woman who wants to help me.

What Karen Kovac could not understand, Mary Jane thought, was that help was not enough. Good intentions were things for children. She was not a child anymore. She could not be touched by words.

She had told her father the same thing on the previous Sunday.

Her father was an attorney in McHenry County. He was an important man to some people there. He was known in the picturesque taverns and old restaurants of the gentrified countryside. He wore three-piece suits, even at home. He had had seven children and Mary Jane had been the last and the most precious. Therefore, she had been most rebellious and had moved away from the family home in Algonquin as soon as she was able and, worse, moved to Chicago. To actually live in the heart of the city.

Karen Kovac drove carefully along Belmont Avenue, taking her time in talking to Mary Jane Caldwell, trying to explain why, in law, nothing could be done.

Her father had said the same things.

Her father had come to Chicago, a city he despised, to talk to her on the previous Sunday. It had been one of those talks that he loved to have with his children. All of his children except Mary Jane had endured them without rebellion, even as they all still lived in McHenry County, scattered to various country towns, all within sound—as it were—of their father's voice.

He had waited until Sunday because he worked every other day. He explained that he had waited only because of the press of business. He explained that he had dispatched her brother, Robert, to the hospital when she had been admitted that Wednesday and that what she saw as Robert's love had been her father's sense of duty. Robert had only been an instrument of his concern. He made her understand that.

She had so much to understand and he had so little time to instruct her.

Her father had explained to her the legal ramifications of the crime of rape. That the woman, rather than the suspect, was more frequently put on trial. That rape was a business in which the woman had to prove that she did not entice the sexual attack.

She had endured that for a while as they sat, over tea, at the mournful table by the window, looking out at the bright city beneath them. When she had endured enough, she told him exactly what had happened on that Wednesday on the elevated-train platform at Jarvis Avenue.

She intended to hurt her father. Her father had the look, the look on the faces of boys, the look on the faces of the policemen. It was not a look you could describe but you knew that look. It was contempt and pity and a certain arrogance and it set you apart when you saw others look at you like that. She told her father everything in every detail, in a plain voice, in a strong clear voice, about how they had thrown her down and torn her clothes from her body in the freezing cold on that El platform and exactly how they had penetrated her vagina, how they had forced her legs apart and thrust their penises into her, long and hard, not in pleasure, not even in seeking release like what those boys had in mind who dated her in high school and college and who were grateful to kiss her and touch her and then, if they pleased her, she would use her hands and give them release; but if they didn't please her, they would have to do it for themselves, later, away from her and that would please her even more, to think of that. She told her father the men on the platform had taken their sex organs and put them in her mouth, one after the other, and she was in pain and fear and humiliation and that when they had released themselves into her twice, after they had beaten her, they decided between themselves whether they would kill her.

Her father said nothing.

Her father watched her as she spoke.

Her father sat very still.

Mary Jane saw that his hand began to shake. His bad hand, the one injured in the war. He was an old man and his cold eyes couldn't protect him this time. The words had gotten through to him. The words were making his hand shake.

Only once had he spoken:

"Come home, baby. Come home with me. Come home, baby."

It was too late for that kind of talk, wasn't it? He should have said those things a long time ago.

Mary Jane pretended to listen to Karen Kovac and her words of kindness. How kind people could be if they thought they were superior to you. It was the same as being kind to black people once you understood they were just niggers and were never going to be anything else. It was easy then to be kind.

She saw it in Karen and in her father.

But she was unmoved by this kind of kindness. And neither of them could understand that. That Mary Jane had become complete in herself and could not be touched by words again. Or by anything.

25
JACK AND
KAREN

Karen called Jack Donovan at home. It was just after 6:00 on the same Sunday.

Jack was not surprised to hear from her. He had thought about her all the way home and thought it was lucky that she had the number from the old case they had worked on years before, when she had been first assigned to Homicide.

Jack Donovan wondered what he would do.

He met her at Kelly's El Tap, an old neighborhood bar three blocks from Jack Donovan's apartment. The tavern was fifty years old and it sat in a building within ten feet of the El tracks. The trains slammed by, north and south, all day and all night. Conversation ceased when the trains rumbled by. Despite this, the old tavern was charming, full of old-timers with old-country stories and full of kids from DePaul University, listening to their first old stories.

Karen and Terry Flynn had gone there many times before.

Karen felt nervous and that made her feel both good and bad. Terry Flynn did not own her. On the other hand, she carefully made up her face before she went to the tavern.

It was Sunday night. Even the trains did not run very often. The bar was quiet. It was basketball season but DePaul Blue Demons were on the road and not playing tonight and the Black

Hawks had played in the afternoon. Tim had seen the game with his father. He was home now.

Jack Donovan wore a sports coat and blue jeans and a white button-down shirt without a tie. He only owned dress shirts. He was not formal—when he had been younger, he had many sports clothes—but now there was only the job and his daughter at night and there was no reason not to close that particular door to that particular closet.

He drank a vodka and tonic at the bar. It was the only drink he ever drank. He explained to his daughter once that the tonic was good for you. They both knew it was a joke. In an odd way, Jack Donovan thought he might be killing himself and that was not a bad idea.

"Hello, Karen."

She smelled fresh, like flowers, and her eyes were bright. She looked right at him as she came to the table and then glanced down and away. She wore her jeans and her sweater and she did not think she looked very glamorous. Her lips were wet from new lipstick.

"What would you like?"

Why had they both known they would meet like this, if not today then tomorrow? When she had gone to his office to talk about law school and get a recommendation from him, they had talked suddenly and freely about the law and about the job. He had talked about when he had been a cop, about the gnawing sense of dissatisfaction that had impelled him into law school, about his wife and how the burden of being married and of having two children in diapers and a husband spending nights at DePaul University law school had cracked her—he had told her too many things in a river of words that spilled out of him. She had been shocked by it at first and then submerged, as though he had waited all his life to tell someone these things. The hurt in him—the enduring and utterly soul-destroying sense of pain at everything he saw and everything he did—tore into her so that they were both floundering after a while in this sea of words. She realized she had his pain now because—now—she had her own.

She ordered a glass of white wine and then changed her order to a glass of Red Label and soda.

"Salut'," he said. They sat at a high table by the front window, where they could see the structure of the elevated cutting across Webster Avenue.

"Salut'." She returned the common Italian toast. It was universal in Chicago where words from every ethnic group were used interchangeably by every other ethnic group. It was pronounced in the Sicilian dialect.

"I took her home," she began. "I talked to her all the way home. Why am I getting this involved with her?"

"It happened for me. Like that," Jack Donovan said, his green eyes glittering in the reflected neon lights of the beer signs. "I was working tactical out of Grand Crossing and we had two kids at home and one of them was still in diapers. I was working afternoons and going to DePaul in the morning, so that I never saw Rita." Rita O'Connor Donovan had been his wife. Was his wife, wherever she was, if she was still alive.

"Woman on the South Side. It was just a stupid nigger case, the kind of case you get thrown in your face every day. It's like digging ditches, after a while you don't notice that you're up to your ass in water." He had a soft, tenor's voice that played the words like songs. Now and then, the tenor would turn down and the words would fall harshly, like unexpected notes at the end of a line of music.

"She compacted one of her children," Jack Donovan said. "She had six kids, your usual welfare momma, and one day she cracked, she couldn't take it anymore, whatever it was that she couldn't take, and she took this squalling brat by one foot and dropped it in the trash compactor and killed it. Not it, it was a her. God. I never forgot the sight of that."

"Oh my God," Karen Kovac said, putting down her drink. She realized her hand was trembling.

"No," Jack Donovan said, turning his green eyes set in that lean Irish face toward her. "You don't understand yet. It was her. She cried and cried and never stopped crying the whole time. I was working with a guy who got sick and then he wanted to kill her. He said he wanted to kill her. I wanted to kill her myself. And that's when it snapped in me; my God, I wanted to kill her so badly and there were all these other children in the apartment, what was going to happen to them now? They would be separated and put in foster homes that might be good or bad but they wouldn't even have each other anymore. No mother no father no sister no brother. There was that and there was this crying woman and there was my partner wanting to kill her. And that's when it snapped."

He stared right at her. "I don't tell that story."

"I know," she said.

"I went home and I saw my own kids. I saw my wife was going crazy day by day. She was going crazy right before my eyes. Poor crazy little Rita O'Connor, the prettiest girl in first grade. I knew her all my life, I grew up with her."

"You closed the door," she said in a very soft voice.

"Yes. That's one way to say it. I closed the door. I keep closing the doors. I can't feel that way about those things, it tears me apart. That's what Mary Jane Caldwell was doing to you."

"You fixed it for yourself," she said.

"Not all the time. I still crack sometimes. I still have to bleed sometimes. You got to deal with it. I never wanted to be a lawyer more than that day the woman compacted her kid. I wanted to get out, to get up and over it, so that it wouldn't ever touch me that way again. I didn't want to kill anyone."

"I would have killed the bastard myself. I had him on the sidewalk, I wanted to put one in his ear, the dirty bastard."

The hate and pain of hating waited between them for a moment.

The night was still and cold. An El train rumbled suddenly overhead, the bright lights of the cars flashing above the street, the sound seeming to shake the building. Someone put money in the jukebox and there was a long and mournful Irish song about a woman who wore the black velvet band. The pub dirge went on and on and it made them sentimental. They knew it was only because they both felt sorry for themselves and they never told anyone about it.

"There are only two ways to deal with it," she said. "You brutalize yourself or you brutalize everyone else."

"Do it to someone else, do it before they do it to you. Be brutal to make it easier on yourself," Jack Donovan said. He said it in a strange cold voice that she had never heard before. It was her own voice.

"There has to be more to it than this," she said at last.

"No. There doesn't have to be. That's the part you finally are going to figure out. Go to law school and pass the bar and start in the business of making money out of this instead of believing that there is something here worth saving, that there's a tough and durable structure of law that frames civilization and that it is worth preserving." The voice had changed. It was flat and sarcastic and the voice was the one he used when he described himself or the office of state's attorney. "There isn't any civilization. There isn't any law. There isn't any justice. Now and then justice gets done but only by accident."

"That's what I want," Karen Kovac said. "When I talked to you last week. I wanted to go to law school, but I had been thinking about it for a long time. I wanted to get a recommendation from you, but it wasn't that. It was something I knew about you. I can't put it in so many words."

"What did you know about me?"

"That you had figured it out."

"No. I never have. I haven't."

"But it's enough. What you've figured out. It's enough."

"And what are you going to do about Terry Flynn?" he said.

"That's the shame of it," she said. "I really love him."

"Yes," Jack Donovan said.

"I love him so much," she said.

Jack Donovan stared at her.

"I'm not going to let it go on anymore," she said.

Jack Donovan said, "Should I wait?"

Karen stared at him. "Yes. Wait a little while. Just a little while."

III

JUSTICE

26
SOLVING WILLIE'S PROBLEM

Willie watched the dude come and go for two days. He watched the dude in the morning leave the apartment building on Lill Street and walk to the Fullerton Avenue El station and catch the El downtown. He was around when the dude came home from work in the afternoon. The first day he had to wait a long time and it was cold, but the second day, when he figured out about the times the dude came and went, he didn't have to wait in the cold as long.

Willie had the sawed-off Remington double-barrel wrapped in a newspaper in the trunk of the Rambler he had picked up off a used-car lot in La Grange.

The Rambler was parked in a no-parking zone on Racine and it had six tickets at the end of two days but Willie knew it would be months before the cops got around to towing it. There were always hundreds of cars abandoned every winter on the streets and the cops ran behind in towing them away.

Willie was back in the city and he didn't need any car. Willie was in his element.

Willie figured he'd hit the dude in the morning, on the third morning, that would be Wednesday morning.

He felt good about making a decision. He went around Seeley and Roscoe looking for Raoul and Slide and he didn't see them. He went around Humboldt Park but the porkies wouldn't give him the time of day, they were all the same, except for Raoul who had been pretty cool for a pork chop.

Willie ran into some friends on Wilson Avenue finally and they were telling him that someone aced Wee Willie Mendota and dumped him in a dumpster and that the cops were around looking for information, when it was as plain as the nose on a Jew's face what Wee Willie Mendota got aced for. It was an interesting story. The cops would never know it.

On Wednesday morning Willie got up on time. He had an alarm clock even. Just like he was going to work. He had a room in the Wellington Arms Hotel, which was a cathouse, except he didn't have time to fuck around with pussy because he had work to do.

Willie took the El down to Fullerton, just like he was going to work.

Willie got off at Fullerton. It was just starting to be light. The day was cloudy and it would probably snow because it smelled that way. He walked against the wind west on Fullerton to Racine, and then he walked north on Racine to the car parked in the no-parking zone. He popped the trunk and took out the sawed-off wrapped in newspapers. He looked around to make sure no one was around and took the sawed-off out of the paper and slipped it under his coat and buttoned his coat over it. He walked to Lill Street and stood in the playlot at the corner for a long time. He lit a Kool with one hand and smoked it, and dropped it when it got too short.

He crossed the street finally. It was light. Lill was a quiet street. He wouldn't have known where the dude lived if Raoul hadn't driven over that first night. It was a good idea that Raoul had had, to ace the dude right away, except the dude had cops around him then. Now it was time to ace him and there weren't any cops around.

Raoul should have done it himself.

Willie wondered where Raoul and Slide were hanging out. Maybe they got out of town like Willie.

He saw the apartment-building door open and he saw Brandon Cale.

Brandon Cale stared at him. Brandon stared right at Willie and Willie opened his coat.

Let the dude check it out, Willie thought. Check out the piece for a minute, let it sink into the dude.

Willie was twenty-five feet away, across the street.

Willie crossed the street, unbuttoning his coat.

The dude saw it all right.

The dude saw the piece all right.

Dude just stood there, staring at the piece. Just stood there.

"Hey, man," Willie said, smiling. He had to admit he was enjoying it. "Bet you never expected to see me again."

Brandon Cale said, "You're going to kill me."

"That's it, stud," Willie said.

He was about ten feet from him now, his coat was open, the piece was ready. When you go to kill someone deliberate, Willie thought, it's very different than when you do it by accident, like that time in Kentucky, in Bowling Green, when the dude had it coming but Willie had not known until the last second that he was going to kill him. Did not know until he actually did kill him.

He looked at the baby face.

There was a red line on one cheek and that must have been where Raoul nicked him.

Little baby face with one red line on one cheek. Pretty little face, Willie saw it too, even though he wasn't like Raoul, he wouldn't fuck anyone, though there was one time when someone inside had wanted to go down on him and there wasn't anything else to do.

It was amazing.

Brandon had a pistol.

A genuine piece. Look like a baby but he had a piece and he was holding it right in front of him. Like they do in the movies.

Willie thought it was comical. The shotgun was loaded but he would have to swing it up. That would take a moment.

Willie heard the shot.

Brandon shot him.

Willie thought about that in a lazy way for about a split second but in Willie's mind, the time went on and on.

The first bullet slammed hard into Willie's right chest, spinning him around, and the second went through his neck and the third hit him in the right eye, chipped off a bone forming the nasal cavity and plowed into the soft matter of the left hemisphere of the brain. Willie (Wilson Madison Thompson, 21, WM) was dead then, but it took a moment for his body to hit the frozen parkway.

27
BRANDON'S PROBLEM

No one knew anything at first. And for a long time after.

The first thing was a lot of questions at the scene, first by a uniform and then by a uniformed sergeant and then by two detectives from Homicide.

The first detective wanted to know where Brandon had gotten his pistol and Brandon refused to say, so they put Brandon in handcuffs and threw him in the backseat of the squadrol and let him wait there while they pawed over the scene of the homicide.

Brandon felt the cuffs bite into his wrists and he was uncomfortable because he wore the cuffs behind his back and his back pressed against the greasy vinyl of the squad and people were coming around the squad to look at the killer. Brandon stared at nothing, saw nothing but Willie and the shotgun. He had not known at first that he had killed anyone.

They drove him to Area Six headquarters on the northwest side of the city.

Quigley called Terry Flynn at home.

"Your boyfriend just shot one of them," Quigley said. "I was working days and they brought him in and I thought you wanted to know."

"Know what? I got no boyfriend."

"Brandon Cale. Your sweetmeat. Little ole Brandon just bumped off Wilson Madison Thompson, who was the third member of the triumvirate that Friday night."

Terry Flynn was groggy with sleep. He fumbled for his watch, which was on the littered coffee table next to the orange couch that was his bed on most days, unless he cleaned the apartment with the expectation that Karen would visit him.

It was 11:03 on Wednesday morning.

"What went down?" Flynn said.

Quigley told him. Two other homicide detectives had Brandon Cale in interview room number 2 and they had gone at him, and eventually Lieutenant Shaffer had figured out this one was involved in the case that Flynn had first investigated.

And Richard Stacy of the Drug Enforcement Administration and Jerry Goldberg of the special investigation team of the state's attorney's office were there as well.

It took Terry Flynn twenty-five minutes to get to Area Six. He felt terrible. He had a cold and his head was stuffed and he felt terrible because he had not spoken to Karen Kovac since Sunday, and he had a bad feeling about what they might say to each other when they talked.

Brandon Cale was in the windowless white room with the massive oak table.

He was cuffed to the chain in the wall.

Terry Flynn looked at Brandon and at Richard Stacy and Jerry Goldberg.

"Take the fucking cuffs off."

"Jesus Christ," Goldberg said.

"Get the fucking mope with the key and take the fucking cuffs off," Terry Flynn said.

"I'm the mope with the keys," said Gerald Rivers, the first homicide detective who had investigated the shooting on Lill Street. He was not in a good mood and he did not like Terry Flynn very much.

"Take the fucking cuffs off," said Terry Flynn in a dangerous and even voice.

"Someone elect you pope?" said Gerald Rivers. "This guy is a prisoner."

Terry Flynn saw the way it was. He took Gerald Rivers by the arm and guided him out to the squad room and he turned to him and spoke very softly and very close to Gerald's large face.

"You know what this is about. You know who this guy is. Why do this thing?"

"You got a real reputation on this guy, you know that, Sergeant?" Gerald Rivers said. He was hot and his eyes seemed too large for his face in that moment. "We got him here because he shot a guy on the street and no one knows what the fuck this is about."

"It's about one of the guys who killed his buddy," Terry Flynn said, trying to be calm.

"His fucking fag lover," Gerald Rivers said. "And a dope dealer. That's what this is about, about this dope-dealing little cocksucker. He suck you off too, Flynn?"

It was stupid. Terry Flynn hit him. It was not a great blow but it was enough to send Rivers back against a table and over it. The others in the immense room—the pair from Auto Theft who were cataloging tires on the other side, the sergeant from Narcotics who was reading the sports section of the *Tribune* in his office, the two Robbery dicks who were buying coffee from the sergeant with the doughnut concession—they were shocked and reacted instantly. They did nothing. After all, the two men fighting carried guns.

Flynn jumped on Rivers and they rolled onto the floor and it was left for the men in Homicide to stop the fight. They did it in the manner of the Chicago Bears defensive team—they just all piled on the combatants until no one could move. The pile unpeeled. It was embarrassing to Homicide. Roughhouse behavior in the station might come at moments of extreme tension—say during a race riot—but never to detectives engaged in the solemn and often dull pursuit of solving homicides.

They made Terry Flynn sit in the inner office where Lieutenant Shaffer kept his photographs in frames on the walls and on the desk. There was a framed certificate noting that Shaffer had successfully completed the course of studies at the FBI school in Virginia.

Terry Flynn stared at Lieutenant Shaffer for a long time and neither of them said anything. Shaffer wasn't particularly against Terry Flynn in this matter; it was just that it all reflected badly on Area Six Homicide and, by turn, his command. Commander Leonard Ranallo had his eye on Shaffer as a potential rival to office; this was not a thing designed to boost Shaffer's chance. That fact colored it for Shaffer but he was, essentially, a fair man to the men under him.

"What was it all about?"

"It was something personal."

"I see. Why didn't you wait until Rivers was off duty and take it out on him then? Why did you come up here to do it?"

"I had an interest in the case. Quigley called me at home."

"Quigley is a troublemaker. Never for himself. Just for other people. Did Quigley tell you that Brandon Cale is being held for the time being? That DEA went in for a writ an hour ago to toss his apartment? It was the excuse we needed."

"No."

"No, Sergeant, Mr. Quigley didn't tell you what was going on. He just called you in off duty and you're one of those meat eaters, you live and breathe and die a cop twenty-four hours a day. This is your case, so you have to be in on it twenty-four hours a day. Don't you have a home life, Sergeant?" The voice was cold, the manner sardonic, the words dropped like stones in a deep well. "The department has more than a few good men. We manage efficiently even while you're off duty."

"This case has been fucked up from the beginning with the DEA. Brandon's not the criminal; the criminal is the guy who rolled him on the El, the guys who iced his buddy. All right, his lover, whatever you call it."

"I call it hot-dogging, the way you come in like John Wayne on this. I call it being a wiener."

Terry Flynn was shocked by that. He began to blush. It was the last thing he ever thought anyone would accuse him of.

"I'm no showboat," he said.

"Sergeant, I know about you. I know about your background. Your chinaman was Matt Schmidt. I like Matt. I know him. I talk to him."

"Do all the loos have a clubhouse where they meet?" Terry Flynn said, and regretted it. His big goddam mouth.

Lieutenant Shaffer's brittle eyes seemed to let it pass. "You're in Leonard Ranallo's doghouse and that's a bad place to be if you want to keep working Homicide. Which I wonder about because of what you just did. It doesn't do me any favors to do you a favor. Being your chinaman is a full-time job. I don't think I could afford you. Matt seemed to put some stock in you and nothing is forever, Sergeant. Even Leonard Ranallo has other things to do than to hate you twenty-four hours a day. But you don't want to let it pass, do you? You just want this to go on and on, don't you? You're like a burr in a horse blanket. You know this is a bigger thing than the hit on the El. There's the whole goddam SAO crawling around on this, and DEA and FBI for all I know. Downtown is aware of what is going on. I mean, above the level of Ranallo, above the deputy supe. I don't know what this drug investigation is about—rather, I think I know, I think it's just another make-work project from the federal cop factory; they'll find a few bags of coke and make a couple of arrests in time to get re-funded by the next congress—but that doesn't matter, Sergeant. Sometimes what matters is to keep your head down as the only way of keeping it attached to your shoulders. Let this pass. This is not important. This is some little mope with a preference for getting butt-fucked and three living examples of human scum floating through, and these four atoms collided one midnight weary and it is too bad about what happened, but that's life. We had eight hundred fourteen homicides last year in Chicago; that's not counting all the kids who were killed in car crashes and the old people who took a tumble down the steps and all the children in Children's Hospital dying of leukemia. You getting the picture, Sergeant, or am I going too fast for you? If you want to save the world, get a pulpit. If you want to see justice done, join the IRA and blow up a department store in Belfast. If you are a true believer, go to church and say the rosary. If you are none of those things and you are not an Oscar Mayer wiener, and if under that crude and stupid exterior there beats the heart of a genuine Chicago police homicide detective *and sergeant*—who wishes to remain a sergeant and a homicide detective—then start learning not to care, start learning that behavior acceptable at midnight in the Slammer Inn has nothing to do with behavior acceptable in the middle of the goddam morning in my goddam office. Now. You got it?"

Flynn stared at Shaffer with embarrassment. He saw the way it was, the way Shaffer was taking the heat on it. He was grateful to Shaffer for saving his ass and he hated himself for needing a favor right now.

"I see the way it is," Terry Flynn said. He swallowed a little more and spit it up. "I apologize, Loo."

"Fuck apologies. Go home. Don't come around this case. Let it go away."

"What about him?" Terry Flynn said. He couldn't let it go that easily. "I mean, that was self-defense, right?"

"Go away," Lieutenant Shaffer said in the same cold and precise voice.

Terry Flynn rose and looked at Shaffer and wanted a word from him but he knew there were no more words. He went to the door. Rivers was in the outer office and he glared at Flynn and Flynn looked right through him. Lieutenant Shaffer said, "OK. Rivers. Come here." The second little boy going to the principal's office. It was exactly like that. And everyone in the room looked superior at the bad boys, especially Terry Flynn, who started it.

Even Quigley.

28
CUTTING
A DEAL

Richard Stacy was excited. His nostrils were wide and flaring like a horse's after a race. His eyes bulged and his voice was high and tense.

This had been his case from the beginning, from the previous spring when a minor drug bust on the Near North Side opened up the can of worms on the Board of Trade and the Options Exchange. Runners and clerks and even some traders were involved in selling more than pork-belly futures and February orange-juice contracts. They were selling hard dope.

The connections had strung out the way such connections are strung, like Christmas tree popcorn. In June, the Chicago Police Department's Narcotics section had stumbled into the investigation with their own bust of a runner caught with two pounds of cocaine in his possession. The runner had run afoul of the police because he had been sampling his own product one afternoon and wondered if his Volkswagen Beetle would fit on the sidewalk that ran along Jackson Boulevard between LaSalle and Clark streets, in the Loop financial district. It did not fit.

The problem in dealing with locals, Stacy felt, was always the same. Local departments had no interest in the big picture. They wanted the quick fix of a quick bust; they did not have patience. Stacy had the authority to go over the heads of the police department to the state's attorney's office to get charges handled differently against the cocaine possessor with the crumpled Volkswagen.

Lee Horowitz smelled a good thing. Lee Horowitz cut the deal—in the name of Bud Halligan—with Stacy and the DEA. To suppress certain charges and overheat other charges. To cover the DEA in exchange for a reasonable amount of recognition when the time came.

From almost the first day, Lee Herran had been fingered as a major dealer on the exchange. Herran's friends and associates led to clues of other members of what appeared to be a loosely organized drug ring.

Lee Herran had been observed in Key West twice, associating with known drug smugglers and wholesalers. A former lover—a bartender at Swallow's named David Parker—also might be involved. And Brandon Cale had been an associate— and presumed lover—of both men.

All of this was at a level far removed from Terry Flynn, who had blundered into the case only because he was the homicide detective on duty the night that Lee Herran was killed. It was a stupid murder, Stacy had thought from the beginning, so stupid and so wanton that there must have been a reason for it. He thought Brandon Cale was part of the reason and thought so more when the killer turned out to be someone like Raoul Macam, a dealer and user, albeit in circles far removed from the glitter of the exchange.

Raoul Macam had been put in protective custody after he was bailed out—using DEA slush money—and been milked for information. Raoul soon proved he didn't know a damned thing about the exchange trade, but he was useful because he was free.

Richard Stacy was a reasonably competent career employee of the federal government and a pioneer member of the Drug Enforcement Administration. He had been in Chicago for two years. A bust like this would enhance his 201 file and would be useful in getting him transferred out of what he considered a dead-end office. Miami was to his liking; or southern California, the narcotics nirvana.

Stacy had no personal animosity toward any of the principals in the case. He hated them all with the professional hatred of a dedicated law-enforcement officer who has to pick out the bad guys quickly in order to function at all. All of his theories in the case were based on the principle of deciding who was guilty and then proving it. It is the operating principle of law enforcement. Even Terry Flynn would have understood that.

Richard Stacy of the Drug Enforcement Administation and a team of investigators said they found nearly fourteen ounces of controlled substance—in this case, cocaine—contained in the cassette-tape cases in the apartment occupied by the late Lee Herran.

After strong dealing with the state's attorney's office, state charges of cocaine possession were placed against Brandon Cale instead of federal charges, as the U.S. attorney preferred. The deal was for the convenience and use of the Cook County state's attorney and a joint press conference in the SAO office in the Civic Center was planned for 10:00 Thursday morning, in which the arrests of six members of an alleged drug-selling ring operated by runners and clerks with the Board of Trade, as well as the Chicago Board Options Exchange, would be announced.

Brandon Cale was unchained at last and taken to one of the criminal courtrooms stuffed into the Civic Center because there was not enough room for all the courts needed in the Criminal Courts Building. Brandon was arraignd on charges related to narcotics possession, as well as being charged with voluntary manslaughter in the shooting death of Wilson Madison Thompson, who had been found shot to death in a brutal manner outside 1178 W. Lill Street. Brandon Cale was given his rights and given the right to an attorney. He had no attorney and one was appointed for him by the court, in accordance with provisions arising out of the *Esposito* and *Miranda* decisions. The attorney—a recent law-school graduate working in the public defender's office—suggested he plead not guilty. Bond was set at $40,000 and 10 percent of bond was needed in cash for Brandon Cale's release. Brandon Cale tried to reach his brother, Michael. On the second call to Decatur, he caught his sister-in-law, Claudine, and told her what had happened to him. She said that Michael was in Peoria and would be home by nightfall.

Night fell.

Brandon was locked in a solitary cell in one of the holding tiers in Cook County Jail.

He had never been so frightened in his life. He heard the night sounds of the beast of the immense jail and shrank into a corner of the dark cell and held his arms across his chest and waited and waited for morning that was so far away from him.

In all of this, Brandon could not understand why cocaine had been found in his apartment. He could not understand it.

Terry Flynn could not understand it either. He felt betrayed when he read the report on Cale when he came on shift at 11:00 P.M.

Sergeant Buchanan ran into Sergeant Flynn at 2:00 A.M. on the street. Buchanan pulled his marked squad alongside Flynn's car at the curb and double-parked. Buchanan rolled down his side window and smirked at Terry Flynn.

"I tole you. I tole you that night, didn't I?"

"What did you tell me?"

"Fags. Your fag. Your fag wastes some guy and it turns out he a fucking drug dealer. I tole you, fags are all the same. I tole you it was a fag killing, I told you that."

"You told me," Terry Flynn said. He was waiting for Glenn, his partner for the night, who had gone into the all-night Snow White Grill across the street to get coffee and doughnuts.

Buchanan laughed out loud. Terry Flynn stared straight ahead of him. He had put himself in enough trouble for one day.

"And you go after the guy that busts the little fag creep. You must have rocks in your fucking head," Sergeant Ernest Buchanan said.

Terry Flynn turned and looked at Buchanan and thought he had to say something.

Except there was nothing to be said anymore.

29
RAOUL AND
RICHARD

Richard Stacy had been made aware, when he was very young, that he had a name he would have to live down. In a strange way, that made him tougher. He was tough on himself, on his wives (he had gone through two of them), on his only daughter (second wife), on the people on the beat, on the job, on his invalid mother, on his prisoners. Particularly on the scum. People like Raoul Macam never had it so tough. Richard Stacy— who was, inevitably, Dick Stacy and Dick Tracy, though not to his face anymore—thought he really poured it on Raoul.

Raoul thought otherwise.

Raoul was having the best time he had had in a long time.

They kept him in an apartment building on Lake Shore Drive, for one thing. It was a nice apartment, there were clean sheets, there was a Mr. Coffee machine. Actually, there was food but no booze, not even beer. That was a fly in the ointment but it didn't ruin it for Raoul. It was better than jail. It was almost as good as sex to wake up in a warm bed in the morning and look out at the sun rising up over Lake Shore Drive and look down at the ants in their cars running off to work. The world looked very foolish from up here, on the twenty-first floor.

And there was always someone to talk to. The night guy was Harry. Harry had a lot of stories and Raoul had a lot of stories.

They traded stories sometimes or they watched "The A-Team" on television and Harry told Raoul that Mr. T used to be a Rush Street bouncer before he got this television gig. That impressed Raoul. Maybe after this was over, he'd go to California, always wanted to see California, maybe get himself in television. How hard could it be? Raoul could be as hard as he had to be. He told Harry that and Harry said anything was possible.

Dick Tracy was on days most days and that's when Raoul had to do a little work. It got easier every day. Dick Tracy wanted to know about Lee Herran and Brandon Cale. Raoul laid some shit on him about Brandon Cale, because that was the part that Dick Tracy seemed most interested in.

Without knowing it, a lot of what he made up about Brandon was corroborated with Slide's desperate and made-up story uttered on the day he was arrested by Terry Flynn. So, thought Dick Tracy from the beginning, there was a connection between Herran and Raoul and Cale. Three swinging dicks.

"I like girls, you know," Raoul said. "But them boys was business. I mean, they want to suck my thang, that's their pleasure, you dig?"

Richard Stacy was sure he understood, as disagreeable as the image might be. He had never allowed fellatio to be performed on his body, by either of his wives or any of his girl friends. He had a horrible fear that someone might bite it. He could see someone biting him. He could see it bitten off.

Raoul wanted to bring Slide into the picture because it would have been great if Slide had been bonded out the way Raoul had been bonded out and Slide had been in the crib with Raoul, they would have been digging the whole scene from the twenty-first floor.

On the day after Brandon Cale was arrested and charged with voluntary manslaughter and was put in Cook County Jail, Dick Tracy lost interest in Raoul.

"It was useful," is the way Richard Stacy put it, staring hard at Raoul Macam, who was lounging in pajamas at 1:00 in the afternoon. "It was useful and it's going to mean something when your case comes up."

"Oh, man, now what did I do?" Raoul whined.

"You didn't do nothing," Richard Stacy said. He liked it when they whined like that. They were monkeys, all the scum, they were in little boxes and they didn't even know it.

"What you gonna do?"

"Put you back in your cage," Richard Stacy said in his John Law voice. "You didn't think you were going to stay here forever, did you?"

"Shit, man, I cooperate. Didn't I cooperate? Now you gonna put me back inside, man, I don't understand you."

"You got charges against you," Richard Stacy said. "You're going to have to wait for your court date."

"But you got me outta jail—"

"I got you out to see what you knew about things I wanted to know and to put heat on a certain little fagola dope pusher and I did it. It worked out different than the way I planned it—I never figured he was going to ice your buddy but your buddy was scum of the earth, it didn't matter—and now we got our dope ring busted and you just don't figure in the picture anymore," Richard Stacy said. "So get dressed, Raoul—"

"Hey. Man. Hey man, look here, my man—"

"Get the fuck dressed," Richard Stacy said in the tough voice. He wore a three-piece gray suit and he carried a small and efficient .32 nickel-plate Smith & Wesson snub-nose in a $315 crocodile-skin holster clipped to his belt. He was a clean person with clean fingers and a vaguely soapy odor.

It just didn't turn out the way everyone expected.

It is usually a very routine matter for the state's attorney's office to have bond revoked on a person charged and bonded. The SAO goes to court and explains that new information received by the office shows that the person allowed bond to roam the free streets of the city is worse than the SAO knew at the time of the original bond hearing and that it is imperative that the accused be locked up to keep society safe.

The routine becomes unusual only often enough to make everyone alert and on edge.

The judge was Henry Winkman and he was a warhorse of the

Democratic machine from whose ranks most judges in the county were selected (because it is an elected office and the judges are slated by the political party in power).

Henry Winkman surprised everyone.

Certainly he surprised Richard Stacy.

And Raoul Macam most of all.

In a long and quiet tirade about the abuse of power by the federal government and the state's attorney's office and about individual human rights and about the ends and means and what justice is supposed to be, Henry Winkman reduced bond on Raoul Macam, refused to return the prisoner to Cook County Jail, ordered his release and set trial date in March. Jerry Goldberg was so surprised that he momentarily lost the gift of speech until he saw Raoul signing a paper and turning and smiling his way out of court, saying "Thank you, judge" to the judge.

"This isn't right," Goldberg sputtered at last.

But Henry Winkman was already descending from the bench.

30
BROTHERS

Michael drove up from Decatur in the morning. He had found the cash but it had been hard and it had been embarrassing. He had to explain to everyone that it was a mistake of some sort, that he knew his brother, Brandon, and that Brandon was a decent man. His friends and neighbors liked Michael Cale and his wife and his children; Michael was a decent and hardworking man. They all knew that Brandon was a homosexual and lived with homosexuals in Chicago, where all the homosexuals and niggers lived, but brothers are brothers and they gave their support to Michael because he asked for it.

Michael had the money in a brown no. 10 envelope on the front seat next to him. He drove a 1981 Ford 150 pickup with a cap over the bed, which he used for hauling, and in the summer they used for camping. As he approached the city from the southwest on the Stevenson Expressway, he had an instinct to slow down but the traffic surged around him and pushed him along in the stream. The light was early and the eastern sky was streaked with red trails against the light clouds. He saw the spread of towers of the Loop and the Near North Side marching along the lakefront. The vision of the city was huge. In all his life, Michael Cale—who was thirty-one years old—had never been to Chicago and had never wanted to go there.

He eventually found the public defender and they eventually went to court and Brandon was eventually bailed out of Cook County Jail. It was nearly 12:30 in the afternoon when all the horrible proceedings were over.

Michael Cale was shocked when he finally saw Brandon Cale. Brandon had aged, just since Thanksgiving. Brandon's light-blue eyes were drained of color. His baby face was old, was coarsened by his beard and by a strange sadness at the corners of his mouth that might be taken as a smile of pity. When he saw Michael, he said hello and then he said nothing else. They took him from the court building. He had been raped in his cell when it was open after breakfast. He knew who did it but he could not say a thing because there was a rule about this sort of thing; you never told anyone what happened inside or you were dead. The penalty was always death.

"Are you all right?" Michael said three or four times.

He drove Brandon home and they sat in Brandon's apartment. The apartment had been torn apart. Everything in the apartment had been opened, tossed, investigated. The apartment had no secrets.

They sat at the table in the kitchen and Michael waited for Brandon.

Brandon finally found a voice. The voice was older and deeper and softer than it had been at Thanksgiving, when Brandon had come to the old house and brought the Christmas presents because he would not be home at Christmas. The kids liked Brandon, Michael knew; Brandon listened to them. And Brandon didn't act queer when he was home with the family. Michael thought it was something about the city that had done this thing to Brandon.

"I'm not a drug dealer, Michael," Brandon said. "I think I didn't know enough about Lee. I hate to say that. But I think I was just naïve. I hate to admit that."

"It's all right to admit you were wrong," Michael said without judgment. He was in no position to judge anyone. He went to Mass on Sunday and he had doubts about God and church, but he never told anyone he had doubts because the family seemed so secure in its belief. He often prayed to God to help him have a stronger faith. He realized that sinners were saved and he believed there was repentance and forgiveness.

"They did find cocaine here. I think they did. I don't know. I don't know what this is all really about. I know this is a nightmare and I can't wake up from it."

"I talked a good while to your lawyer. He seemed very young."

"Yes. I don't know what this is going to be about. I mean, I can't tell you about jail." He squinted back tears. That was weak. He wasn't going to cry for anyone anymore. "I'll kill myself before I go back to jail."

"Jesus Christ," Michael said in a solemn and sudden voice. "Don't ever say that, Bran. Don't ever say that. No matter how bad it is, you gotta have hope. You can't talk about doing something like that, don't say it. My God, Bran, what's happened to you in this damned city? I mean, what's happened to you?"

"Something is going on and it doesn't involve me. I don't know what they want me to do. I would do it if I knew what they want me to do. They keep telling me that I'm just a small fish, they want to flip me, that's the way they say it, they say they're after big fish. And I don't know a thing about what they want. I worked on the exchange, I wasn't dealing in dope, I never used dope except we would smoke some marijuana sometimes at a party. Lee. And me."

"We'll clean this matter up somehow. You got to believe that. And I think you ought to come home."

"No. I can't go home. And this just gets worse and worse."

"Dammit, Bran, you got to be strong."

"I killed a man yesterday morning. Just like that. He had a shotgun and I said to him, 'Are you going to kill me?' And he said, 'You got it, stud.' And I wanted him to say that." Brandon paused. "See, Mick, I wanted him to say that because I wanted to kill him so damned bad. I really did murder him."

"You didn't murder nobody. That's self-defense, that's plain as the nose on your face."

"So why am I in jail? And why is the man who killed Lee and

cut me, why is he out of jail? I don't understand how this is supposed to work."

"This isn't right," Michael said. "At home, it would be righter."

"But I'm not home, Mick. I'm caught here. You can't do anything and I can't do anything because I don't even know what they want me to do." There was a little silence between them.

"I believe you, Bran. You know I believe you. You know Claudine believes you. She was frantic, trying to find me all over Peoria, she was calling around and she was putting together some of the money when I finally showed up at home. I got to let her know where I am. I admit I was through with business, I went over to Oakwood Tavern and had a couple of beers with the locals. I should have let her know I would be late for supper. I'm sorry, Bran, I really am."

"God, Mick, if I didn't have a brother," said Brandon.

"But you got one," Michael Cale said. "You got a brother and that's what counts."

31
BREAKING

"This isn't going to be easy," Karen Kovac said.

They were sitting at a table in the back of the Corona Cafe on Rush Street. The big room was lit softly, from the tables up. White linen was on the tables. The murmur of conversations was the only sound in the room. No Muzak and no shticks: It was a grown-up place to hold a grown-up conversation.

"Why isn't it going to be easy?" Terry Flynn said.

"We're drifting. We've been drifting," she said. Her voice was nervous. She picked up the water glass and took a swallow. The waiter appeared with a pencil and a smile.

"Stoli," she said. "Straight up."

"This *is* serious," Terry Flynn said. He was smiling. Everything was a joke. She frowned and it was for his benefit.

"All right," he said to the waiter. "I'll play grown-up too. Red Label on the rocks and bring a little water on the side."

The waiter went away.

"I'm going to law school," she said.

"I know."

"How do you know."

"Because you decided to grow up," Terry Flynn said.

"Is this a joke? If this is a joke, let's just drop it and let's eat and then get out of here," she said.

"Am I supposed to take law school seriously?"

"You drive me crazy."

He thought about that. You could do it with anyone, you could push anyone just so far and they had to turn on you. Even the kicked dog bares its teeth.

"I don't want to be with you anymore," she said.

The waiter brought the drinks and left menus.

Terry Flynn did not put any water in his drink after all. He tasted the Scotch and it numbed the roof of his mouth.

"I'm sorry," he said. "I didn't mean to rag at you. The last couple of weeks. I'm sorry, Karen. I was bringing it home and you're not supposed to bring it home. And it was law school. It had to be law school. And you asked Jack Donovan for a letter, so you could get in, even if you're too old for law school. I'm tired of clout, letters, chinamen and aldermen and all the rest of it. And it had to be Donovan you asked."

"This isn't about Jack," she said.

"Come on, Karen. We're all playing grown-up tonight. This is about Jack because it's about law school and it's about me. You look at me different. Before, it was fun. We sort of fell into something like love and we didn't have to call it anything. We just liked each other."

"And I like you," she said.

He didn't like that at all. He made a face.

"I like you," she said again. "I do."

"What's this about, Karen?"

"You know, don't you?"

"You say it. Put it in words. Forget the 'read my mind' stuff," he said.

"That's right, Terry. Make it easy."

"Why should I? I love you," he said.

It was between them in those words. It lay on the white tablecloth and it was heavy and you couldn't ignore it. He wasn't supposed to say that.

"This makes it worse," she said.

"I love you," he said. The words were used like weapons. When you got into a fight, you used every means to win. His

194

hard blue eyes stared at her and she couldn't look back. She looked down at the table and saw the words lying between them.

"I don't love you," she said. "For a long time, I thought I might love you and that it would stay the way it was. It was fun. It was fun to play hooky that time in the room at the motel. I loved that. I love that. I love sex, that part of it. But that isn't where this is going. Was going. You want love and I don't love you and it keeps heading toward the same train station and I don't want to go along for the ride. Not again."

"Who do you love?"

"Tim," she said.

"His father?"

"No."

"Did you ever love him?"

"Yes."

"Why did you leave him?"

"That's not part of this."

"Sure it is. Everything is part of this."

"What you want is a cop's wife. You want someone who shops at Old Orchard and stays home in Sauganash and doesn't get in the way. You want a clean house. God, you could use a clean house."

They weren't supposed to laugh.

When they finished laughing, it was as though the release had been painful as well. And he had tears in his eyes. She saw the tears and it broke her heart. It might have been tears from laughter, she told herself. But it broke her heart anyway.

"Terry, we're not going the same way. It wasn't law school and it wasn't Jack Donovan," she said. "It wasn't your case either. What they did to that boy. It stinks and we know it happens, it happens not often but it happens just enough to make you aware of how awful it really is. And Mary Jane Caldwell. It isn't her fault, it isn't anyone's fault, and everyone is terribly sorry, but the system works that way. I just got depressed, I got into it too much. I carried the job home, just the way you did. We both carried it to each other."

Terry Flynn saw it then. It wasn't going to work but at least he saw the way it was going.

Karen looked him in the face then. Her eyes were so clear. "I wanted comfort from you and I couldn't get it from you. Not that you didn't try. We all try. But I couldn't get it from you and I couldn't give it to you. We both brought it home to each other and neither of us wanted to share it. That's what happened, Terry. I couldn't help you and you couldn't help me."

"You think it's automatic? You think it works out clean? It doesn't," he said. "Why do a big scene? Why do a breaking up? We're not in high school. I didn't give you my fraternity pin. Why make words that only make trouble?"

"I can't stand it anymore is why," she said. "You wear me out. I think about you. I get a guilty feeling I'm failing you."

"So you don't want to think about me anymore?"

"That's it, Terry. That's what it's about."

They didn't speak again for a while. The waiter came and Terry Flynn ordered a butt steak, rare. And she ordered linguine with clam sauce. And both of them ordered another drink. The waiter asked if Terry wanted to see a wine list.

"No, that's over now," he said to the waiter. The waiter went away. Karen smiled.

Terry Flynn caught the smile. "No more burgundy. No more chablis. No more rosé. Free at last, free at last."

"You never pretended very hard."

"I would do anything for you," he said. "I would drink zinfandel for you."

"Oh, Terry," she said. Almost a sigh. Her eyes closed a moment and Terry Flynn thought she might cry as well. But she didn't. She was being grown-up.

They ate and didn't talk.

When the meal was over, they had coffee. A sober little meal on a Monday night in a big room downtown.

"Think about it," he said.

It was a way out.

"I'll think about it," she said. For him.

"I have a lot of time invested in you," he said.

"It wasn't time wasted," she said. "It was you and me and we had fun. We had a lot of fun."

"The time we went out to the arboretum. The first time. You never were there."

"You wanted to make love in the grass," she said. "Remember when we went to Milwaukee that Sunday?"

"Milwaukee. We sure did a lot. We went to the arboretum to look at trees and we went to Milwaukee and ate in a German restaurant. I wanted to give you Paris."

That did it. She was crying then.

"Oh, honey," he said. He never called her that. "I'm sorry." So gently. Perhaps he had been too much for her after all, he thought. The guilt set in with the coffee.

They parted at the front door of the place. Rush Street was quiet, the streets were dry, the night air full of damp and chill. He kissed her and she let him. It was supposed to be hard.

"This doesn't mean we never talk to each other," he said.

She understood what he wanted her to say. "No."

"But don't tell anyone we're just good friends," he said.

"It's our secret," she said.

"Because it wouldn't be true," he said.

"Why, Terry?"

"Because I love you. And, maybe, in a while down the way, I can say I loved you and put it behind me. But you can't be friends when you're in love with someone. It doesn't work that way, not when you break it off."

"That hurts," she said.

He smiled at her with his hard face and tough blue eyes. "It was supposed to," he said. And when he saw the hurt on her face, it was good enough. Just good enough. He turned around and walked away, up Hubbard Street, back toward Michigan Avenue. He left her standing there, hurting.

32
DEAD OF
WINTER

You see, these guys think they can get away with it. Get away with anything they want to do. It's funny to see them on the street all of a sudden, just like this. The same guy with another of his buddies. A couple of bad guys. Funny to see them on the street just like this. And to be following them without them knowing they're being followed. They don't know a thing.

A block farther down and they start again. There's the hassling. They love it, they love to hassle people. The one guy grabs the girl and the other guy grabs her purse.

Sure, it's midnight. Women aren't supposed to be on the sidewalks at midnight. She was asking for it. See, she's really scared and she's backing away and the one guy is making little kissing sounds at her. He's got her around the waist.

The other guy is telling him to stop fucking around, to get out of there.

The first guy is the one. He's the troublemaker. He's the one who enjoys it so much, the power of it. He wants to make sure she's really scared, really frightened so that she'll never forget what happened. Not just about losing the purse but about the feeling she had of being so helpless.

Stand here in the gangway and watch them and don't make a

move to stop them. Let them go as far as they want to go. Let them think they are getting away with something.

The taller guy says to the one who's got the girl by the coat and is making kissing sounds, he says to get the fuck out of here. They open the purse and take out the wallet and the little one says that they know her name and her address and if she says anything to anyone about this, they'll come to her and cut her tits off. She is crying. You'd think there would be someone on the street to stop this, but that's the way it goes. No one is supposed to be on the streets in the middle of the night except the animals who escape every night from the zoo.

Every goddam night. It makes you sick to your stomach to think about it.

The girl is running away without her purse and the two of them are laughing, really enjoying it, having it all their own way.

Guys who think they can get away with anything. You see something like that and it makes you boil inside and you want to cry. You want to cry because there's not a damned thing you can do about it. And if it comes down to it and the cops catch them, what's going to happen to them. Not a thing. She'll be brought downtown and told to identify them and then there'll be delays in court and when the case finally goes to trial, the judge'll give them probation because the jails are too damned crowded and, after all, this was only a purse-snatching case, it was hardly a major crime.

Wait, Your Honor. What about the humiliation and the fear and the pain of remembering how afraid you were and how you pleaded for your life when they threatened to kill you? What about those things?

But the judge can't take time to consider all the little pains inflicted on all the little people in the world. If he did, the courts would be blocked and nothing would ever be done. Don't you see that?

Besides, there might be a technicality here and the state will pay for a lawyer to defend the scum so that you're not even sure that the case will come to trial. Besides, honey, what did you lose? Your purse? Your credit cards? A few dollars? A few nights' sleep?

That'll teach you not to take the El home at night and walk down Belmont Avenue from the station to your home.

And now the two dudes are going into the station and they are going up the stairs. Two guys who did it again. It's easy to do, to be the fox in the chicken coop. All those chickens.

They're going up to the southbound platform. Maybe going to get someone else before the night is over. Those guys figure they can do anything.

So go up the northbound stairs to the northbound platform and watch them. See what they're going to do. It's ironic, in a way. The irony shouldn't be lost on them. On either of them.

So take it out now.

The pistol is really heavy and really ugly, the way a pistol should be. There's beauty in ugly things. Like a hammer.

The pistol. Hold it straight out, two hands, one hand bracing the wrist of the other. Cock it. Be calm and slow. That's the way to do it.

But they won't look this way.

Make them know who you are.

The first shot is good. It makes a good sound, just like a whip-crack on a smart horse's ass. Slap the leather and the horse starts and begins the gallop across the meadow fields. There is power in that beast beneath your seat, dumb power controlled by spurs and a riding crop that stings the flesh.

Whip-crack again and the big one turns and makes a dancer's leap and falls on the wooden platform.

Hold the pistol out straight and keep the sightline clear. A big guy like him. He's crawling on the platform, in the slush, he's trying to get up but that little bullet in him is too large. And look at the other one. He's standing there, staring right at you, petrified, in shock, he can't believe this is happening to him. He's the one who's supposed to be making people afraid. He's the one who killed on the El. He's the one who makes people afraid to go out at night. And now he's being made afraid because he sees the pistol.

An ugly, beautiful pistol sparkling in the light. See the pistol and hear the crack of the whip again. This time, the little one jumps and he is trying to crawl out of the way. Crack the whip again and make him jump.

The big one is up. Crack the whip again.

The big one falls onto the tracks. Why isn't there a train coming? Crack the whip again, for the little one this time.

Whip-crack!

There, that does it. The little one caught it and gave a dancer's leap just like the big one did and he's down too, on the platform, crawling around, crying. What is he saying?

Help me. He's asking for help. He's begging for help and mercy. Beg on your knees, scum, and lick my shoes while you're at it. Cry and swear on your mother's grave.

Crack the whip again.

But that's all the cracks left. Click and click the pistol to make sure. All right. Good enough. They won't forget this night any more than that poor little boy on the El. The big one is on the tracks and he reaches out for help and—look at it!—he touched the third rail. Look at him leap and look at the sparks! He broke his back with that leap, he really had to break his back.

Beautiful. Just beautiful. Stare at those guys until tears come into your eyes because it is so beautiful to see their pain and dying.

33
LUCKY
RAOUL

"Remember me?"

"You shot me."

"I only shot you the first time."

"Sheet. I hurt bad this time."

"Lucky Raoul. You got a nick."

"How come they got a tube in my nose? It itches."

"You got an infection. You're a sick boy, Raoul. You shouldn't play around with dirty needles."

"I wanna know who da fuck shot me."

"Unfortunately, we want to know too. I'd like to give him a medal."

"You fuckin' cops, you steenk, man."

"But I don't have a tube in my nose, Raoul. You look like a trussed turkey."

Raoul was in the hospital bed in the secure ward at Cook County Hospital. He was handcuffed to the bed. His right arm was attached to a glucose bottle by an IV tube and needle. The other tube was down his nose.

"Where I got shot?"

"In the ass. Nicked your testicles."

"Ma balls? Ma balls! What you sayin', I got no balls?"

Terry Flynn smiled. "Unfortunately, you still have balls. But they are big and infected. In fact, you are something of a medical marvel, Raoul. The doctors say you don't seem to have any immunity. You're fading fast, Raoul."

And he managed to scare Raoul and that was something. He felt good about it. Maybe he could scare Raoul to death if he tried hard enough.

Terry Flynn had drawn the assignment by chance and whim of the watch commander. "You're our expert at El murders," the commander had said. And Flynn had been surprised, and then not surprised, to find Raoul wounded on the platform.

"Where's Freddie?" Raoul said.

The hospital was full of night sounds and sour smells.

"Where's Freddie?" Raoul said.

"Freddie bought it."

"He dead?"

"He fried himself on the third rail."

"Man. That wasn't fair."

"Well, it's a pretty stiff penalty for purse snatching."

"She tole you. We tole her not to tell you—"

"You said you'd cut her tits off. You're a tough guy, Raoul. Lucky for you you're dying."

"I ain't dying."

"You're dying, Raoul. All those dirty needles are catching up to you. I told you, you got no immunity."

"OK. OK." Raoul was sweating. He felt very strange, felt bad in a way he had never felt before. "OK, so get the state's attorney and I make a deal to get immunity. I give him whoever he wants."

"Not that kind of immunity, Raoul. The kind you can't deal for. You're dying."

"I ain't dying."

"Who shot you?"

"Some dude."

"Tell me."

"Some dude. Wearing one of those navy coats. You know.

Some dude. I didn't see him too good. He was on the other side. He was on the other side and he pulls out his piece and he starts capping. Poor Freddie."

Terry Flynn's eyes were bright with interest. "Didn't say a thing."

"Just started capping. Man. I went down, Freddie went down, the dude keeps capping until he's capped out. Then he just walks away like it was nothing. I watch him. Funny dude."

"How funny?"

"Funny. Small. Skinny dude, little, skinnier than me. Little. You know."

"I don't know."

"Look funny. You know. I don't know. I wanna doctor."

"You got the best the welfare system can buy. You got doctors but they say they never seen anything like you. You got pneumonia, you know that?"

"I caught cold?"

"You got pneumonia and infection in your nuts. You been out of it for three days."

"Man, don't talk that way—"

"You're dying, Raoul." Terry Flynn was not smiling now. The voice was lower, softer. "You got family, Raoul? You got someone?"

"You trying to scare me."

"I'm telling you the way it is."

"I ain't gonna die of pneumonia."

"You got all kinds of things wrong with you."

Raoul felt very strange. He was afraid, really afraid for a change. The cop was staring at him like he was already dead. He seen that look in people's faces when his grandfather was dying of cancer. People look at his grandfather like he was already dead and it was amazing that he was still walking around, talking, living.

"Don't look at me like that. I'm only twenty-two."

"You won't be twenty-three," Terry Flynn said.

"Man, do something for me."

"I can get hold of your family. You got family?"

"Everybody's got family."

"Tell me. Where can I reach them?"

"In Miami, man. I don't . . ."

The guy was taking out a notebook. He was playing a game. Man, this guy was trying to sucker Raoul, scare him.

"This is a game. Get outta here, man, I got nothin' to say to you."

"You wanna talk to your doctor?"

"Yeah, I wanna doctor."

"You wanna priest?"

Raoul closed his eyes and was afraid. He opened his eyes. "I don't need no priest 'cause I ain't dying. You got that?"

"Suit yourself," Terry Flynn said. He got up. "You tell the doc if you want to see me. I can get your family for you. It doesn't make it easier dying alone like this."

"How'm I gonna die?"

"I don't know. I'm no doctor."

"Man, nobody dies of pneumonia. Gimme a shot or something."

"They been giving you shots. All kinds of things. You fucked up your body somehow. You got no defenses. That last hit, the bullet hit your balls and—"

"Man, this city is full of crazy people, crazy people. They shooting people they don't even know. It's crazy, people shootin' people like this."

"Better they stick them, Raoul? Stick them like you stuck Lee Herran."

"Man, I tole you, that was self-defense."

"You're a half-ass junkie and fag and you got shot twice and beat it because you're lucky. But your luck is running out. I want you to come clean to me, I'll get your family up here if I gotta pay their way—"

"Fuck you," Raoul said. "I don't need you."

"You're dying, Raoul. You need me."

34
WHAT THIS
IS ABOUT

The telephone rang three times before Terry Flynn realized it was the telephone. The telephone had been part of a half-asleep dream.

He was on the couch as usual. He rarely slept in his bedroom. He fell asleep on the couch on purpose because he felt terribly alone in the bedroom. Karen had said he would be better off in a studio apartment. She was right but he was too lazy to move.

He reached for the telephone on the coffee table and picked up the receiver.

He listened to Jack Donovan's voice.

"What do you want?"

"I wanted to tell you we're going to drop the charges on Brandon Cale. I thought you wanted to know."

Terry Flynn blinked, wiped his eyes, sat upright. "Why?"

"Because justice triumphs in the long run," Jack Donovan said.

"You use that line on Karen? You're a smooth talker, Jack. You oughta run for state's attorney."

"Yeah. I ought to. I can count on your vote?"

"Sure."

It was three days after Raoul Macam had been shot on the El

platform at Belmont Avenue. Terry Flynn had been to the hospital each day, working on Raoul a little more each time, trying to push Raoul through fear of death and even remorse to clearing Brandon with some sort of confession. And now Jack Donovan said it wasn't necessary.

"Look, Terry—"

"Yeah, Jack? Look at what?"

"Nothing." Silence. When Donovan resumed, his voice was dull. "Stacy at DEA called over and they arrested a guy named David Parker. They went through his apartment and they found everything. Everything."

"Who the hell is David Parker?"

"He knew Brandon. He knew Lee Herran. You know who he is? Bartender at a fag bar on Broadway called Swallow's."

"Nice name for a fag bar," Terry Flynn said.

"He knew Brandon through Lee Herran. He and Lee were asshole buddies, you might say. And they did dope."

"In the trade?"

"In the trade. The wonderful thing about the exchange is that everything is a commodity," Jack Donovan said.

Now the silence lasted longer between them. There was a sense of emptiness in it. Most of the time cases did not break. There was no snap to this one and no climax. It just ran down and neither man had had anything to do with it. A jerk in DEA had found the key to the puzzle without even knowing he was looking for it.

"Shit," Terry Flynn said in a long sigh.

"Come down."

"It's my day off."

"I'll buy you lunch. I owe you lunch."

"You don't owe me a thing," Terry Flynn said. He was getting angry all over again.

But Donovan's voice was soft. "You did it, Terry. You pushed on this thing. You said all along that Brandon was the innocent."

"I say a lot of things."

"So you were right. Congratulations."

"Fuck you."

"I wanted to tell you all about it. It was your day off but I figured you wanted to know. It's nearly eleven in the morning, I let you sleep; Karen said you were still on nights."

That was a cheap shot and it was intended. Terry Flynn thought about it, held the receiver tight in his left hand. And then he smiled.

"Prick."

"You got to be hard-nosed in the SAO," Jack Donovan said. He was smiling as well.

"Prick in DEA wraps this up. You wouldn't think those guys would know a clue if it hit them over the head."

"Don't you believe in detective work?"

"Sure. And Santa Claus. OK. You buy me breakfast. I like spaghetti for breakfast. I meet you over at Tuscano's around, what? Noon?"

"OK. I meet you there."

"Bring Karen. We can have a threesome," Terry Flynn said.

"Go fuck yourself."

"Yeah. That's what it comes down to."

"I want to tell you about Brandon and this Parker guy. You want to hear, OK. You want to be an asshole, which is what you sound like, that's OK too. You were interested in this."

"You could say that."

"Don't you know when to stop pushing, Terry?"

"What are you? Someone elect you patrol boy?"

"Forget it," Jack Donovan said.

"Noon," Terry Flynn said.

Tuscano's was on South Oakley Street, in the tiny Italian ghetto surrounded by railroad yards and factories, not far from the Criminal Courts Building. All the restaurants on the two blocks south of Twenty-fourth Street were good and cheap and usually filled at lunchtime with cops and lawyers and crooks and judges who were taking their noon meals between trials.

They didn't say much to each other at first. There was this sense of pain between them and that was because they had known each other for a long time. And Jack Donovan had been there the night they found Karen in the gangway on the North Side with the body of the psychopath who had stalked her to rape and kill her. They had both had a feeling for Karen for a long time and Karen had chosen between them. Twice.

Karen had shifted and the earth moved and they were Freemasons, groping for a sign beween them that would let them be brothers again.

"David Parker," Jack Donovan said. He had tried the linguine in clam sauce. It was good but his stomach hurt again. He ate some bread and then quit trying.

"He had an arsenal in his place and some very heavy shit."

"How heavy?"

"Twenty kilos of coke."

"Stacy'll go on the television and say it was the biggest drug bust of the century."

"They always are. That was just in the apartment. He was carrying another ten on his body when they stopped him at O'Hare last night."

"This our crack O'Hare Airport detail?"

"No. Customs got a feeling and then DEA came into it. He was flying in from Colombia."

"And he wasn't bringing coffee."

"You gotta give Stacy credit."

Terry Flynn swallowed a forkful of spaghetti. "I gotta do nothing. Stacy is an asshole, a regular federal creep. He made a deal with you guys. He sprung Raoul, the living embodiment of a scumbag. So now you can congratulate yourselves on another job well done and I gotta keep looking for the guy who shot Raoul. And Raoul is gonna die so I suppose that makes it homicide."

"Is that what they say?"

"That is not what they say. Don't tell me you still believe in doctors at your age. I look at Raoul and Raoul's got the death look."

"You gonna look hard?"

"I give a fuck who shot Raoul. Raoul has got some kind of

infection he can't shake. Doctor says his immune system ain't working, I don't know what the fuck it means, but it comes from the shooting, he's got an infection. Doctor says there's been a couple of cases like Raoul, fags all of them. Maybe it comes from butt-fucking. It's nice to think Raoul is dying, except that it means someone is a killer."

"Let me tell you about David Parker."

"Yeah. Tell me."

"David Parker knew Brandon. He knew Lee Herran from a way back, through the bar on Broadway. There was shit going through that bar, that's what Stacy says. Well, Parker and Herran are lovers and then they're dealing in dope together because Herran has good connections on the various stock exchanges, good place to deal dope."

"The high life."

"Very. Now, Herran gets stuck by accident at Fullerton Avenue and you got to see it from Stacy's point of view, this doesn't look so accidental. And when he finds dope in Brandon's apartment—"

"Dope that was Lee Herran's—"

"Yeah, but you see why he was making the connect. He wanted to see where it led back to. And it was Parker, and the connection was made by accident, just because the bastard got caught going through customs at O'Hare."

"So we all get a break and Brandon doesn't have to face doing time."

"It turned out that David and Lee took trips together. Down to Key West; it's a big fag resort. Took these trips that were part pleasure and part business. Take boats out to other boats and take stuff back home. They were dealing and Lee kept some of the stash in his apartment. And you thought Stacy planted it there."

Terry Flynn tore off another piece of Italian bread and sopped up the meat sauce on the plate. "The thought occurred to me."

"You think you're the Lone Ranger."

"Sure."

"Everyone is wrong, Terry Flynn is right."

"Something like that."

"It must be a burden to be God."

"I never asked Him."

"Look, I'm going out of my way for you," Jack Donovan said, and he realized he was angry now, a profound and deep anger that did not raise its voice.

Terry Flynn looked up from the plate. His eyes were cold and mild, like the lake on the first warm day of spring when all the ice is out of it but the water is freezing.

"You go out of your way for yourself. This isn't about telling me that you're dropping charges on Brandon Cale. This is about your guilt trip. This is about Karen. You went out of your way, all right. But it wasn't to do me no favor. It was to do you a favor."

"Anybody knock that chip off your shoulder?"

"They do it all the time. And I keep picking it up and putting it back on."

"It's not me. I mean, about Karen. It's not me she's crazy about."

"Is that right?"

"You asshole. You make it too hard on her. You make it too hard on everyone."

"Maybe life is hard."

"And you're the first guy who figured that out?"

"I learn slow," Terry Flynn said. "I didn't even know my old man was shaking down taverns in his district until I became a cop. I just thought he was the big man, big Captain Flynn, everyone's friend. He was a pal of Monsignor Duffy at St. Alma's. They'd drink whiskey together in the rectory after twelve o'clock Mass on Sunday. Terry Flynn is the fair-haired boy, all right. Got it made. My old man said before he died that he'd make me a captain, because that's what a father did for his son. Everything is a gift. The house we lived in was a gift. People loved my father and I was so fucking stupid that it wasn't till I was on the department that I figured out what a fucking crook he was. The trouble with learning things slow and the hard way

211

is that the lessons stick. Nothing is ever what it seems to be, you know that? I knew you awhile, Jack. I figured we were friends. I learn slow."

"And if Karen had picked me? If she had picked me a long time ago?"

"Then she picked you and I would be picking my nose."

"I really believe that," Jack Donovan said.

Terry Flynn threw the fork on the plate so that it made a loud sound in the loud restaurant.

"You fucking right you believe it. You moved on her—"

And Jack Donovan smiled. Sadly. "No. You're wrong. You got it all wrong."

Terry Flynn stared at him.

"I tried to tell you. You do learn slow, you got that right. Your old man took some petty graft along the way and you want to make it a federal case. He lived in a different time. You think the department is church and you're Martin Luther. You're not going to change anything, you're just going to set up your own church."

Terry Flynn waited.

"I got a feeling from Karen. But I figured it out right away, but you still haven't figured it out. It has nothing to do with me, I was just a warm body around. She wants to get rid of you but she can't do it. You're driving her crazy. You're too much for her. You never stop fighting. Karen needs a rest from you. She thinks she's going to get rid of you but she can't. She talks about you to me, for Christ's sake."

It was like ice breaking after winter on the lake. Terry Flynn started to eat again. "She does, huh?" Softly.

"You were right, that's the bad part of it. About fighting. About Brandon. About pushing us around as though you could do it and God elected you patrol boy of the world. What we did was dirty but that was the deal we had to make with the G. We make deals all the time. You don't make deals, the thing falls apart. I heard Raoul got capped three days ago on the El platform and what did I think about? About you. About how scum like Raoul got the chance to be on the street again in the first place."

Silence between them.

"Maybe because of scum like me."

And more silence.

Jack Donovan picked up the piece of bread, looked at it, put it down again.

"I can't stand to fight like that. Karen can't. No one can. But you just keep pushing and pushing and you don't give a shit. Is this because your father was taking? Is that what this fighting all the time is about?"

"I don't have to fight now," Terry Flynn said. "Brandon got off. They did let him know, didn't they?"

"Yes."

"You gonna make it all right with his employers and all?"

"We'll make some calls," Jack Donovan said.

"Some guy who didn't even figure in this." Terry Flynn shook his head. "Some kid from left field I never heard of, it turns out he's the guy—"

"Dave Parker, your friendly neighborhood fag dealer."

"So what about Raoul? Was he connected in all this? In the dealing? Was it a fag killing?"

"No. Just one of those things. Random." Jack Donovan looked at the congealed linguine on his plate. "God was playing Lotto."

35
VICTIM

Dawn broke. Red light streaked the purple eastern sky. The streets were empty and wet beneath the light. Snow was piled in grubby little hills along the miles of curb.

The city is early to rise because it sits at the eastern edge of the Central Time Zone. The sun rises here first.

Mary Jane Caldwell woke with the first light.

She slept on her daybed. The daybed was a place to fall asleep as though by accident. The purposeful idea of going to sleep in a dark bedroom, in a bed, spread out like a victim waiting for sleep and death, frightened her so that she was glad she lived in a studio and had no bedroom. She slept with a lamp on, as though she were a child. The room was full of bright things and if she woke during her restless sleep—and she woke often— she could be reassured immediately by her surroundings.

She studied the morning light filling the single window, gradually filling the room and making the lamplight pale. She reached up and turned off the lamp. She listened to the steam clanging up through the pipes into the radiators. The radiators hissed warmth. The room was still cold, but in a little while the suffocating and comforting warmth of the radiators would fill the little apartment.

She threw off the blanket and swung her legs on the floor.

Her cotton nightgown was wrapped tightly around her body. The bare floor was cold to the touch; her feet were cold. She shivered and got up.

She went into the bathroom and turned on the shower. The warmth filled the sticky room. She took off her gown and hung it on the hook behind the door. She stepped into the shower and let the warmth envelop her. She stood in the shower and closed her eyes and let the water warm her. After a little while, she began to bathe herself.

When she was finished, she stepped out of the shower and stood naked before the mirror. She rubbed at the steam condensed on the mirror and saw her body. The bruises were healed, even the slight cut on her arm had disappeared. No marks on her body; unmarked person. She studied her face and particularly, her eyes. Her eyes were deep, innocent, unquestioning. Her face was beautiful. She was beautiful. She knew this. And her body was unmarked.

Sometimes, very suddenly so that her body would jerk awake, she would see both of them in her nightmares. They would be doing those things to her again and they would be talking to each other about killing her. And she would be crying to them: Don't kill me. Please don't kill me.

She despised that person.

That person on her knees, begging them. Doing what they wanted her to do.

She had developed a slight tremor in her left hand in the last few weeks. She thought it was part of the legacy of that afternoon on the El platform. The tremor came and went with a life of its own.

One afternoon two weeks ago, she had gone into a little shop on Halsted Street and purchased some things they sold there.

When she got back to her apartment, she had put the clothes on. Crotchless black panties and a sheer black garter belt and sheer seamed stockings and a black peignoir. She had gone into the bathroom and made up her face so that she resembled her idea of what a whore looked like. She had seen them on Broadway, the tired and washed-out streetwalkers in their tight skirts and garish sweaters. She tried to think of herself as a whore that afternoon, to exorcise something in her that had been on its knees, begging for life, praying to God, doing those things those men demanded that she do.

It was finished then.

She threw the clothes away.

It was finished just like that.

She had purchased the pistol the next morning in a gun shop on Mannheim Road in the western suburbs. The gun shop was attached to a shooting gallery.

The owner of the shooting gallery thought she had purchased too much pistol. He said so. He said a lot of things but in the end, it didn't matter. No one listened. This was a new world and a new trend among women who were teaching themselves how to shoot pistols in order to defend themselves. It was nonsense, of course. Shooting at a paper target was not the same thing as shooting at a man.

When she fired—it was her passion now, she went to the range four days a week, she had dropped out of college—she did not wear earplugs. She wanted to hear the sound of the pistol reverberate on the range, to hear the sounds of others firing guns, to hear the power of the piece bucking in her hand. The sound was part of the power.

When she fired, the tremor in her hand ceased. The tremor waited for the weight of the pistol in her hands to still it. The sound deafened her and lasted for hours.

She thought she was very good.

The ugly, brutish weapon had frightened her at first. The purchase of it had been an act of courage. But after she fired it, the weapon did not frighten her. The power of the piece became part of her.

Even the owner finally said, "You're very good. You handle it well."

She did handle it well. Her eyes were steady, gray and cold. She fired and she was not striking a paper target but she was tearing flesh from sinew and bone.

When she lay on the daybed in the afternoons, she would stare at the pistol on the bare dining table near the window. The pistol caught the afternoon light. It shone a steady light in the afternoon. She stared at it with fond eyes, as a lover watches the beloved.

She would daydream about the two of them now. They were surprised she had a gun. She told the one to get down on his knees and suck the other one and they were begging for their lives. She held the pistol to his head and he sank to his knees and opened the fly of the other one and when he began the act, she fired and blew the top of his head off. And, in that moment of death, he bit the other one. It was funny, it was comical and she would smile in her daydream to think of it.

The one who was still living was writhing in agony on the El platform, the corpse of the other one still attached to him.

The pistol was the power in her.

It was heavy, heavier than she imagined it would have been when she saw it. It was ugly in a wonderful way. The snubby snout of the barrel almost formed a face.

She went out without fear. She rode the El without fear. She had no fear because of the power in her.

She wore her peacoat and stocking cap and jeans and the pistol was in her jacket pocket. It was always ready. When she walked down the street, men did not leer at her as they did at other women. They knew she had the power. She knew her eyes frightened them. She had the power and it infused her whole body with strength.

She was strong; the power made her strong.

But not when she finally surrendered to sleep late at night, on the daybed in the studio in the middle of a large building full of such apartments and apartment sounds. When sleep came, she fought against it; but when sleep insisted, she felt herself falling, felt herself in surrender again, and all the forces of darkness were around her again.

Every day, she cleaned the pistol with care. The smell of the cleaning oil filled the apartment and pleased her. The pistol was a presence in the room, like living with a man. The presence and the smell of the presence dominated her when they were alone; the presence protected her and made her strong when she was on the street.

She cleaned the pistol every afternoon, before the light failed, before it was night and the jewelbox of the city was opened.

36
THAT KIND OF A DAY

They were just driving around, killing time. It had been that kind of a day, when witnesses aren't home and suspects are otherwise employed and every street is a dead end.

Sid Margolies was driving because he was careful and Karen was not. They had been teamed off and on all winter and they could spend a lot of time in each other's company without talking. It gets that way between partners who share a police car eight hours a day.

"The funny thing I heard," Sid said.

The fragment of sentence was followed by a period of silence.

"What was that?" Karen said. She stared out the side window at an old man with white whiskers, sitting on a slushy stoop, drinking from a bottle wrapped in a paper bag.

"What was what?"

"You heard something funny."

"I heard about Terry Flynn going to ask for a transfer out of Homicide," said Sid Margolies.

"That'll be the day."

"Yeah," Sid said, turning into Lawrence Avenue, heading east. The big battered Dodge sedan was unmarked. "You want to go to that place on Belmont and Broadway?"

"I'm not hungry," she said. "I'll have a cup of coffee."

"You on a diet again?"

"I'm always on a diet. You go out with Terry Flynn and you end up drinking beer all night."

Sid looked at her sideways. "You go out with Terry Flynn still?"

"Before, I meant," she said.

"Yeah," said Sid. He always drove with both hands on the steering wheel. He was the most careful man anyone knew.

"Winter. The snow is melting and now we find all the dead bodies we couldn't find last winter," she said.

"Terry always said that."

"I must have picked it up from him."

"Well, you don't have to go on diets anymore," Sid Margolies said.

"Yeah."

Silence.

"Maybe what I heard is true after all?"

"Look at that," Karen said. "The city primitive." A man with a dark coat was putting out kitchen chairs in the street to reserve a parking place for his car. "Asshole lives three blocks from the El, he drives a car, and will kill to protect his space."

"I figure he's getting out of Homicide to ease off. You know, he's been driving pretty hard—"

"Nobody asked him."

"He sure went crazy on that Brandon Cale business, didn't he?" Sid was smiling. "Terry. I wish he was back with us. Matt wishes he was back."

"So he can drive everyone else crazy? This is peaceful, Sid. Enjoy it."

"He never got to me."

"You're the only one."

"I admire that. You know. Principles."

"Principles don't have to make you loud."

"Sometimes they do."

Sid said this last so softly that it startled both of them. What

220

was he talking about? But she knew and she turned to the side window again when she spoke: "Forget it, Sid. You're Jewish but you're no matchmaker."

"I was just talking about Terry. He's a friend of mine," Sid said.

They didn't speak for a long time, all the way down to Rick's on Broadway. The coffee-shop lights were bright against the gloomy day. The sky was gray, bleak, full of the smell of damp. Would it rain or snow? It was that kind of a day.

Sid parked in a NO PARKING NO STOPPING NO STANDING zone, marked by a red-and-white sign. He turned off the ignition and they both got out and slammed the doors. The gutters were slushy and Karen stepped gingerly to the sidewalk in her high boots. Sid wore rubbers.

"Mary Jane," Karen Kovac said.

It was her. She had turned the corner from Broadway into Belmont. She stopped, looked startled. Her eyes were wide, focused on some middle distance. Then she seemed to see Karen and tried on a smile.

"Hello," she said.

"How're you doing? You remember Sid?"

"Hello, Detective," she said.

"How're you doing?" Sid said.

"Oh. OK. I'm doing OK." The voice was flat all of a sudden. "What are you doing?"

Karen looked hard at her face and the smile. Mary Jane was dressed in black from head to foot. She wore black slacks. She wore a wool beret on her head.

"What do you mean?"

"I mean, what are you doing here?" Mary Jane said.

"Doing?" Sid said. He seemed confused.

"Taking a break," Karen said. "Coffee. You want some coffee?"

"Oh. Coffee. No. No, I don't want coffee. Oh, I see. It was just— This was the place where those men—"

"Oh, I see," Karen said. It was the same corner, the same

coffee shop. It hadn't occurred to her. "And you live right down the street anyway," Karen said, explaining why Mary Jane was here. Why was she explaining?

"You doing all right?" Karen said again.

"I'm all right." And her voice was chill and very sure. "I heard that someone was shot on the Belmont El the other night. It was in the paper. He was a suspect in that killing. The one on the El."

Again, Karen looked hard at her. On the narrow sidewalk, the three of them blocked the way. "Yes," she said at last. "He was shot."

"Good," Mary Jane Caldwell said. Her eyes were bright. "Good. I hope he dies."

"Yeah," said Sid. He thought he understood. He seemed embarrassed. "Well, we gotta go," he said.

"Yes," Mary Jane said to Karen Kovac. "Maybe people like him will stop preying on people."

"Like who?"

"This one that was shot. On the El platform. Worthless. Worthless people. You wonder why God lets worthless people be born. Maybe it's just a test to see if the rest of us are going to put up with them. See how long people will put up with them."

It was such a strange thing to say in the middle of a city sidewalk and Karen felt the same embarrassment that Sid had felt a moment before. It was such a strange thing to say.

"Don't—" Karen began. Don't what? "Take it easy. How's school going?"

"School?"

Again, Karen thought Mary Jane was seeing something beyond the three of them. Karen almost turned around to see what was holding Mary Jane's eyes.

But Mary Jane blinked. "Oh. School. School is fine. Just fine. Going along." Her eyes narrowed. "I'm doing fine now. Just fine."

"Immigration," Sid said suddenly. "They're working on one of them to deport him. It's a slow process but they'll deport him."

"Oh. Deport him. The one who raped me, you mean." She stared very hard at Sid. "That's a big punishment, isn't it?"

"Mary Jane—"

"Oh, nothing," she said. "Nothing. Just forget it. I'm trying to forget it. I really am. Nothing. I have to go now. I've got to get to the bank before it closes."

"All right," Karen said, but she didn't move. "Take it easy."

The good-byes took longer than that and Karen said something about staying in touch. And then Mary Jane Caldwell was gone.

"She's as bad off as she was the first day," Sid Margolies said.

Karen felt cold in her greatcoat. She felt small and cold and weak. "Damn," she said. "Sometimes you just want to get out. Sometimes with something like that, what happened to that girl."

"Yeah," said Sid Margolies. "I suppose that's part of what got to Terry. Maybe he just has to get out."

37
CONNECTIONS

"Flynn."

Terry Flynn walked across the big room from the coffee machine to the glass office used by Area Six Homicide in the squat brick building at Belmont and Western. He was on nights still but not for long. That's what Ranallo had said down at headquarters. Ranallo was as anxious to transfer him out of Homicide as Flynn thought he was to leave.

"It's your boyfriend," said Sergeant Marcos, making a kissy-kissy face.

Flynn didn't even frown. It rolled off his back. He was working on taking it easy. That's what he told guys like Hauptman when they went out drinking all night in O'Sullivan's, trading cop stories above the brass sound of the nightly band. Life is too short to work that hard at it, he would tell Hauptman in a loud voice to be heard above the band. And no one seemed to believe him, that this was a new Terry Flynn they were seeing.

He picked up the phone and said, "Sergeant Flynn."

"Sergeant? This is Brandon Cale. I was meaning to get to you before this. I called a couple of times but you were off. I guess we weren't making connections or something. I was home for a while. After they . . . they dropped the charges. I wanted to tell you."

"I know they dropped the charges."

"There's still Raoul Macam but—"

"Don't worry about Raoul," Terry Flynn said. "He's not going anywhere soon. Unless it's feet first, like they say in Westerns."

"I—I wanted to tell you."

"Tell me what?"

"I wanted to tell you, well, I wanted to say thanks. So, thanks. I just wanted to say thanks," Brandon Cale said.

"Yeah." Terry Flynn felt awkward. "Yeah," he said again as though it might lead someplace. "Well, don't worry about it. You doing OK?"

"Yes."

"You were talking once about going back to your hometown—"

"No. I don't think so. I thought about it. I don't think so. I think I'll stick it out."

"City isn't as bad as it looks sometimes." Terry Flynn frowned. Why was he saying such idiotic things? "Well, good luck to you."

"Yeah. Well. I'll see you around."

"Not if you stay out of trouble," Terry Flynn said. It was the kind of joke his father might have made.

"Yeah. OK." A kind of chuckle. "Well, OK, Sergeant, and thanks for everything."

"Sure," said Sergeant Terry Flynn.

Commander Ranallo of Homicide was on line 2.

It was the next night or the night after. Terry Flynn picked up the phone and said his name.

"You got a lot of fucking nerve," Ranallo began.

Terry Flynn waited.

"You got your fucking transfer all right. You got it, mister. You can take your leave right after we finish this conversation for all I care, I'd like to get the smell of you outta Homicide. I oughta fumigate."

Terry Flynn smiled.

"You there?"

"I'm here," he said.

"You rotten son of a bitch," Lieutenant Ranallo said. "You're so slick."

"So I had to do it. You could of just let me go but that wasn't good enough for you. So you had to fuck me around some more," Terry Flynn heard himself saying. "I want to get out, I want a little peace and quiet and mostly, I want days. So I suggest review downtown but you don't want me downtown, so you are going to fuck me around and put me in uniform nights in Grand Crossing so I can chase niggers and play cowboy on Friday nights. I did that already, Loo. I don't have to do that again. I did my time, now I want a little time off."

Ranallo was, in fact, a lieutenant in civil-service rank but a commander in title. Reminder of rank was meant to needle him. Not that it took much to set Ranallo off.

"I want to know what your clout is. I thought Matt Schmidt was your chinaman."

"Maybe he is."

"So how could Matt Schmidt get you airport detail?"

Flynn's grin broke ear to ear. "I got the airport? I got the fucking airport? I can't believe it. Write parking tickets and take two hours for lunch. Fucking airport. Terrific. He swung it."

"Who is he? I just want to know what your clout is?"

"No, that would be telling."

"Well, I'll tell you this. You got an enemy now. You got an enemy in me. You watch me every fucking minute, you son of a bitch."

"I'm trembling, Lennie," said Terry Flynn. "You know how easily I get frightened. All I want is to get away from you for a while. I know about you, Lennie. You aren't a keeper. You got no rhythm. You don't know when to leave well enough alone. Shoving me out to Grand Crossing, that was it, I wasn't gonna stand for that. Yeah, I talked around, I got some IOUs in the department."

"You got clout from your old man."

"My old man is dead," Terry Flynn said.

226

"He was a fucking Mick scumbag grafting son of a bitch," Ranallo said. The words choked.

Terry Flynn said nothing. He might have said something but he didn't want to let it go that far. "When do I go?"

"Go now. Go now for all I care, I give a fuck when you go," Ranallo said. He never swore. He was probably drinking, Terry Flynn thought. Ranallo never drank.

Kelly's Tap was below the El tracks. Every time the trains rumbled overhead, conversation stopped in the place. It had been that way for nearly fifty years. Kelly himself was the son of the Irish immigrant who started the place. He had a wide face and childlike blue eyes and a whisky voice. He was explaining the facts of life to Terry Flynn at the end of the bar when Karen Kovac walked in. The El passed overhead and conversation stopped.

Karen Kovac saw Terry Flynn and seemed to be surprised. She said hello in a little voice that was lost in the sound of the rumbling train.

The phone rang behind the bar and Kelly picked it up and spoke. The phone rang all day and all night and it was always for Kelly. He was the most connected man in the city.

"I didn't expect to see you here."

"I was drowning my sorrows. I was trying to watch basketball and see if I could learn to like it. I really think it's a stupid game."

"So's football."

"Football is not stupid," he said. "It's sick but it's not stupid. There is something nice about twenty-two men on a field wearing padding and helmets, trying to beat each other up with their bare hands. But this is stupid."

"Then why do you watch it?"

"DePaul girls come in here all the time. I told Kelly I want a piece of ass, he said I had to understand basketball."

"They wouldn't appreciate your sense of humor."

"Who wants to tell jokes? I can drink with Hauptman if I want jokes." He paused. "You want a drink?"

It was the kind of question that meant more. She hesitated. And then:

"Sure."

She ordered beer this time, not vodka.

"I thought you were on a diet," he said.

"I'm always on a diet."

"Not me. I am learning to let it go with the flow. I tell you I'm going to the airport?"

She stared at him. "I heard about it. From Matt."

"Matt did all right for me."

"You rubbed it in. To Ranallo. I heard that."

"Not from me. Ranallo should learn to keep his mouth shut. You go around telling people that you got fucked, pretty soon, everyone's going to think you're bragging about it." He finished the stein and signaled for another. "How are you, Karen? You getting ready for school?"

"Summer. Start in summer."

"How long you figure it's gonna take for you to be a lawyer?"

"I got time," she said.

"I turned over Raoul Macam," said Terry Flynn. "Nice not to have to think about that scumbag. I feel clean, you know? Like I was changing jobs. Or getting married. Or better, getting divorced."

"Breaking old ties," she said.

"Making new connections. I talked to the Loo at O'Hare. A guy named Breaker. He seems OK, we'll watch out for each other."

"This is not a step up," she said. "You go to the airport to retire."

"So maybe I'm retiring," he said. "I'm tired of Raoul Macams and I'm tired of talking to guys like Jack Donovan. I need to rest it awhile. And how is Jack, now that I brought him up?"

"He's fine," she said in a fine tough voice. "Just fine."

"I'm sorry. That is not part of my go-with-the-flow. I bought a book by Leo Buscaglia but it made me gag. I'm going to try Kahlil Gibran next."

And that made her laugh out loud.

"I ain't kidding," Terry Flynn said. "I'm a changed man."

"Yeah," she said. She was still smiling. "I heard about that too. About Jack Donovan's little talk with you."

"Jack Donovan told you? Everyone is getting confessional. Don't people know how to keep secrets? Jack Donovan has nothing to do with this."

"No," she said.

"I just want a change," he said.

"No," she said.

"All right. What is it?"

"I'm a lot tougher than you think I am," Karen Kovac said.

"What has that got to do with anything?"

She considered it. She stared at him for a long time without saying anything to him. "I came looking for you."

"Is that right?"

"You don't make it easy."

"You're the one who's the tough guy. You don't make it easy either, Karen." The voice dropped into gentleness. "I like you enough to think about changing my act. That counts for something. When Jack Donovan went after you, it was like a kick in the nuts."

"He didn't."

They thought about that.

"I have to talk to you. I'm getting as crazy as you are. I kept thinking about Brandon Cale the last couple of days. You were like a wild man. I couldn't take it. No, that's not it; I could take it but I wasn't going to. Women who let themselves be abused deserve everything they get."

"Was I abusing you?"

"You abuse yourself. It's the same thing when someone gets close to you."

"Well, Brandon Cale is over."

"But Mary Jane Caldwell isn't."

"Sure it is. She fucked up her own case, there's nothing you can do about it now. She's an unreliable witness."

"She was talking about Raoul Macam," Karen said.

A train rumbled overhead, heading south for the Loop. When the silence returned, Terry said: "What about him?"

"We met her by accident one afternoon, Sid and I. We were going for coffee at Rick's on Broadway. She was strange, I thought. I asked her about school and she said it was fine. I called the school. She isn't in school anymore. She brought up the shooting at Belmont station. She brought it up, I checked with Sid, we didn't say anything about it. She said booga stuff like 'I hope he dies' and 'That should be a lesson for scum who prey on people' and stuff like that. I wasn't listening for it at the time but then it stayed with me. I kept thinking about her. Could she be involved? So what did I do?"

Terry Flynn did not speak or move. He stared at her. Her face was white, as though she might be ill.

"What did you do, Karen?"

"Goddammit," Karen Kovac said.

Terry waited.

"The trouble is that everything happened to her."

"What did you do?"

"I talked to her father. He was a sad old man. I went up to see him on my day off. I talked to him about Mary Jane."

"What did he say?"

"He just had a lot of silences after a while. He started off, showing me pictures of her. She was what you call a horsey girl. Horseback riding. Shooting. She probably would have been a fox hunter if she was English."

"Shooting," Terry Flynn said.

"Yes."

They understood each other.

"So what was I going to do next?"

"Check firearm registrations."

"Yes. I felt almost dirty doing it."

"Sure. She was raped, beaten, almost killed and now her killers are free."

"She has a weapon."

"I know. That's what you were going to tell me, so I knew it already." Very quiet. "And what are you going to do about it?"

"I don't know. She shot someone, didn't she? You see it too?"

"Sure. She shot Raoul Macam. It is kind of crazy, like poetic justice, isn't it?" But Terry Flynn was not smiling.

"And who else is she going to shoot?"

"Maybe herself."

"And if she's got rid of the gun?"

"Anything is possible," Terry Flynn said.

"And I get a warrant, we search her apartment, we find the piece, the ballistics match up, we make the arrest. Then what happens? We go to court."

"We ask our mutual friend Jack Donovan what to do," Terry Flynn said. His eyes were very cold now. "He says 'justice is justice.' We move to trial. She gets a lawyer and we get a lawyer. A jury is asked to convict a strange girl who was raped on an El platform by two pieces of living scum and who, in rage at the failure of the system, goes on another El platform one night and guns down a man—this is our charge—who is a murderer and drug dealer and all-around three-legged alligator. The jury finds her not guilty by reason of insanity. Or, our friend Jack Donovan makes a deal and she does not go to court at all, but they put her in one of our wonderful state institutions for the criminally insane, where she can defecate in the day room and walk around with a glazed look on her face and get taken by whoever wants her to spread her legs for them."

Karen Kovac looked at the bartender and said, "Vodka. A glass of vodka and ice."

"Two," said Terry Flynn.

The drinks came and they drank them.

"You go to her apartment and she does not have the pistol anymore. That's the best scenario," Terry Flynn said.

"But I know she has it."

"How do you know?"

"Because I have a feeling about her. That this isn't over yet."

"So what are you going to do, then?"

"Do what I have to do," Karen said. "I just had to tell you. To see it clearly."

"Bullshit," Terry Flynn said. "Why don't you ask Jack Donovan? He makes deals. You ask him what to do and he's going to stick his neck out and tell you to do nothing, do not follow up on your sworn duty as an officer of the law? Do not send Mary Jane Caldwell into the maws of our criminal justice system? Do not pass go? Do not collect two hundred dollars?"

"It wasn't about Jack Donovan," she said.

"But it could have been," Terry Flynn said. "You know what the right thing is, don't you? You know what you got to do, don't you?"

"Yes, goddam you, Terry, I know."

"So do it."

"You push."

"The world pushes. You gotta push back or you get flattened."

"I can't do it."

"You know what the right thing is," he said.

"I can't do it," Karen said.

And then Terry Flynn understood why she had come to tell him these things.

38
THE RIGHT THING

Mary Jane Caldwell opened the door.

Terry Flynn filled the doorway for a moment and then stepped inside before she could say anything. She stood at the open door and looked into the dark hall.

"What are you doing here?"

"Just a courtesy visit by the police."

"It's ten o'clock at night."

"Yeah. We work around the clock."

"What is this about?"

"Close the door."

"What is this about?"

"Close the door, Mary Jane."

"I will not. You have no right to be in my apartment."

"You let me in."

"You said it was the police on the intercom."

"Well, it is. You want to see my star?"

"You've been drinking. I can smell you."

"That's beer for you. A dead giveaway." He walked around the bare room on the bare floor. The dark night penetrated. He saw the daybed was made up. Just like his couch.

He stopped at the window and looked down at the sullen

street. Some nights seemed darker than others.

"So. How you doing, Mary Jane?"

"Why?"

"I was talking to Karen. You remember Karen?"

"Karen?"

"Karen the cop. You remember her."

"Of course."

"I was talking to Karen and we were talking about you."

"Is that right?"

"Karen says she saw you the other day."

"I don't remember."

"It was just the other day. You remember stuff that happened a couple of days ago."

"I don't remember."

"She was worried about you."

"She doesn't have to worry about me. She could spend more time worrying about getting some of those perverts on the streets off the streets, that's what she could spend more time worrying about."

Terry Flynn looked at her in her blue robe. Her face was severe and her eyes were very beautiful. And strange.

"Yeah. Well, that part comes with the job. The part about you doesn't. So you worry her when you tell her things that aren't so."

Mary Jane caught her breath.

"See, you told her you were in school and you aren't in school anymore."

"It's none of her goddam business what I am doing. You don't have any right to interfere with my life."

He was moving again, looking at the bookshelf, running his hand over the tops of the books. She saw this and felt the pistol in the pocket of her robe. She formed her fingers around the trigger and grip.

"So she went up and talked to your dad," Terry Flynn said.

"She did that? She has no right—"

"Come on, people got the right to talk to people. She talked to him about you. He was worried about you."

"He's worried about himself. He's worried about dying. He's getting old and he worries about dying because he's going to have to see God someday and explain how he made all his money and how he cheated people and how—"

"Well, we'll leave that to God."

"Yes. We'll leave that to God. But I'm surprised he found time to talk about me. I mean, it must be part of creeping senility, for him to talk about me. What did he say about me?"

"I don't know. Usual stuff, I suppose. You know, about loving and worrying about you."

"Fine. The usual stuff all right."

"You can't judge people that hard, you know, Mary Jane."

"What are you doing? You're all over my apartment. What are you looking for?"

"I'll know when I find it."

And she was very cold inside herself and she thought she knew what she would have to do.

"Why are you here?"

"I want the piece, Mary Jane."

"I beg your pardon."

"I want the gun. The cap pistol. You know you got it."

"Are you searching my apartment without a warrant?"

"Yeah."

"I see. I see." Her voice rose a notch. "The right of the criminals, that's what you people think about, but if two men terrorize a girl on the streets, take her purse, practically threaten to rape her—"

Terry Flynn stopped. He turned. "How do you know about that? How come you know they did that?"

"It was in the paper. It was on the news—"

"Bullshit. It was not. The papers got the story wrong, about a porkie being snuffed by another porkie who wounded a third in what they call a gang-related shooting. That's what was in the papers. You were right there, Mary Jane. This is what you call a gotcha. I gotcha."

"You have no right to be here." Very cold, the lady-of-the-manor voice.

"Yeah. I know that better than you think." He stared at her. "You got a beer in the icebox?"

"Get out of here."

Terry Flynn walked into the kitchen with his broad back to her. It wouldn't be that hard, she thought. She felt the cold thing in her hand in the pocket.

He opened the refrigerator.

"Light beer? Ugh. But in an emergency." He popped the can and came back into the room and he was smiling. "Sometimes they put it in the icebox. I never figure that at all, why someone would put a piece in an icebox but it happens a lot. One guy put it in the freezer."

"You do this all the time."

"I've done everything once," he said.

"I threw it away."

"Sure, you did."

"I threw it away. After. What are you going to do about it?"

Terry Flynn said, "Someone appoint you Charles Bronson? You on a mission from God? You hear voices?"

"I don't know what you're talking about."

"You shot those guys on the El platform. That's what I'm talking about. You may have done society a service but that still is not permitted. It is not permitted for private persons to shoot other private persons within the city limits unless they are in danger of their life and even then, we frown on it. We are up to two hundred eleven homicides so far, according to the count they keep, and that is too many. The mayor doesn't even like it because it makes him look bad."

"I'm sorry about the image of Chicago. I didn't know it was so fragile."

"Stop fucking around with me, Mary Jane, and give me the piece."

"I have a right to have a pistol."

"But you don't have any right to use it."

"I have a right to defend myself."

"You capped them on the El."

"I never go out at night."

"Let me have the pistol."

"Do you know what it's like to be a woman in this city? Do you know about men always looking at you like you were meat, like you were a whore? You wear certain clothes and you're a whore. You walk a certain way. Your breasts are too large or your fanny is too curved. You know what I mean? I went through the criminal justice system and it stinks. It's worse than not working. It stinks. The cops stink and when you say you've been raped, then the cops want to make sure that you didn't ask for it. What do you think it's like to live in a world where you're the object all the time, where everyone is undressing you all the time, where everyone figures that you're nothing but a piece of cake, just a piece of ass, just something to fuck and walk away from—"

Her voice had been rising. Now it broke.

"You know, don't you?" she said. "You look at me and you wonder what it would be like to be on top of me and putting your penis in me, making me take it—"

Terry Flynn held the can of beer very still. He felt sick. It was the unexpectedness of it. "You're crazy, aren't you, Mary Jane? You are really crazy inside, aren't you?"

"Oh, God, I'm so sick inside," she said. And she suddenly vomited and the vomit spilled down the dressing gown and she staggered toward the bathroom in the little hall. Terry Flynn took a step toward her, and the bathroom door shut. He heard retching sounds inside the bathroom. He pushed the door but it was locked.

"Are you all right, Mary Jane?"

It was eerie. The silence of the building almost made a buzzing sound in his ears. He knocked on the door.

"I'm coming out," said the weak voice.

He went back into the main room. He felt very uncertain. He did this all the time, she said. He felt the way he felt once in a dead-end gangway on the South Side, full of shadows and little stabs of light and, somewhere, a man hiding with a gun. He heard the bathroom door open.

He turned and looked at her.

She was completely naked. Her body was pale and formed by long, curving lines. Her nipples were pink and large and her pubic hair was thick. She was beautiful and pale. She held the pistol in her right hand and was braced with her left hand. It was a good position and no shooting instructor would have found a flaw in it

Terry Flynn thought of his father in that moment and thought to say: It's all right. It wasn't for me to say anything to anybody. It was between you and God, if there was God in it somewhere.

"What are you going to do, Mary Jane?"

The instructor said that in such situations, it was important to make your voice as calm as possible. Establish eye contact and keep it. Don't look at the weapon, look only at the person. Don't let the weapon come between you. Except the pistol was at eye level and it was clear that Mary Jane intended to kill him.

"You came here at night, in the middle of the night," she said. Her voice was describing a dream. It had an unnatural softness to it. "You came at night and when I asked you what you wanted, you said it was police business. You forced yourself on me and you tried to rape me. You had been drinking and you wanted to rape me."

"I told people I was coming here."

"Oh, stop that. You know that isn't true."

"Mary Jane—"

"You don't have a warrant and you broke into my place and you were drinking and you told me you wanted to sleep with me. I told you to get out and then you turned nasty and you said you were going to fuck me whether I liked it or not and I had to get this pistol—I have a firearms card—I got my pistol and you—"

"Why did you shoot those men on the El?"

The question broke the trance. Mary Jane blinked. She did not lower the pistol.

"I had to do something. You would have done something. I went to a movie and I was on Sheffield and I saw that one, that Raoul, the one who had killed that homosexual boy. You remember when we were in the Records section at police headquarters that day? And I saw the picture and remembered it. So I felt angry and frightened. And then the two of them grabbed that girl on the street. What would you have done?"

"I would have shot them," Terry Flynn said.

She smiled. "You're a policeman. You could do anything you wanted to do. I can't do what you would do. You see how crazy that is."

Terry Flynn said nothing. He still held the can of beer in hand.

"They fondled her. They took her purse. Just a girl on the street at night. Except women have no right to walk on the street at night."

"It was a purse snatching," he said. "Try to have a little perspective."

"I don't care. It was terrorism. It was as much terrorism as anything is. These people terrorize people. They push down old people and they fondle women and when they feel like it, they rob you or kill you or rape you because they are animals. Animals. And animals have to be killed sometime."

"So it goes back to you being Charles Bronson. That's a movie, Mary Jane. It isn't real."

"Maybe it should be."

"Maybe you should kill your old man."

She blinked. "What did you say?"

"You told me he was a crook. Maybe you should kill him."

"Kill my father?"

"You should kill the old man for being a crook and for cheating people. When you're done with that, I think you should kill yourself."

"What are you saying?"

Terry Flynn stared at her. "You found out your old man was a crook and what did you do? You kept living in his house, using his money to go to school, you kept driving a car on his crooked money because you could despise him and that was good enough. So kill your old man if you want to equalize things. And then kill yourself for—"

"I'm going to kill you. I don't want to but I have to."

"With what? Your pistol? Not for five minutes, honey. That was used in commission of a felony. We got crack scientists who will take that piece and compare the slugs with the El shooting and—"

"Why would they?"

"Because I told you, I told people I was coming here."

"In a bar somewhere? Are you trying to fool me?" She bit her lip. "Take out your pistol, carefully, and put it on the floor and kick it over here."

"I don't have a pistol."

"Yes, you do," she said.

He waited.

"With your left hand."

"Maybe I'm left-handed," he said.

"With your left hand."

He reached for the .357 in his belt. The trouble was, this was going to be the end of it. She was good. She had been standing there for two minutes holding the pistol and her hand never trembled. This was going to be the end of it. Karen would figure it out right away and Mary Jane would never get away with it. But this was going to be the end of it.

"Catch," he said.

And threw the can of beer up in the air, foam spraying across the room.

She moved to the object for a split second and fired, striking white plaster above the living-room window. It was just enough.

Flynn fell on her and pounded her gun hand on the floor very hard. She cried in pain and the pistol fell out of her hand. He hit her and pushed the pistol aside. His own pistol was on the floor behind him where he had dropped it. There was the sound of heavy breathing. Her naked body yielded beneath him. He stared at her. Her face was beautiful, fevered, her eyes were clear and gray. He could smell her beneath him. He felt his bulk upon her breasts. Her body was beautiful. They were breathing very hard and then she kissed him and wrapped her arms up around him and held his mouth and probed his mouth with her wide, wet tongue and her legs opened beneath him and she was pulling him toward her.

Damn, he thought. It was all true, all of it, even when you looked at it from what you thought was the outside.

He pushed himself up from her. "Stop it, Mary Jane," he said. "Get your clothes on."

"Come on," she said. She smiled at him. "I want you."

"Get up and get your clothes on, Mary Jane. Stop acting crazy."

He picked up the pistols and had his back to her.

She struck him on the back with her hands and the blows were hard and they hurt.

He turned and she struck him in the face again and again. The blows were hard. He pushed her away, across the room. His lip was bleeding. He said again: "Get some clothes on."

When she came out of the bathroom, he was putting down the telephone. She looked washed-out, as though she had survived an illness. She looked pale in the dark, formless clothes.

"What are you going to do now?" she said. Her voice was dull.

"Wait awhile," he said. "Let's go in the kitchen. You want me to get you something? You want a beer or something?"

"You can't do anything. You obtained the weapon without a search warrant."

"You're a lawyer too," Terry Flynn said. "Everyone's a lawyer."

"So there's nothing you can do."

"You'd be surprised. I could get a warrant if I wanted one or needed one. I get it and I get you. Except that's the hard part. What do I do with you?"

"I'll do anything you want," Mary Jane said.

Flynn slammed his fist down on the kitchen table. "You are a monster, Mary Jane, you know that? You're a fucking monster and you probably always were a monster, and sometimes a monster finds his world breaks and it is like letting the monster out of a glass cage. You got to be locked up again."

"You won't. My father is a lawyer, I won't spend day one in jail."

"No. No, you won't. Pretty monsters don't get thrown in jail too often," Terry Flynn said. It was all pure hate.

"There's nothing you can do—"

"But there are state institutions for people like you—"

Just a flicker of a smile on her face. "The law works both ways, officer. I won't go to any place like that. You should know that."

"It happens."

"But not to me. I have money."

"Your father's crooked money."

"It's still money," she said.

"And you're still a monster," he said. "I am sorry when bad things happen to ordinary people but I don't have sympathy for monsters. I hope your father has more—"

"He does. I can take care of him."

"Good. Good," Terry Flynn said. "Because he's coming to take care of you. I called him up. He'll be down here in an hour. We'll just wait for him, you and me. He'll be coming for you in an hour."

"You called my father?"

"You were a bad girl, Mary Jane. You can't have guns anymore and you've got to go home."

"I can do anything I want to do."

"You can't shoot people."

"I can have you killed."

"No. Not anymore," said Terry Flynn.

"My father? You called my father?" She stared at him. "You can't do that. He's a bad man. He's a crook. I can tell you how he stole from his clients."

"All lawyers are crooks," Terry Flynn said. "When they lose."

"You can't do this," she said. "Do you know who I am?"

"No," Terry Flynn said. And now his voice was gentle again. He sat down at the kitchen table across from Mary Jane Caldwell and they stared at each other in the night, without speaking.

And the old man came at midnight. He was thin and his face was mean and his eyes were in pain. It was a late hour for an old man. He stared at Mary Jane sitting at the kitchen table.

"You can't make me do anything," she said.

"Is there going to be . . . any more trouble?" he said to Terry Flynn.

"Keep her in her cage," Terry Flynn said. "Keep her away from people she can hurt and from people who can hurt her."

"You can't do anything to me," she said.

The old man spoke as though she wasn't there. "It's like my life is just empty now. She was the only one left. Her mother gone. No one left. And now—"

"Yeah," Terry Flynn said because he did not want to hear this. "You got a driver?"

"Yes, like you said."

"You get up, Mary Jane."

"I won't go."

"Goddammit, I'm sick of this shit. Get up and go downstairs or I'll carry you downstairs."

"Don't you touch me," she said. She looked at her father. "I want to go home with you. Do you know what he did to me? He took all my clothes off and he made me suck his penis. He made me do it and he said he would kill me if I told anyone. Remember Robert Hughes in high school when I told you he tried to rape me? It was like that only it was worse. What are you going to do to him, Daddy?"

But she went downstairs with the old man and crawled into the backseat of the Lincoln Continental with him, and a man named Fergus started up the car and it crept out of the neighborhood of the city. The old man said once, "My poor little girl."

And Terry Flynn said nothing at all.

39
TELL ME

The ice began to crack on the lake. The ice cracked more and more every day, and if you stood on the rocks off Diversey Harbor, you could see the cracks running all the way across the patterns of ice to the open gray sea. The first freighters of the new season were moving again on the lake, bringing iron ore down to Gary at the south end of the lake, where it would become steel. The freighters drifted in the open gray sea on the horizon line.

"Spring," Karen Kovac said, staring across the rocks to the open sea.

"When we find all the dead bodies unaccounted for beneath the snow," Terry Flynn said.

"I like it like this. It's warm today and you can feel it really is going to be spring someday and there'll be leaves on the trees again."

"Yeah. The four seasons in Chicago. Six months of winter. Two weeks of spring. Five months of heat. Two weeks of fall."

"Only the tough survive," Karen said.

"That's me."

"I'm not tough enough."

"Sure you are. You'll do in a pinch," he said. He pinched her.

"Is that any way to treat a friend?"

He smiled at her. His eyes were not as cold as they had been in winter. "I got to get my bike fixed. I'm going to ride a bike this summer and work off this winter fat."

"I'm going on a diet," she said.

"You drink too much beer."

"That's because I'm with you."

They walked on the rocks for a while. The rocks are large, square slabs piled into the lakeshore at intervals to keep back the sea. All the land along the lake has been reclaimed from the lake. The park was dull and muddy brown in this first spring. The snow was all gone, except for a few stubborn dirty piles of ice. People were walking in the park like survivors emerging from the end of a battle. There was a stunned quality to the warm, blustery day.

"I never asked you," Karen said.

"You never asked me."

"Did you keep it?"

"I thought about it. I kept it for a while."

"In case she came back."

"I wasn't worried about that. I kept it because it was a nice piece."

"So you kept it."

"No. I came over one day and found a spot where the ice was broken up good and I dropped it in."

"I knew you would."

"I know."

"It was the right thing and I couldn't do it."

"That's all right. Don't talk about it, Karen."

"I should have been able to do it."

"Well, it got done."

"I should thank you. I should be thanking you."

"No. Don't talk about it."

"Why not?"

"Because it isn't good. I like you and we get along again. So don't talk about it. Don't ever mention it again."

She understood then. She took his arm and they walked awhile without speaking. It was a warm day and they talked finally about going back to his apartment and making love to each other.